SIX FOOTPRINTS TO SATAN

SEVEN FOOTPRINTS TO SATAN
Abraham Merritt
ISBN 978-1-902197-56-2
A Scorpionic Book
Published 2013 by Creation Oneiros, London UK
Copyright © Creation Oneiros

SEVEN FOOTPRINTS TO SATAN

5

THROUGH THE DRAGON GLASS

209

CHAPTER ONE

The clock was striking eight as I walked out of the doors of the Discoverers' Club and stood for a moment looking down lower Fifth Avenue. As I paused, I felt with full force that uncomfortable sensation of being watched that had both puzzled and harassed me for the past two weeks. A curiously prickly, cold feeling somewhere deep under the skin on the side that the watchers are located; an odd sort of tingling pressure. It is a queer sort of a sensitivity that I have in common with most men who spend much of their lives in the jungle or desert. It is a throwback to some primitive sixth sense, since all savages have it until they get introduced to the white man's liquor.

Trouble was I couldn't localize the sensation. It seemed to trickle in on me from all sides. I scanned the street. Three taxis were drawn up along the curb in front of the Club. They were empty and their drivers busy talking. There were no loiterers that I could see. The two swift side-rubbing streams of traffic swept up and down the Avenue. I studied the windows of the opposite houses. There was no sign in them of any watchers.

Yet eyes were upon me, intently. I knew it.

The warning had come to me in many places this last fortnight. I had felt the unseen watchers time and again in the Museum where I had gone to look at the Yunnan jades I had made it possible for rich old Rockbilt to put there with distinct increase to his reputation as a philanthropist; it had come to me in the theater and while riding in the Park; in the brokers' offices where I myself had watched the money the jades had brought me melt swiftly away in a game which I now ruefully admitted I knew less than nothing about. I had felt it in the streets, and that was to be expected. But I had also felt it at the Club, and that was not to be expected and it bothered me more than anything else.

Yes, I was under strictest surveillance. But why?

That was what this night I had determined to find out.

At a touch upon my shoulder, I jumped, and swept my hand

halfway up to the little automatic under my left armpit. By that, suddenly I realized how badly the mystery had gotten on my nerves. I turned, and grinned a bit sheepishly into the face of big Lars Thorwaldsen, back in New York only a few days from his two years in the Antarctic.

"Bit jerky, aren't you, Jim?" he asked. "What's the matter? Been on a bender?"

"Nothing like it, Lars," I answered. "Too much city, I guess. Too much continual noise and motion. And too many people," I added with a real candor he could not suspect.

"God!" he exclaimed. "It all looks good to me. I'm eating it up – after those two years. But I suppose in a month or two I'll be feeling the same way about it. I hear you're going away again soon. Where this time? Back to China?"

I shook my head. I did not feel like telling Lars that my destination was entirely controlled by whatever might turn up before I had spent the sixty-five dollars in my wallet and the seven quarters and two dimes in my pocket.

"Not in trouble, are you, Jim?" he looked at me more keenly. "If you are, I'd be glad to – help you."

I shook my head. Everybody knew that old Rockbilt had been unusually generous about those infernal jades. I had my pride, and staggered though I was by that amazingly rapid melting away of a golden deposit I had confidently expected to grow into a barrier against care for the rest of my life, make me, as a matter of fact, independent of all chance, I did not feel like telling even Lars of my folly. Besides, I was not yet that hopeless of all things, a beachcomber in New York. Something would turn up.

"Wait," he said, as some one called him back into the Club.

But I did not wait. Even less than baring my unfortunate gamble did I feel like telling about my watchers. I stepped down into the street.

Who was it that was watching me? And why? Some one from China who had followed after the treasure I had taken from the ancient tomb? I could not believe it. Kin-Wang, bandit though he might be, and accomplished graduate of American poker as well as of Cornell, would have sent no spies after me. Our, well – call it transaction, irregular as it had been, was finished in his mind when he had lost. Crooked as he might be with the cards, he was not the man to go back on his word. Of that I was sure. Besides, there had been no need of letting me get this far before striking. No, they were no emissaries of Kin-Wang.

There had been that mock arrest in Paris, designed to get me quickly out of the way for a few hours, as the ransacked condition of my room and baggage showed when I returned. A return undoubtedly much earlier than the thieves had planned, due to my discovery of the ruse and my surprise sally which left me with an uncomfortable knife slash under an arm but, I afterwards reflected pleasantly, had undoubtedly left one of my guards with a broken neck and another with a head that would not do much thinking for another month or so. Then there had been the second attempt when the auto in which I was rushing to the steamer had been held up between Paris and the Havre. That might have been successful had not the plaques been tucked among the baggage of an acquaintance who was going to the boat by the regular train, thinking, by the way, that he was carrying for me some moderately rare old dishes that I did not want to trust to the possible shocks of fast automobile travel, to which the mythical engagement on the day of sailing had condemned me.

Were the watchers this same gang? They must know that the jades were now out of my hands and safe in the museum. I could be of no further value to these disappointed gentlemen, unless, of course, they were after revenge. Yet that would hardly explain this constant, furtive, patient watching. And why hadn't they struck long before? Surely there had been plenty of opportunities.

Well, whoever the watchers were, I had determined to give them the most open of chances to get at me. I had paid all my bills. The sixty-six dollars and ninety-five cents in my pocket comprised all my worldly goods, but no one else had any claim on it. Whatever unknown port I was clearing for with severely bare sticks and decks, it was with no debts left behind.

Yes, I had determined to decoy my enemies, if enemies they were, out into the open. I had even made up my mind as to where it should be.

In all New York the loneliest spot at eight o'clock of an October night, or any night for that matter, is the one which by day is the most crowded on all the globe. Lower Broadway, empty then of all its hordes and its canyon-like cleft silent, its intersecting minor canyons emptier and quieter even than their desert kin. It was there that I would go.

As I turned down Fifth Avenue from the Discoverers' Club a man passed me, a man whose gait and carriage, figure and clothing, were oddly familiar.

I stood stock still, looking after him as he strolled leisurely up the steps and into the Club.

Then, queerly disturbed, I resumed my walk. There had been something peculiarly familiar, indeed disquietingly familiar, about that man. What was it? Making my way over to Broadway, I went down that street, always aware of the watchers.

But it was not until I was opposite City Hall that I realized what that truly weird familiarity had been. The realization came to me with a distinct shock.

In gait and carriage, in figure and clothing, from light brown overcoat, gray soft hat, to strong Malacca cane that man had been – Myself!

CHAPTER TWO

I stopped short. The natural assumption was, of course, that the resemblance had been a coincidence, extraordinary enough, but still – coincidence. Without doubt there were at least fifty men in New York who might easily be mistaken for me at casual glance. The chance, however, that one of them would be dressed precisely like me at any precise moment was almost nil. Yet it could be. What else could it be? What reason had any one to impersonate me?

But then, for that matter, what reason had any one to put a watch on me?

I hesitated, of half a mind to call a taxi, and return to the Club. Reason whispered to me that the glimpse I had gotten had been brief, that perhaps I had been deceived by the play of light and shadow, the resemblance been only an illusion. I cursed my jumpy nerves and went on.

Fewer and fewer became the people I passed as I left Cortlandt Street behind me. Trinity was like a country church at midnight. As the cliffs of the silent office buildings hemmed me I felt a smothering oppression, as though they were asleep and swaying in on me; their countless windows were like blind eyes. But if they were blind, those other eyes, that I had never for an instant felt leave me, were not. They seemed to become more intent, more watchful.

And now I met no one. Not a policeman, not even a watchman. The latter were, I knew, inside these huge stone forts of capital. I loitered at corners, giving every opportunity for the lurkers to step out, the invisible to become visible. And still I saw no one. And still the eyes never left me.

It was with a certain sense of disappointment that I reached the end of Broadway and looked out over Battery Park. It was deserted. I walked down to the Harbor wall and sat upon a bench. A ferryboat gliding toward Staten Island was like some great golden water bug. The full moon poured a rivulet of rippling silver fire upon the waves. It was very still – so still that I could faintly hear Trinity's bells chiming nine o'clock.

I had heard no one approach, but suddenly I was aware of a man sitting beside me and a pleasant voice asking me for a match. As the flame flared up to meet his cigarette, I saw a dark, ascetic face, smooth-shaven, the mouth and eyes kindly and the latter a bit weary, as though from study. The hand that held the match was long and slender and beautifully kept. It gave the impression of unusual strength – a surgeon's hand or a sculptor's. A professional man certainly, I conjectured. The thought was strengthened by his Inverness coat and his soft, dark hat. In the broad shoulders under the cloak of the coat was further suggestion of a muscular power much beyond the ordinary.

"A beautiful night, sir," he tossed the match from him. "A night for adventure. And behind us a city in which any adventure is possible."

I looked at him more closely. It was an odd remark, considering that I had unquestionably started out that night for adventure. But was it so odd after all? Perhaps it was only my overstimulated suspicion that made it seem so. He could not possibly have known what had drawn me to this silent place. And the kindly eyes and the face made me almost instantly dismiss the thought. Some scholar this, perhaps, grateful for the quietness of the Park.

"That ferryboat yonder," he pointed, seemingly unaware of my scrutiny. "It is an argosy of potential adventure. Within it are mute Alexanders, inglorious Caesars and Napoleons, incomplete Jasons each almost able to retrieve some Golden Fleece – yes, and incomplete Helens and Cleopatras, all lacking only one thing to round them out and send them forth to conquer."

"Lucky for the world they're incomplete, then," I laughed. "How long would it be before all these Napoleons and Caesars and Cleopatras and all the rest of them were at each other's throats – and the whole world on fire?"

"Never," he said, very seriously. "Never, that is, if they were under the control of a will and an intellect greater than the sum total of all their wills and intellects. A mind greater than all of them to plan for all of them, a will more powerful than all their wills to force them to carry out those plans exactly as the greater mind had conceived them."

"The result, sir," I objected, "would seem to me to be not the super-pirates, super-thieves and super-courtesans you have cited, but super-slaves."

"Less slaves than at any time in history," he replied. "The personages I have suggested as types were always under control of Destiny – or God, if you prefer the term. The will and intellect I have in mind would profit, since its house would be a human brain, by the mistakes of blind, mechanistic Destiny or of a God who surely, if he exists, has too many varying worlds to look after to give minute attention to individuals of the countless species that crawl over them. No, it would use the talents of its servants to the utmost, not waste them. It would suitably and justly reward them, and when it punished – its punishments would be just. It would not scatter a thousand seeds haphazardly on the chance that a few would find fertile ground and grow. It would select the few, and see that they fell on fertile ground and that nothing prevented their growing."

"Such a mind would have to be greater than Destiny, or, if you prefer the term, God," I said. "I repeat that it seems to me a super-slavery and that it's mighty lucky for the world that no such mind exists."

"Ah!" he drew at his cigarette, thoughtfully, "but, you see – it does."

"Yes?" I stared at him, wondering if he were joking. "Where?"

"That," he answered, coolly, "you shall soon know – Mr. Kirkham."

"You know me!" for one amazed moment I thought that I could not have heard aright.

"Very well," he said. "And that mind whose existence you doubt knows – all of you there is to know. He summons you! Come, Kirkham, it is time for us to go!"

So! I had met what I had started out to find! They, whoever they were, had come out into the open at last.

"Wait a bit." I felt my anger stir at the arrogance of the

hitherto courteous voice. "Whoever you may be or whoever he may be who sent you, neither of you knows me as well as you seem to think. Let me tell you that I go nowhere unless I know where it is I'm going, and I meet no one unless I choose. Tell me then where you want me to go, who it is I'm to meet and the reason for it. When you do that, I'll decide whether or not I'll answer this, what did you call it – summons."

He had listened to me quietly. Now his hand shot out and caught my wrist. I had run across many strong men, but never one with a grip like that. My cane dropped from my paralyzed grasp.

"You have been told all that is necessary," he said, coldly. "And you are going with me – now!"

He loosed my wrist, and shaking with rage I jumped to my feet.

"Damn you," I cried. "I go where I please when I please–" I stooped to pick up my cane. Instantly his arms were around me.

"You go," he whispered, "where he who sent me pleases and when he pleases!"

I felt his hands swiftly touching me here and there. I could no more have broken away from him than if I had been a kitten. He found the small automatic under my left armpit and drew it out of its holster. Quickly as he had seized me, he released me and stepped back. "Come," he ordered.

I stood, considering him and the situation. No one has ever had occasion to question my courage, but courage, to my way of thinking, has nothing whatever to do with bull-headed rashness. Courage is the cool weighing of the factors of an emergency within whatever time limit your judgment tells you that you have, and then the putting of every last ounce of brain, nerve and muscle into the course chosen. I had not the slightest doubt that this mysterious messenger had men within instant call. If I threw myself on him, what good would it do? I had only my cane. He had my gun and probably weapons of his own. Strong as I am, he had taught me that my strength was nothing to his. It might even be that he was counting upon an attack by me, that it was what he hoped for.

True, I could cry out for help or I could run. Not only did both of these expedients seem to me to be ridiculous, but, in view of the certainty of his hidden aides, useless.

Not far away were the subway stations and the elevated road. In that brilliantly lighted zone I would be comparatively safe from any concerted attack – if I could get there. I began to walk away across the Park toward Whitehall Street.

To my surprise he made neither objection nor comment. He paced quietly beside me. Soon we were out of the Battery and not far ahead were the lights of the Bowling Green Station. My resentment and anger diminished, a certain amusement took their place. Obviously it was absurd to suppose that in New York City anyone could be forced to go anywhere against his will, once he was in the usual close touch with its people and its police. To be snatched away from a subway station was almost unthinkable, to be kidnapped from the subway once we got in it absolutely unthinkable. Why then was my companion so placidly allowing each step to take me closer to this unassailable position?

It would have been so easy to have overpowered me just a few moments before. Or why had I not been approached at the Club? There were a dozen possible ways in which I could have been lured away from there.

There seemed only one answer. There was some paramount need for secrecy. A struggle in the Park might have brought the police. Overtures at the Club might have left evidence behind had I disappeared. How utterly outside the mark all this reasoning was I was soon to learn.

As we drew closer to the Bowling Green entrance of the subway, I saw a policeman standing there. I admit without shame that his scenic effect warmed my heart.

"Listen," I said to my companion. "There's a bluecoat. Slip my gun back into my pocket. Leave me here and go your way. If you do that, I say nothing. If you don't I'm going to order that policeman to lock you up. They'll have the Sullivan Law on you if nothing else. Go away quietly and, if you want to, get in touch with me at the

Discoverers' Club. I'll forget all this and talk to you. But don't try any more of the rough stuff or I'll be getting good and mad."

He smiled at me, as at some child, his face and eyes again all kindness. But he did not go. Instead, he linked his arm firmly in mine and led me straight to the officer. And as we came within earshot he said to me, quite loudly:

"Now come, Henry. You've had your little run. I'm sure you don't want to give this busy officer any trouble. Come, Henry! Be good!"

The policeman stepped forward, looking us over. I did not know whether to laugh or grow angry again. Before I could speak, the man in the Inverness had handed the bluecoat a card. He read it, touched his hat respectfully and asked:

"And what's the trouble, doctor?"

"Sorry to bother you, officer," my astonishing companion answered. "But I'll ask you to help me a bit. My young friend here is one of my patients. War case – aviator. He hurt his head in a crash in France and just now he thinks he is James Kirkham, an explorer. Actually, his name is Henry Walton."

The bluecoat looked at me, doubtfully. I smiled, in my certain security.

"Go on!" I said. "What else do I think?"

"He's quite harmless," he gently patted my shoulder, "but now and then he manages to slip away from us. Yes, harmless, but very ingenious. He evaded us this evening. I sent my men out to trace him. I found him myself down there in the Battery. At such times, officer, he believes he is in danger of being kidnapped. That's what he wants to tell you – that I am kidnapping him. Will you kindly listen to him, officer, and assure him that such a thing is impossible in New York. Or, if possible, that kidnappers do not conduct their captives up to a New York policeman as I have."

I could but admire the deftness of the story, the half humorous and yet patient, wholly professional manner in which he told it. Safe now as I thought myself, I could afford to laugh, and I did.

"Quite right, officer," I said. "Only it happens that my name really is James Kirkham. I never even heard of this Henry Walton. I never saw this man here until tonight. And I have every reason in the world to know that he is trying to force me to go somewhere that I have no intention whatever of going."

"You see!" My companion nodded meaningly to the policeman, who, far from answering my smiles, looked at me with an irritating sympathy.

"I wouldn't worry," he assured me. "As the good doctor says, kidnappers don't hunt up the police. Ye couldn't be kidnapped in New York – at least not this way. Now go right along wit' the doctor, an' don't ye worry no more."

It was time to terminate the absurd matter. I thrust my hand into my pocket, brought out my wallet and dipped into it for my card. I picked out one and with it a letter or two and handed them to the bluecoat.

"Perhaps these identifications will give you another slant," I said.

He took them, read them carefully, and handed them back to me, pityingly.

"Sure, lad," his tone was soothing. "Ye're in no danger. I'm tellin' ye. Would ye want a taxi, doctor?"

I stared at him in amazement, and then down to the card and envelopes he had returned to me. I read them once and again, unbelievingly.

For the card bore the name of "Henry Walton," and each of the envelopes was addressed to that same gentleman "in care of Dr. Michael Consardine" at an address that I recognized as a settlement of the highest-priced New York specialists up in the seventies. Nor was the wallet I held in my hand the one with which I had started this eventful stroll a little more than an hour before.

I opened my coat and glanced down into the inner pocket for the tailor's label that bore my name. There was no label there.

Very abruptly my sense of security fled. I began to realize that it might be possible to force me to go where I did not want to, after all. Even from a New York Subway station.

"Officer," I said, and there was no laughter now in my voice, "you are making a great mistake. I met this man a few minutes ago in Battery Park. I give you my word he is an utter stranger to me. He insisted that I follow him to some place whose location he refused to tell, to meet some one whose name he would not reveal. When I refused, he struggled with me, ostensibly searching for weapons. During that struggle it is now plain that he substituted this wallet containing the cards and envelopes bearing the name of Henry Walton in the place of my own. I demand that you search him for my wallet, and then whether you find it or not, I demand that you take us both to Headquarters."

The bluecoat looked at me doubtfully. My earnestness and apparent sanity had shaken him. Neither my appearance nor my manner was that of even a slightly unbalanced person. But on the other hand the benign face, the kindly eyes, the unmistakable refinement and professionalism of the man of the Battery bench were as far apart as the poles from the puzzled officer's conception of a kidnapper.

"I'm perfectly willing to be examined at Headquarters – and even searched there," said the man in the Inverness. "Only I must warn you that all the excitement will certainly react very dangerously on my patient. However – call a taxi–"

"No taxi," I said firmly. "We go in the patrol wagon, with police around us."

"Wait a minute," the bluecoat's face brightened. "Here comes the Sergeant. He'll decide what to do." The Sergeant walked up.

"What's the trouble, Mooney?" he asked, looking us over. Succinctly, Mooney explained the situation. The Sergeant studied us again more closely. I grinned at him cheerfully.

"All I want," I told him, "is to be taken to Headquarters. In a patrol wagon. No taxi, Dr. – – what was it? Oh, yes, Consardine. Patrol wagon with plenty of police, and Dr. Consardine sitting in it with me – that's all I want."

"It's all right, Sergeant," said Dr. Consardine, patiently. "I'm quite ready to go. But as I warned Officer Mooney, it means delay and excitement and you must accept the responsibility for the effect upon my patient, whose care is, after all, my first concern. I have said he is harmless, but tonight I took from him – this."

He handed the Sergeant the small automatic.

"Under his left arm you will find its holster," said Consardine. "Frankly, I think it best to get him back to my sanatorium as quickly as possible."

The Sergeant stepped close to me and throwing back my coat, felt under my left arm. I knew by his face as he touched the holster that Consardine had scored.

"I have a license to carry a gun," I said, tartly.

"Where is it?" he asked.

"In the wallet that man took from me when he lifted the gun," I answered. "If you'll search him you'll find it."

"Oh, poor lad! Poor lad!" murmured Consardine. And so sincere seemed his distress that I was half inclined to feel sorry for myself. He spoke again to the Sergeant.

"I think perhaps the matter can be settled without running the risk of the journey to Headquarters. As Officer Mooney has told you, my patient's present delusion is that he is a certain James Kirkham and living at the Discoverers' Club. It may be that the real Mr. Kirkham is there at this moment. I therefore suggest that you call up the Discoverers' Club and ask for him. If Mr. Kirkham is there, I take it that will end the matter. If not, we will go to Headquarters."

The Sergeant looked at me, and I looked at Consardine, amazed.

"If you can talk to James Kirkham at the Discoverers' Club," I said at last, "then I'm Henry Walton!"

We walked over to a telephone booth. I gave the Sergeant the number of the Club.

"Ask for Robert," I interposed. "He's the desk man."

I had talked to Robert a few minutes before I had gone out. He would still be on duty.

"Is that Robert? At the desk?" the Sergeant asked as the call came through. "Is Mr. James Kirkham there? This is Police Sergeant Downey."

There was a pause. He glanced at me.

"They're paging Kirkham," he muttered – then to the phone – "What's that? You are James Kirkham! A moment, please – put that clerk back. Hello – you Robert? That party I'm talking to Kirkham? Kirkham the explorer? You're certain? All right – all right! Don't get excited about it. I'll admit you know him. Put him back – Hello, Mr. Kirkham? No, it's all right. Just a case of – er – bugs! Man thinks he's you–"

I snatched the receiver from his hand, lifted it to my ear and heard a voice saying:

"–Not the first time, poor devil–"

The voice was my very own!

CHAPTER THREE

The receiver was taken from me, gently enough. Now the Sergeant was listening again. Mooney had me by one arm, the man in the Inverness by the other. I heard the Sergeant say:

"Yes – Walton, Henry Walton, yes, that's the name. Sorry to have troubled you, Mr. Kirkham. Goo'-by."

He snapped up the 'phone and regarded me, compassionately.

"Too bad!" he said. "It's a damned shame. Do you want an ambulance, doctor?"

"No, thanks," answered Consardine. "It's a peculiar case. The kidnapping delusion is a strong one. He'll be quieter with people around him. We'll go up on the subway. Even though his normal self is not in control, his subconscious will surely tell him that kidnapping is impossible in the midst of a subway crowd. Now, Henry," he patted my hand, "admit that it is. You are beginning to realize it already, aren't you–"

I broke out of my daze. The man who had passed me on Fifth Avenue! The man who had so strangely resembled me! Fool that I was not to have thought of that before! "Wait, officer," I cried desperately. "That was an impostor at the Club – some one made up to look like me. I saw him–"

"There, there, lad," he put a hand on my shoulder reassuringly. "You gave your word. You're not going to welch on it, I'm sure. You're all right. I'm telling you. Go with the doctor, now."

For the first time I had the sense of futility. This net spreading around me had been woven with infernal ingenuity. Apparently no contingency had been overlooked. I felt the shadow of a grim oppression. If those so interested in me, or in my withdrawal, wished it, how easy would it be to obliterate me. If this double of mine could dupe the clerk who had known me for years and mix in with my friends at the Club without detection – if he could do this, what could he not do in my name and in my guise? A touch of ice went through my blood. Was that the plot? Was I to be removed so this double could take my place in my world for a time to perpetrate some villainy that would blacken forever my memory? The situation was no longer humorous. It was heavy with evil possibilities.

But the next step in my involuntary journey was to be the subway. As Consardine had said, no sane person would believe a man could be kidnapped there. Surely there, if anywhere, I could escape, find some one in the crowds who would listen to me, create if necessary such a scene that it would be impossible for my captor to hold me, outwit him somehow.

At any rate there was nothing to do but go with him. Further appeal to these two policemen was useless.

"Let's go – doctor," I said, quietly. We started down the subway steps, his arm in mine.

We passed through the gates. A train was waiting. 1 went into the last car, Consardine at my heels. It was empty. I marched on. In the second car was only a nondescript passenger or two. But as I neared the third car I saw at the far end half a dozen marines with a second lieutenant. My pulse quickened. Here was the very opportunity I had been seeking. I made straight for them.

As I entered the car I was vaguely aware of a couple sitting in the corner close to the door. Intent upon reaching the leathernecks, I paid no attention to them.

Before I had gone five steps I heard a faint scream, then a cry of–

"Harry! Oh, Dr. Consardine! You've found him!"

Involuntarily, I halted and turned. A girl was running toward me. She threw her arms around my neck and cried again:

"Harry! Harry! dear! Oh, thank God he found you!"

Two of the loveliest brown eyes I had ever beheld looked up at me. They were deep and tender and pitying, and tears trembled on the long black lashes. Even in my consternation I took note of the delicate skin untouched by rouge, the curly, silken fine bobbed hair under the smart little hat – hair touched with warm bronze glints, the nose a bit uplifted and the exquisite mouth and elfinly pointed chin. Under other circumstances, exactly the girl I would have given much to meet; under the present circumstances, well – disconcerting.

"There! There, Miss Walton!" Dr. Consardine's voice was benignly soothing. "Your brother is all right now!"

"Now, Eve, don't fuss any more. The doctor found him just as I told you he would."

It was a third voice, that of the other occupant of the corner seat. He was a man of about my own age, exceedingly well dressed, the face rather thin and tanned, a touch of dissipation about his eyes and mouth.

"How are you feeling, Harry?" he asked me, and added, somewhat gruffly, "Devil of a chase you've given us this time, I must say."

"Now, Walter," the girl rebuked him, "what matter, so he is safe?"

I disengaged the girl's arms and looked at the three of them. Outwardly they were exactly what they purported to be – an earnest, experienced, expensive specialist anxious about a recalcitrant patient with a defective mentality, a sweet, worried sister almost overcome with glad relief that her mind-sick runaway brother had been found, a trusty friend, perhaps a fiance, a bit put out, but still eighteen-carat faithful and devoted and so glad that his sweetheart's worry was over that he was ready to hand me a wallop if I began again to misbehave. So convincing were they that for one insane moment I doubted my own identity. Was I, after all, Jim Kirkham? Maybe I'd only read about him! My mind rocked with the possibility that I might be this Henry Walton whose wits had been scrambled by some accident in France.

It was with distinct effort that I banished the idea. This couple had, of course, been planted in the station and waiting for me to appear. But in the name of all far-seeing devils how could it have been foretold that I would appear at that very station at that very time?

And suddenly one of Consardine's curious phrases returned to me:

"A mind greater than all to plan for all of them; a will greater than all their wills–"

Cobwebs seemed to be dropping around me, cobwebs whose

multitudinous strands were held by one master hand, and pulling me, pulling me – irresistibly...where...and to what?

I turned and faced the marines. They were staring at us with absorbed interest. The lieutenant was on his feet, and now he came toward us.

"Anything I can do for you, sir?" he asked Consardine, but his eyes were on the girl and filled with admiration. And at that moment I knew that I could expect no help from him or his men. Nevertheless, it was I who answered.

"You can," I said. "My name is James Kirkham. I live at the Discoverers' Club. I don't expect you to believe me, but these people are kidnapping me–"

"Oh, Harry, Harry!" murmured the girl and touched her eyes with a foolish little square of lace.

"All that I ask you to do," I went on, "is to call up the Discoverers' Club when you leave this car. Ask for Lars Thorwaldsen, tell him what you have seen, and say I told you that the man at the Club who calls himself James Kirkham is an impostor. Will you do that?"

"Oh, Dr. Consardine," sobbed the girl. "Oh, poor, poor brother!"

"Will you come with me a moment, lieutenant?" asked Consardine. He spoke to the man who had called the girl Eve – "Watch; Walter – look after Harry–"

He touched the lieutenant's arm and they walked to the front of the car.

"Sit down, Harry, old man," urged Walter.

"Please, dear," said the girl. A hand of each of them on my arms, they pressed me into a seat.

I made no resistance. A certain grim wonder had come to me. I watched Consardine and the lieutenant carry on a whispered conversation to which the latter's leathernecks aimed eager ears. I knew the story Consardine was telling, for I saw the officer's face soften, and he and his men glanced at me pityingly; at the girl, compassionately. The lieutenant asked some question, Consardine nodded acquiescence and the pair walked back.

"Old man," the lieutenant spoke to me soothingly, "of course I'll do what you ask. We get off at the Bridge and I'll go to the first telephone. Discoverers' Club, you said?"

It would have been wonderful if I had not known that he thought he was humoring a lunatic.

I nodded, wearily.

"'Tell it to the marines,'" I quoted. "The man who said that knew what he was talking about. Invincible but dumb. Of course, you'll not do it. But if a spark of intelligence should miraculously light up your mind tonight or even tomorrow, please phone as I asked."

"Oh, Harry! Please be quiet!" implored the girl. She turned her eyes, eloquent with gratitude, to the lieutenant. "I'm sure the lieutenant will do exactly as he has promised."

"Indeed I will," he assured me – and half winked at her.

I laughed outright, I couldn't help it. No heart of any marine I had ever met, officer or otherwise, could have withstood that look of Eve's – so appealing, so grateful, so wistfully appreciative.

"All right, lieutenant," I said. "I don't blame you a bit. I bet myself I couldn't be kidnapped under a New York cop's eye at a subway entrance. But I lost. Then I bet myself I couldn't be kidnapped in a subway train. And again I've lost. Nevertheless, if you should get wondering whether I'm crazy or not, take a chance, lieutenant, and call up the Club."

"Oh, brother," breathed Eve, and wept once more.

I sank back into my seat, waiting another opportunity. The girl kept her hand on mine, her eyes, intermittently, on the leatherneck lieutenant. Consardine had seated himself at my right. Walter sat at Eve's side.

At Brooklyn Bridge the marines got out, with many backward looks at us. I saluted the lieutenant sardonically; the girl sent him a beautifully grateful smile. If anything else had been needed to make him forget my appeal it was that.

Quite a crowd piled on the car at the Bridge. I watched them hopefully, as they stampeded into the seats. The hopefulness faded steadily as I studied their faces. Sadly I realized that old Vanderbilt had been all wrong when he had said, "The public be damned." What he ought to have said was "The public be dumb."

There was a Hebraic delegation of a half dozen on their way home to the Bronx, a belated stenographer who at once began operations with a lipstick, three rabbit-faced young hoods, an Italian woman with four restless children, a dignified old gentleman who viewed their movements with suspicion, a plain-looking Negro, a rather pleasant-appearing man of early middle age with a woman who might have been a school teacher, two giggling girls who at once began flirting with the hoods, a laborer, three possible clerks and a scattering dozen of assorted morons. The typical New York subway train congregation. A glance at right and left of me assayed no richer residue of human intelligence.

There was no use in making an appeal to these people. My three guardians were too far ahead of them in gray matter and resourcefulness. They could make it abortive before I was half finished. But I might drop that suggestion of calling up the Club. Someone, I argued, might have their curiosity sufficiently developed to risk a phone call. I fixed my gaze on the dignified old gentleman – be seemed the type who possibly would not be able to rest until he had found out what it was all about.

And just as I was opening my mouth to speak to him, the girl patted my hand and leaned across me to the man in the Inverness.

"Doctor," her voice was very clear and of a carrying quality that made it audible throughout the car. "Doctor, Harry seems so much better. Shall I give him – you know what?"

"An excellent idea, Miss Walton," he answered. "Give it to him."

The girl reached under her long sport coat and brought out a small bundle.

"Here, Harry," she handed it to me. "Here's your little playmate – who's been so lonely without you."

Automatically I took the bundle and tore it open.

Into my hands dropped out a dirty, hideous old rag-doll!

As I looked at it, stupefied, there came to me complete perception of the truly devilish cunning of those who had me in their trap. The very farcicality of that doll had a touch of terror in it. At the girl's clear voice, all the car had centered their attention upon us. I saw the dignified old gentleman staring at me unbelievingly over his spectacles, saw Consardine catch his eye and tap his forehead significantly – and so did every one else see him. The Negro's guffaw suddenly stopped. The Hebraic group stiffened up and gaped at me; the stenographer dropped her vanity case; the Italian children goggled at the doll, fascinated. The middle-aged couple looked away, embarrassed.

I realized that I was on my feet, clutching the doll as though I feared it was to be taken from me.

"Hell!" I swore, and lifted it to dash it to the floor.

And suddenly I knew that any further resistance, and further struggle, was useless.

The game was rigged up against me all the way through the deck. For the moment I might as well throw down my hand. I was going, as Consardine had told me, where the "greater intellect and will" pleased, whether it pleased me or not. Also I was going when it pleased. And that was now.

Well, they had played with me long enough. I would throw my hand down, but as I sat back I would have a little diversion myself.

I dropped into my seat, sticking the doll in my upper pocket where its head protruded grotesquely. The dignified old gentleman was making commiserating clucking noises and shaking his head understandingly at Consardine. One of the rabbit-faced youths said "Nuts" and the girls giggled nervously. The Negro hastily got up and retreated to the next car. One of the Italian children pointed to the doll and whined, "Gimme."

I took the girl's hand in both of mine.

"Eve, darling," I said, as distinctly as she had spoken, "you know I ran away because I don't like Walter there."

I put my arm around her waist.

"Walter," I leaned over her, "no man like you just out of

prison for what was, God knows, a justly deserved sentence, is worthy of my Eve. No matter how crazy I may be, surely you know that is true."

The old gentleman stopped his annoying clucking and looked startled. The rest of the car turned its attention like him, to Walter. I had the satisfaction of seeing a slow flush creep up his cheeks.

"Dr. Consardine," I turned to him, "as a medical man you are familiar with the stigmata, I mean the marks, of the born criminal. Look at Walter. The eyes small and too close together, the mouth's hardness deplorably softened by certain appetites, the undeveloped lobes of the ears. If I ought not be running loose – how much less ought he to be, doctor?"

Every eye in the car was taking in each point as I called attention to it. And each happened to be a little true. The flush on Walter's face deepened to a brick red. Consardine looked at me, imperturbably.

"No," I went on, "not at all the man for you, Eve."

I gripped the girl closer. I drew her tightly to me. I was beginning to enjoy myself – and she was marvelously pretty.

"Eve!" I exclaimed. "All this time I've been away from you – and you haven't even kissed me!"

I lifted up her chin and – well, I kissed her. Kissed her properly and in no brotherly manner. I heard Walter cursing under his breath. How Consardine was taking it I could not tell. Indeed I did not care – Eve's mouth was very sweet.

I kissed her again and again – to the chuckles of the hoods, the giggles of the girls, and horrified exclamations of the dignified old gentleman.

And the girl's face, which at the first of my kisses had gone all rosy red, turned white. She did not resist, but between kisses I heard her whisper:

"You'll pay for this! Oh, but you'll pay for this!"

I laughed and released her. I did not care now. I was going to go with Dr. Consardine wherever he wanted to take me – as long as she went with me.

"Harry," his voice broke my thought, "come along. Here is our station."

The train was slowing up for the Fourteenth Street stop. Consardine arose. His eyes signaled the girl. Her own eyes downcast, she took my hand. Her hand was like ice. I got up, still laughing. Consardine at my other side, Walter guarding the rear, I walked out upon the platform and up the steps to the street. Once I looked behind me into Walter's face, and my heart warmed at the murder in it.

It had been touche for me with two of them at any rate – and at their own game.

A chauffeur in livery stood at the top of the steps. He gave me a quick, curious glance and saluted Consardine.

"This way – Kirkham!" said the latter, curtly.

So I was Kirkham again! And what did that mean?

A powerful car stood at the curb. Consardine gestured. Eve's hand firmly clasped in mine, I entered, drawing her after me. Walter had gone ahead of us. Consardine followed. The chauffeur closed the door. I saw another liveried figure on the driver's seat. The car started.

Consardine touched a lever and down came the curtains, closeting us in semi-darkness.

And as he did so the girl Eve wrenched her hand from mine, struck me a stinging blow across the lips and huddling down in her corner began silently to weep.

CHAPTER FOUR

The cab, one of expensive European make, sped smoothly over to Fifth Avenue and turned north. Consardine touched another lever and a curtain dropped between us and the driving seat. There was a hidden bulb that shed a dim glow.

By it I saw that the girl had recovered her poise. She sat regarding the tips of her shapely narrow shoes. Walter drew out a cigarette case. I followed suit.

"You do not mind, Eve?" I asked solicitously.

She neither looked at me nor answered. Consardine was apparently lost in thought. Walter stared icily over my head. I lighted my cigarette and concentrated upon our course. My watch registered a quarter to ten.

The tightly shaded windows gave no glimpse of our surroundings. By the traffic stops I knew we were still on the Avenue. Then the car began a series of turns and twists as though it were being driven along side streets. Once it seemed to make a complete circle. I lost all sense of direction, which, I reflected, was undoubtedly what was intended.

At 10:15 the car began to go at greatly increased speed and I judged we were out of heavy traffic. Soon a cooler, fresher air came through the ventilators. We might be either in Westchester or Long Island. I could not tell.

It was precisely 11:20 when the car came to a stop. After a short pause it went on again. I heard from behind us the clang of heavy metal gates. For perhaps ten minutes more we rolled on swiftly and then halted again. Consardine awoke from his reverie and snapped up the curtains. The chauffeur opened the door. Eve dropped out, and after her Walter.

"Well, here we are, Mr. Kirkham," said Consardine, affably. He might have been a pleased host bringing home a thrice-welcome guest instead of a man he had abducted by outrageous wiles and falsehoods.

I jumped out. Under the moon, grown storm-promising and watery as a drunkard's eye, I saw an immense building that was like some chateau transplanted from the Loire. Lights gleamed brilliantly here and there in wings and turrets. Through its doors were passing the girl and Walter. I glanced around me. There were no lights visible anywhere except those of the chateau. I had the impression of remoteness and of wide, tree-filled spaces hemming the place in and guarding its isolation.

Consardine took my arm and we passed over the threshold. On each side stood two tall footmen and as I went by them I perceived that they were Arabs, extraordinarily powerful. But when I had gotten within the great hall I stopped short with an involuntary exclamation of admiration.

It was as though the choicest treasures of medieval France had been skimmed of their best and that best concentrated here. The long galleries, a third of the way up to the high vaulted ceiling, were exquisite Gothic arrases and tapestries whose equals few museums could show hung from them and the shields and arms were those of conquering kings.

Consardine gave me no time to study them. He touched my arm and I saw beside me an impeccably correct English valet.

"Thomas will look after you now," said Consardine. "See you later, Kirkham."

"This way, sir, if you please," bowed the valet, and led me into a miniature chapel at the side of the hall. He pressed against its fretted back. It slid away and we entered a small elevator. When it stopped, another panel slipped aside. I stepped into a bedroom furnished, in its own fashion, with the same astonishing richness as the great hall. Behind heavy curtains was a bathroom.

Upon the bed lay dress trousers, shirt, cravat, and so on. In a few minutes I was washed, freshly shaved and in evening clothes. They fitted me perfectly. As the valet opened a closet door a coat hanging there drew my sharp attention. I peered in.

Hanging within that closet was the exact duplicate of every garment that made up my wardrobe at the Club. Yes, there they were, and as I looked into the pockets for the tailor's labels I saw written on them my own name.

I had an idea that the valet, watching me covertly, was waiting for some expression of surprise. If so he was disappointed. My capacity for surprise was getting a bit numb.

"And now where do I go?" I asked.

For answer he slid the panel aside and stood waiting for me to enter the lift. When it stopped I expected of course to step out into the great hall. Instead of that the opening panel revealed a small anteroom, oak paneled, bare and with a door of darker oak set in its side. Here was another tall Arab, evidently awaiting me, for the valet bowed me out of the elevator and re-entering, disappeared.

The Arab salaamed. Opening the door, he salaamed again. I walked over its threshold. A clock began to chime midnight.

"Welcome, James Kirkham! You are punctual to the minute," said some one.

The voice was strangely resonant and musical, with a curious organ quality. The speaker sat at the head of a long table where places were laid for three. That much I saw before I looked into his eyes, and then for a time could see nothing else. For those eyes were of the deepest sapphire blue and they were the alivest eyes I had ever beheld. They were large, slightly oblique, and they sparkled as though the very spring of life was bubbling up behind them. Gem-like they were in color, and gem-like were they in their hardness. They were lashless, and as unwinking as a bird's – or a snake's.

It was with distinct effort that I tore my gaze from them and took note of the face in which they were set. The head above them was inordinately large, high and broad and totally bald. It was an astonishing hemisphere whose capacity must have been almost double that of the average. The ears were long and narrow and distinctly pointed at the tips. The nose was heavy and beaked, the chin round but massive. The lips were full, and as classically cut and immobile as of some antique Greek statue. The whole huge, round face was of a marble pallor, and it was unwrinkled, unlined and expressionless. The only thing alive about it were the eyes, and alive indeed they were –

uncannily, terrifyingly so.

His body, what I could see of it, was unusually large, the enormous barrel of the chest indicating tremendous vitality.

Even at first contact one sensed the abnormal, and the radiation of inhuman power.

"Be seated, James Kirkham," the sonorous voice rolled out again. A butler emerged from the shadows at his back and drew out for me the chair at the left.

I bowed to this amazing host of mine and seated myself silently.

"You must be hungry after your long ride," he said. "It was good of you, James Kirkham, thus to honor this whim of mine."

I looked at him sharply but could detect no sign of mockery.

"I am indebted to you, sir," I answered, as urbanely, "for an unusually entertaining journey. And as for humoring what you are pleased to call your whim, how, sir, could I have done otherwise when you sent messengers so – ah – eloquent?"

"Ah, yes," he nodded. "Dr. Consardine is indeed a singularly persuasive person. He will join us presently. But drink – eat."

The butler poured champagne. I lifted my glass and paused, staring at it with delight. It was a goblet of rock crystal, exquisitely cut, extremely ancient I judged – a jewel and priceless.

"Yes," said my host, as though I had spoken. "Truly one of a rare set. They were the drinking glasses of the Caliph Haroun-al-Raschid. When I drink from them I seem to see him surrounded by his beloved cup-companions amid the glories of his court in old Bagdad. All the gorgeous panorama of the Arabian Nights spreads out before me. They were preserved for me," he went on, thoughtfully, "by the late Sultan Abdul Hamid. At least they were his until I felt the desire to possess them."

"You must have exercised great – ah – persuasion, sir, to have made the Sultan part from them," I murmured.

"As you have remarked, James Kirkham, my messengers are – eloquent," he replied, suavely.

I took a sip of the wine and could not for the life of me hide my pleasure.

"Yes," intoned my strange host, "a rare vintage. It was intended for the exclusive use of King Alfonso of Spain. But again my messengers were – eloquent. When I drink it my admiration for its excellences is shadowed only by my sympathy for Alfonso in his deprivation."

I drank that wine, worshipfully. I attacked with relish a delicious cold bird. My eye was caught by the lines of a golden compote set with precious stones. So exquisite was it that I half arose to examine it more closely.

"Benvenuto Cellini made it," observed my host. "It is one of his masterpieces. Italy kept it for me through the centuries."

"But Italy would never voluntarily have let a thing like that go from her!" I exclaimed.

"No, quite involuntarily, oh quite, I assure you," he answered, blandly.

I began to glance about the dimly lighted room and realized that here, like the great hall, was another amazing treasure chamber. If half of what my eyes took in was genuine, the contents of that room alone were worth millions. But they could not be – not even an American billionaire could have gathered such things.

"But they are genuine," again he read my thoughts. "I am a connoisseur indeed – the greatest in the world. Not alone of paintings, and of gems and wines and other masterpieces of man's genius. I am a connoisseur of men and women. A collection of what, loosely, are called souls. That is why, James Kirkham, you are here!"

The butler filled the goblets and placed another bottle in the iced pail beside me; he put liqueurs and cigars upon the table and then, as though at some signal, he withdrew. He disappeared, I noted with interest, through still another wall panel that masked one of the hidden lifts. I saw that he was a Chinese.

"Manchu," observed my host. "Of princely rank. Yet he thinks to be my servant the greater honor."

I nodded casually, as though the matter were commonplace and butlers who were Manchu princes, wine lifted from King Alfonso, goblets of an Arabian Nights' Caliph and Cellini compotes everyday affairs. I realized that the game which had begun in Battery Park a few hours before had reached its second stage and I was determined to maintain my best poker face and manner.

"You please me, James Kirkham," the voice was totally devoid of expression, the lips scarcely moved as it rolled forth. "You are thinking – 'I am a prisoner, my place in the outer world is being filled by a double whom even my closest friends do not suspect of being other than I; this man speaking is a monster, ruthless and conscienceless, a passionless intellect which could – and would – blow me out if he desired as carelessly as he would blow out a candle flame.' In all that, James Kirkham, you are right."

He paused. I found it better not to look into those jewel-bright blue eyes. I lighted a cigarette and nodded, fixing my attention on the glowing tip.

"Yes, you are right," he went on. "Yet you ask no questions and make no appeals. Your voice and hands are steady, your eyes untroubled. But back of all, your brain is keenly alert, poised on tiptoe to seize some advantage. You are feeling out for danger with the invisible antennae of your nerves like any jungleman. Every sense is alive to catch some break in the net you feel around you. There is a touch of terror upon you. Yet outwardly you show no slightest sign of all this – only I could detect it. You please me greatly, James Kirkham. Yours is the true gambler's soul!"

He paused again, studying me over the rim of his goblet. I forced myself to meet his gaze and smile.

"You are now thirty-five," he continued. "I have watched you for years. I was first attracted to you by your work in the French Espionage Service during the second year of the war."

My fingers stiffened involuntarily about my glass. None, I had thought, had known of that hazardous work except the Chief and myself.

"It happened that you ran counter to no plans of mine," the toneless voice rolled on. "So you – lived. You next came to my notice when you undertook to recover the Spiradoff emeralds from the

Communists in Moscow. You ingeniously left with them the imitations and escaped with the originals. I did not care for them, I have much finer ones. So I allowed you to return them to those who had commissioned you. But the audacity of your plan and the cool courage with which you carried it out entertained me greatly. I like to be entertained, James Kirkham. Your indifferent acceptance of the wholly inadequate reward showed that it had been the adventure which had been the primal appeal. It had been the game and not the gain. You were, as I had thought, a true gambler."

And now despite myself I could not keep astonishment from my face. The Spiradoff affair had been carried out in absolute secrecy. I had insisted upon none except the owner knowing how the jewels had been recovered. They had been resold for their value as gems and not with their histories attached...not even the Communists had as yet discovered the substitution, I had reason to believe, and would not until they tried to sell them. Yet this man knew!

"It was then I decided I would – collect – you," he said. "But the time was not fully ripe. I would let you run awhile. You went to China for Rockbilt on the strength of a flimsy legend. And you found the tomb wherein, true enough, the jade plaques of that legend lay on the moldering breast of old Prince Sukantse. You took them and were captured by the bandit Kin-Wang. You found the joint in that cunning thief's armor. You saw, and took, the one chance to escape with your loot. Gambler he was, and you knew it. And there in his tent you played him for the plaques with two years' slavery to him as your forfeit if you lost.

"The idea of having you as a willing slave amused him. Besides, he recognized of what value your brain and courage would be to him. So he made the bargain. You detected the cards he had cunningly nicked before the game had gone far. I approve the dexterity and skill with which you promptly nicked others in the identical fashion. Kin-Wang was confused. Luck was with you. You won."

I half arose, staring at him, fascinated.

"I do not wish to mystify you further." He waved me back into my seat. "Kin-Wang is sometimes useful to me. I have many men in many lands who do my bidding, James Kirkham. Had you lost, Kin-Wang would have sent me the plaques, and he would have looked after you more carefully than his own head. Because he knew that at any time I might demand you from him!"

I leaned back with a sigh, the feeling that some inexorable trap had closed upon me, oppressive.

"Afterwards," his eyes never left me, "afterwards, I tested you again. Twice did my messengers try to take the plaques from you. Purposely, in neither of those efforts had I planned for sure success. Else you would have lost them. I left in each instance a loophole that would enable you to escape had you the wit to see it. You had the wit – and again I was vastly entertained. And pleased.

"And now," he leaned forward a trifle, "we come to tonight. You had acquired a comfortable sum out of the jades. But there seemed to be a waning interest in the game you know so well. You cast your eyes upon another – the fool's gamble, the stock market. It did not fit in with my plans to let you win at that. I knew what you had bought. I manipulated. I stripped you, dollar by dollar, leisurely. You are thinking that the method I took was more adapted to the wrecking of some great financier than the possessor of a few thousands. Not so. If your thousands had been millions the end would have been the same. That was the lesson I wished to drive home when the time came. Have you learned the lesson?"

I repressed with difficulty a gust of anger.

"I hear you," I answered, curtly.

"Heed!" he whispered, and a bleakness dulled for a breath the sparkling eyes.

"So too," he went on, "it was of tonight. I could have had you caught up bodily and carried here, beaten or drugged, bound and gagged. Such methods are those of the thug, the unimaginative savage in our midst. You could have had no respect for the mind behind such crude tactics. Nor would I have been entertained.

"No, the constant surveillance which at last forced you out into the open, your double now enjoying himself at your Club – a splendid actor, by the way, who studied you for weeks – in fact, all your experiences were largely devised to demonstrate to you the extraordinary character of the organization to which you have been called.

"And I say again that your conduct has pleased me. You could have fought Consardine. Had you done so you would have shown yourself lacking in imagination and true courage. You would have come here just the same, but I would have been disappointed. And I was greatly diverted by your attitude toward Walter and Eve – a girl whom I have destined for a great work and whom I am training now for it.

"You have wondered how they came to be in that particular subway station. There were other couples at South Ferry, the elevated station and at all approaches to the Battery within five minutes after you had seated yourself there. I tell you that you had not one chance of escape. Nothing that you could have done that had not been anticipated and prepared for. Not all the police in New York could have held you back from me tonight.

"Because, James Kirkham, I had willed your coming!"

I had listened to this astonishing mixture of subtle flattery, threat and colossal boasting with ever-increasing amazement. I stood back from the table.

"Who are you?" I asked, directly. "And what do you want of me?"

The weird blue eyes blazed out, intolerably.

"Since everything upon this earth toward which I direct my will does as that will dictates," he answered, slowly, "you may call me – Satan!

"And what I offer you is a chance to rule this world with me – at a price, of course!"

CHAPTER FIVE

The two sentences tingled in my brain as though charged with electricity. Absurd as they might have sounded under any other circumstances, here they were as far removed from absurdity as anything I have ever known.

Those lashless, intensely alive blue eyes in the immobile face were – Satanic! I had long sensed the diabolic touch in every experience I had undergone that night. In the stillness of the huge body, in the strangeness of the organ pipe voice that welled, expressionless, from the almost still lips was something diabolic too – as though the body were but an automaton in which dwelt some infernal spirit, some alien being that made itself manifest through eyes and voice only. That my host was the exact opposite of the long, lank, dark Mephisto of opera, play and story made him only the more terrifying. And it has long been my experience that fat men are capable of far greater deviltries than thin men.

No, this man who bade me call him Satan had nothing of the absurd about him. I acknowledged to myself that he was – dreadful.

A bell rang, a mellow note. A light pulsed on a wall, a panel slid aside and Consardine stepped into the room. Vaguely, I noted that the panel was a different one than that through which the Manchu butler had gone. At the same time I recalled, aimlessly it seemed, that I had seen no stairway leading up from the great hall. And on the heels of that was recollection that I had noticed neither windows nor doors in the bedroom to which I had been conducted by the valet. The thoughts came and went without my mind then taking in their significance. That was to come later.

I arose, returning Consardine's bow. He seated himself without salutation or ceremony at Satan's right.

"I have been telling James Kirkham how entertaining I have found him," said my host.

"And I," smiled Consardine. "But I am afraid my companions did not. Cobham was quite upset. That was really cruel of you,

Kirkham. Vanity is one of Cobham's besetting sins."

So Walter's name was Cobham. What was Eve's, I wondered.

"Your stratagem of the rag-doll was – demoralizing," I said. "I thought I was rather restrained in my observations upon Mr. Cobham. There was so much more opportunity, you know. And after all, so much provocation."

"The rag-doll was a diverting idea," observed Satan. "And effective."

"Diabolically so," I spoke to Consardine. "But I find that was to have been expected. Just before you entered I discovered that I have been dining with – Satan."

"Ah, yes," said Consardine, coolly. "And you are no doubt expecting me to produce a lancet and open a vein in your wrist while Satan puts in front of you a document written in brimstone and orders you to sign away your soul in your blood."

"I am expecting no such childish thing," I replied with some show of indignation.

Satan chuckled; his face did not move but his eyes danced.

"Obsolete methods," he said. "I gave them up after my experiences with the late Dr. Faustus."

"Perhaps," Consardine addressed me, blandly, "you think I may be the late Dr. Faustus. No, no – or if so, Kirkham," he looked at me slyly, "Eve is not Marguerite."

"Let us say, not your Marguerite," amended Satan.

I felt the blood rush up into my face. And again Satan chuckled. They were playing with me, these two. Yet under that play the sinister note persisted, not to be mistaken. I felt uncomfortably like a mouse between a pair of cats. I had a sudden vision of the girl as just such another helpless mouse.

"No," it was Satan's sonorous voice. "No, I have become more modern. I still buy souls, it is true. Or take them. But I am not so rigorous in my terms as of old. I now also lease souls for certain periods. I pay well for such leases, James Kirkham."

"Is it not time that you ceased treating me like a child?" I asked coldly. "I admit all that you have said of me. I believe all that you have said of yourself. I concede that you are – Satan. Very well. What then?"

There was a slight pause. Consardine lighted a cigar, poured himself some brandy and pushed aside a candle that stood between us, so I thought, that he could have a clearer view of my face. Satan for the first time turned his eyes away from me, looking over my head. I had come to the third stage of this mysterious game.

"Did you ever hear the legend of the seven shining footsteps of Buddha?" he asked me. I shook my head.

"It was that which made me change my ancient methods of snaring souls," he said gravely. "Since it caused the beginning of a new infernal epoch, the legend is important. But it is important to you for other reasons as well. So listen.

"When the Lord Buddha, Gautama, the Enlightened One," he intoned, "was about to be born, he was seen gleaming like a jewel of living light in his Mother's womb. So filled with light was he that he made of her body a lantern, himself the holy flame."

For the first time there was expression in the voice, a touch of sardonic unctuousness.

"And when the time came for him to be delivered, he stepped forth from his Mother's side, which miraculously closed behind him.

"Seven footsteps the infant Buddha took before he halted for the worship of the devis, genü, rishis and all the Heavenly hierarchy that had gathered round. Seven shining footsteps they were, seven footsteps that gleamed like stars upon the soft greensward."

"And, lo! Even as Buddha was being worshipped, those shining footsteps of his stirred and moved and marched away, beginning the opening of the paths which later the Holy One would traverse. Seven interesting little John the Baptists going before him – Ho! Ho! Ho!" laughed Satan, from unchanged face and motionless lips.

"West went one and East went one," he continued. "One North and one South – opening up the paths of deliverance to the whole four quarters of the globe."

"But what of the other three? Ah – alas! Mara, the King of

Illusion, had watched with apprehension the advent of Buddha, because the light of Buddha's words would be a light in which only the truth had shadow and by it would be rendered useless the snares by which mankind, or the most of it, was held in thrall by Mara. If Buddha conquered, Mara would be destroyed. The King of Illusion did not take kindly to the idea, since his supreme enjoyment was in wielding power and being entertained. In that," commented Satan, apparently quite seriously, "Mara was much like me. But in intelligence much inferior, because he did not realize that truth, aptly manipulated, creates far better illusions than do lies. However–"

"Before those laggard three could get very far away, Mara had captured them!"

"And then by wile and artifice and sorcery Mara seduced them. He taught them naughtiness, schooled them in delicious deceptions – and he sent them forth to wander!"

"What happened? Well, naturally men and women followed the three. The paths they picked out were so much pleasanter, so much more delectable, so much softer and more fragrant and beautiful than the stony, hard, austere, cold trails broken by the incorruptible four. Who could blame people for following them? And besides, superficially, all seven footprints were alike. The difference, of course, was in the ending. Those souls who followed the three deceitful prints were inevitably led back into the very heart of error, the inner lair of illusion, and were lost there: while those who followed the four were freed."

"And more and more followed the naughty prints while Mara waxed joyful. Until it seemed that there would be none left to take the paths of enlightenment. But now Buddha grew angry. He sent forth a command and back to him from the four quarters of the world came hurrying the shining holy quartette. They tracked down the erring three and made them prisoners."

"Now arose a problem. Since the erring three were of Buddha, they could not be destroyed. They had their rights, inalienable. But so deep had been their defilement by Mara that they could not be cleansed of their wickedness."

"So they were imprisoned for as long as the world shall last. Somewhere near the great temple of Borobudur in Java, there is a smaller, hidden temple. In it is a throne. To reach that throne, one must climb seven steps. On each of these steps gleams one of Buddha's seven baby footprints. Each looks precisely like the other – but, oh, how different they are. Four are the holy ones, guarding the wicked three. The temple is secret, the way to it beset with deadly perils. He who lives through them and enters that temple may climb to the throne."

"But – as he climbs he must set his foot on five of those shining prints!"

"Now, after he has done this, hear what must befall. If of those five steps he has taken he has set his feet upon the three naughty prints, behold, when he reaches the throne, all of earthly desire, all that the King of Illusion can give him, is his for the wishing. To the enslavement and possible destruction of his soul, naturally. But if, of the five, three have been the holy prints, then is he freed of all earthly desire, freed of all illusion, free of the wheel, a Bearer of the Light, a Vessel of Wisdom – his soul one with the Pure One, eternally."

"Saint or sinner – if he steps on the three unholy footprints, all worldly illusions are his, willy-nilly."

"And sinner or saint – if he treads on three of the holy footprints, he is freed of all illusion, a blessed soul forever in Nirvana!"

"Poor devil!" murmured Consardine.

"Such is the legend." Satan turned his gaze upon me again. "Now I never tried to collect those interesting footprints. They could have served no purpose of mine. I have no desire to turn sinners into saints, for one thing. But they gave me the most entertaining idea I have had for – shall I say – centuries?

"Life, James Kirkham, is one long gamble between the two inexorable gambles of birth and death. All men and all women are gamblers, although most are very poor ones. All men and all women have at least one desire during their lives for which they would willingly stake their souls – and often even their lives. But life is such a crude game, haphazardly directed, if directed at all, and with such confusing, conflicting, contradictory and tawdry rules.

"Very well, I would improve the game for a chosen few, gamble with them for their great desire, and for my own entertainment would use as my model these seven footsteps of Buddha.

"And now, James Kirkham, listen intently, for this directly concerns you. I constructed two thrones upon a dais up to which lead not seven but twenty-one steps. On each third step there shines out a footprint – seven of them in all.

"One of the thrones is lower than the other. Upon that I sit. On the other rests a crown and a scepter.

"Now then. Three of these footsteps are – unfortunate. Four are fortunate in the aggregate. He who would gamble with me must climb to that throne on which are crown and scepter. In climbing he must place a foot on four, not five of these seven prints.

"Should those four upon which he steps prove to be the fortunate ones, that man may have every desire satisfied as long as he lives. I am his servant – and his servant is all that vast organization which I have created and which serves me. His, my billions to do as he pleases with. His, my masterpieces. His, anything that he covets – power, women, rule – anything. What he hates I punish or – remove. His is the crown and scepter upon that throne higher than mine. It is power over earth! He may have – everything!"

I glanced at Consardine. He was nervously bending and unbending a silver knife in his strong fingers, his eyes glittering.

"But if he treads on the others?"

"Ah – that is my end of the gamble. If he treads upon the first of my three – he must do me one service. Whatever I bid him. If he treads on two – he must do my bidding for a year. They are my – minor leases.

"But if he treads on all my three" – I felt the blaze of the blue eyes scorch me, heard a muffled groan from Consardine – "if he treads on all my three – then he is mine, body and soul. To kill at once if it is my mood – and in what slow ways I please. To live – if I please, as long as I please, and then to die – again as I please. Mine! body and soul! Mine."

The rolling voice trumpeted, grew dreadful. Satanic enough

was he now with those weird eyes blazing at me as though behind them were flames from that very pit whose Master's name he had taken.

"There are a few rules to remember," the voice abruptly regained its calm. "One need not take the whole four steps. You may stop, if you desire, at one. Or two. Or three. You need not take the next step.

"If you take one step and it is mine, and go no farther, then you do my service, are well paid for it, and after it is done may ascend the steps again.

"So if you go farther and touch the second of my steps. After your year – if you are alive – you again have your chance. And are well paid during that year."

I considered. Power over all the world! Every desire granted. An Aladdin's lamp to rub! Not for a moment did I doubt that this – whatever he was – could do what he promised.

"I will explain the mechanism," he said. "Obviously the relative positions of the seven steps cannot remain the same at each essay. Their combination would be too easy to learn. That combination I leave to chance. Not even I know it. Through that I get the cream of my entertainment.

"I sit upon my throne. I touch a lever that spins a hidden wheel over which roll seven balls, three marked for my steps, four marked for the fortunate ones. As those balls settle into place, they form an electrical contact with the seven footprints. As the balls lie, so lie the prints.

"Where I can see – and others if they are present – but not to be seen by the climber of the steps, is an indicator. As the – aspirant – sets his foot on the prints this indicator shows whether he has picked one of my three or one of his four.

"And there is one final rule. When you climb you may not look back at that indicator. You must take the next step in ignorance of whether that from which you have come was good for you or – evil. If you do weaken and look behind, you must descend and begin your climb anew."

"But it seems to me that you have the better end of the game,"

I observed. "Suppose one steps upon a fortunate step and stops – what does he get?"

"Nothing," he answered, "but the chance to take the next. You forget, James Kirkham, that what he stands to win is immeasurably greater than what I win if he loses. Winning, he wins me and all I stand for. Losing, I win only one man – or one woman. Besides, for my limited leases I pay high. And give protection."

I nodded. As a matter of fact I was profoundly stirred. Everything that I had experienced had been carefully calculated to set my imagination on fire. I thrilled at the thought of what I might not be able to do with – well, admit he was Satan – and his power at my beck and call. He watched me, imperturbably; Consardine, understandingly, with a shadow of pity in his eyes.

"Look here," I said abruptly, "please clear up a few more things. Suppose I refuse to play this game of yours – what happens to me?"

"You will be set back in Battery Park tomorrow," he answered. "Your double will be withdrawn from your club. You will find he has done no harm to your reputation. You may go your way. But–"

"I thought, sir, there was a but," I murmured.

"But I will be disappointed," he went on, quietly. "I do not like to be disappointed. I am afraid your affairs would not prosper. It might even be that I would find you such a constant reproach, such a living reminder of a flaw in my judgment that–"

"I understand," I interrupted. "The living reminder would strangely cease some day to be a reminder – living."

He did not speak – but, surely, I read the answer in his eyes.

"And what is to prevent me from taking your challenge," I asked again, "going partly through with it, enough to get away from here, and then – ah – ?"

"Betray me?" again the chuckle came through the motionless lips. "Your efforts would come to nothing. And as for you – better for you, James Kirkham, had you remained unborn. I, Satan, tell you so!"

The blue eyes scorched; about him in his chair seemed to grow a shadow, enveloping him. From him emanated something diabolic, something that gripped my throat and checked the very pulse of my heart.

"I, Satan, tell you so!" he repeated.

There was a little pause in which I strove to regain my badly shaken poise.

Again the bell sounded.

"It is time," said Consardine. But I noticed that he had paled, knew my own face was white.

"It happens," the organ-like voice was calm again, "it happens that you have an opportunity to see what becomes of those who try to thwart me. I will ask you to excuse certain precautions which it will be necessary to take. You will not be harmed. Only it is essential that you remain silent and motionless and that none read your face while you see – what you are going to see."

Consardine arose, I followed him. The man who called himself Satan lifted himself from his chair. Huge I had guessed him to be, but I was unprepared for the giant that he was. I am all of six feet and he towered over me a full twelve inches.

Involuntarily I looked at his feet.

"Ah," he said, suavely. "You are looking for my cloven hoof. Come, you are about to see it."

He touched the wall. A panel slipped away revealing a wide corridor, not long, and windowless and doorless. He leading, Consardine behind me, Satan walked a few yards and pressed against the wainscoting. It slid back, soundlessly. He stepped through.

I walked after him and halted, staring blankly, into one of the most singular – rooms, chambers, no, *temple* is the only word that its size and character deserve to describe it – I stood staring, I repeat, into one of the most singular temples that probably man's eyes had ever looked upon.

CHAPTER SIX

It was suffused with a dim amber light from some concealed source. Its domed roof arched a hundred feet above me. Only one wall was straight; the others curved out from it like the inner walls of a vast bubble. The straight wall cut across what was the three-quarter arc of a huge hemisphere.

That wall was all of some lustrous green stone, malachite, I judged. And upon its face was carved in the old Egyptian style a picture.

The subject was the Three Fates, the Moerae of the ancient Greeks, the Parcse of the Romans, the Norns of the Norsemen. There was Clotho with the distaff upon which were spun the threads of human destiny, Lachesis guiding the threads, and Atropos with her shears that cut the threads when the trio so willed. Above the Fates hovered the face of Satan.

One of his hands grasped that of Clotho, he seemed to whisper to Lachesis, his other hand guided that of the Fate who wielded the shears. The lines of the four figures were lined in blues, vermilions and vivid green. The eyes of Satan were not upon the threads whose destinies he was controlling. They were looking out over the temple.

And whoever the unknown genius who had cut that picture, he had created a marvelous likeness. By some trick, the eyes blazed out of the stone with the same living, jewel-like brilliancy of those of the man who called himself Satan.

The curved walls of some black wood – teak or ebony. There was shimmering tracery upon them – like webs. I saw that they were webs; spider webs traced upon the black wood and glimmering like those same silken traps beneath the moon. By the hundreds and thousands they were interlaced upon the walls. They shimmered over the ceiling.

The floors of the temple lifted toward the back in row upon row of seats carved out of black stone and arranged like those of the old Roman amphitheaters.

But all of this I noted only after I had forced my gaze away from the structure that dominated the whole strange place. This was a flight of semicircular steps that swept out in gradually diminishing arcs from the base of the malachite wall. There were twenty-one of them, the lowest, I estimated, a hundred feet wide and the highest about thirty. They were each about a foot high and some three feet deep. They were of inky black stone.

At their top was a low dais upon which stood two elaborately carved thrones – one of black wood, and the other, resting on a pedestal which brought its seat well above the first, apparently of dull, yellow gold.

The black throne was bare. Over the back of the golden throne was a strip of royal purple velvet; upon its seat was a cushion of the same royal purple.

And upon that cushion rested a crown and scepter. The crown was ablaze with the multicolored fires of great diamonds, the soft blue flames of huge sapphires; red glowings of immense rubies and green radiances that were emeralds. The orb of the scepter was one enormous diamond. And all its jeweled length blazed like the crown with gems.

Ranged down each side of the one and twenty steps were seven men in white robes shaped like the burnooses of the Arabs. If they were Arabs they were of a tribe I had never come across; to me they appeared more like Persians. Their faces were gaunt and of a peculiar waxen pallor. Their eyes seemed pupilless. Each carried in his right hand a snake-like rope, noosed like a lariat.

From every third ebon step a footprint shone out, the footprint of a child outlined as though by living fire.

There were seven of them, shining out with an unearthly brilliancy as though they themselves were alive and poised to march up those steps.

I had looked first at the crown and scepter, and the sight of them had fanned within me such desire as I had never known; a burning lust for possession of them and the power that went with them; a lust that shook me like a fever.

I had looked next at those gleaming marks of a babe's feet, and the sight of them had stirred within me an inexplicable awe and terror and loathing as great as had been the desire which the sight of them had swiftly numbed.

And suddenly I heard Satan's voice.

"Sit, James Kirkham!"

There was an armed chair, oddly shaped, almost against the circular wall and close beside the edge of the first curving step. It was somewhat like a lesser throne. I dropped into it, glad at the moment of its support.

Instantly, bands of steel sprang from the arms and circled my elbows; other bands bound my ankles, and from the back where my head rested a veil dropped, covering my face. Its lower edge, thick and softly padded, was drawn tight across my lips.

I was held fast, gagged, my face hidden all in an instant. I made no attempt to struggle. These, I realized, were the "precautions" of which my host had warned me. The bonds held but did not constrict, the silencing pad was not uncomfortable, the veil was of a material which, though it hid my face, enabled me to see as clearly as though it were not enveloping my head.

I saw Satan at the foot of the steps. His enormous body was covered from neck to feet by a black cloak. He paced slowly up the flight. As he trod upon the first step the white-robed, rope-bearing men bent before him, low. Not until he had seated himself upon the black throne did they straighten.

The amber light dulled and went out. Before there could be anything but a thin slice of darkness, a strong white light beat down upon thrones and steps. Its edge formed a sharp semicircle three yards away from the curve of the first. It bathed Satan, the fourteen guardians and myself. Under it the seven footprints leaped out more brilliantly, seeming to be straining against some invisible leash and eager to follow their master. The unwinking eyes of the man on the black throne and their counterparts in the stone behind him glittered.

I heard a movement at the rear of the temple among the seats of stone. There were rustlings as of many people seating themselves, faint whisperings of panels sliding back and forth in the black walls, opening of hidden entrances through which this unseen audience was streaming.

Who they were, what they were – I could not see. The semicircle of light glaring upon the steps and thrones formed an impenetrable curtain beyond which was utter darkness.

A gong sounded. Silence fell. Whatever that audience, the doors were now closed upon them; the curtain ready to rise.

Now I saw, high up and halfway between roof and floor, a globe gleam forth like a little moon. It was at the edge of the white light and as I watched its left half darkened. The right half shone undimmed, the black half was outlined by a narrow rim of radiance.

Abruptly the greater light went out again. For an instant only was the temple in darkness. The light blazed forth once more.

But now he who called himself Satan was not alone on the dais. No. Beside him stood a figure that the devil himself might have summoned from hell!

It was a black man naked except for a loin cloth. His legs were short and spindly; his shoulders inordinately wide, his arms long, and upon shoulders and arms the muscles and sinews stood out like blackened withes of thick rope. The face was flat-nosed, the jaw protruding, brutish and ape-like. Ape-like too were the close-set, beady eyes that burned like demon-lights. His mouth was a slit, and upon his face was the stamp of a ravening cruelty.

He held in one hand a noosed cord, thin and long and braided as though made of woman's hair. In his loin cloth was a slender knife.

A sighing quavered out of the darkness beyond me as from scores of tightening throats.

Again the gong clanged.

Into the circle of light came two men. One was Consardine; the other a tall, immaculately dressed and finely built man of about forty. He looked like a highly bred, cultured English gentleman. As he faced the black throne I heard a murmur as of surprise and pity well up from the hidden audience.

There was a debonair unconcern in his poise, but I saw his face twitch as he glanced at the horror standing beside Satan. He drew a cigarette from his case and lighted it; in that action was a touch of bravado that betrayed him; nor could he control the faint tremor of the hand that held the match. Nevertheless, he took a deliberate inhalation and met the eyes of Satan squarely.

"Cartright," the voice of Satan broke the silence. "You have disobeyed me. You have tried to thwart me. You have dared to set your will against mine. By your disobedience you almost wrecked a plan I had conceived. You thought to reap gain and to escape me. You even had it in your mind to betray me. I do not ask you if all this is so. I know it is so. I do not ask you why you did it. You did it. That is enough."

"I have no intention of offering any defense, Satan." answered the man called Cartright, coolly enough. "I might urge, however, that any inconvenience to which I have put you is entirely your own fault. You claim perfection of judgment. Yet in me you picked a wrong tool. Is the tool to blame or the artisan if that tool which he picks cannot stand up under the task for which that artisan selects it?"

"The tool is not to blame," answered Satan. "But what does the artisan do with such a tool thereafter? He does not use it again. He destroys it."

"The perfect artisan does not," said Cartright. "He uses it thereafter for work for which it is fit."

"Not when he has more than enough good ones to choose from," said Satan.

"You have the power," Cartright replied. "Nevertheless, you know I have answered you. I am simply an error of your judgment. Or if your judgment is perfect as you boast, then you deliberately picked me to fail. In either event, punish yourself, Satan – not me!"

For a long minute the black-robed figure regarded him. Cartright met the gaze boldly.

"I ask only for justice," he said. "I ask no mercy of you. Satan."

"Not – yet!" answered Satan, slowly, and the flaming eyes grew bleak and cold and once more a sighing passed me from the darkness of the temple.

There was another interminable minute of silence.

"Cartright, you have given me an answer," the organ voice rolled out, emotionless. "For that answer you shall be credited. You have reminded me that a wise artisan uses a faulty tool only for work it can do without breaking. That too I set down for you.

"Now, Cartright, this is my decree. You shall take the four steps. Now. And all of them. You shall have, first of all, your chance to win that crown and scepter and the empire of earth that they carry with them. This if the four footprints that you tread upon are the four fortunate ones.

"And if you place your foot on three of the fortunate prints and on but one of mine – I forgive you. This in recognition of a certain justice in your parable of the artisan and the faulty tool."

I saw Cartright's tenseness slacken, a shadow of relief pass over his face.

"If you tread upon two of the fortunate prints and upon two of mine then I will give you a choice of a swift and merciful death or of joining my slaves of the kehjt. In brief, Cartright, you pick between the destruction of your body or slow annihilation of your soul. And that mercy I hold out to you in recognition of your claim that the wise artisan chooses some other use for the untrustworthy tool."

Once more the sighing, and Cartright's face paled.

"We come now to the last possibility – that on your journey upward you tread upon all three of my dainty little servants. In that case" – the voice chilled – "in that case, Cartright, you die. You die at the hands of Sanchal here by the cord. Not one death, Cartright. No, a thousand deaths. For slowly and with agony Sanchal's cord shall drag you to the threshold of the gates of death. Slowly and with agony he shall drag you back to life. Again and again...and again... and again...until at last your torn soul has strength to return no more and crawls whimpering over that threshold whose gates shall close upon it...forever! Such is my decree! So is my will! So shall it be!"

The black horror had grinned evilly as he heard his name and had shaken with a ghastly gesture the cord of braided woman's hair. As for Cartright, at that dreadful sentence the blood had drained from his face, the cigarette fallen from his fingers. He stood, all bravado gone. And Consardine, who all the while had been beside him, slipped back into the shadow, leaving him alone. Satan pressed down a lever which stood like a slender rod between the two thrones. There was a faint whirring sound. The seven gleaming prints of a child's bare foot flashed as though fire had shot from them.

"The steps are prepared," called Satan. "Cartright – ascend!"

The white-robed men stirred; they unslung the loops of their ropes and held the nooses ready, as though to cast swiftly. The black horror thrust his head forward, mouth slavering, his talons caressing his cord.

The silence in the temple deepened – as though all within had ceased to breathe Now Cartright walked forward, moving slowly, studying the gleaming footprints. Satan leaned back in his throne, hands hidden beneath his robe, his huge head having disconcertingly the appearance of being bodiless, floating over the dais as the head in the stone floated above the three Norns.

And now Cartright had passed by the first print and had walked up the two intervening steps. He set without hesitation his foot upon the second gleaming mark.

Instantly a glittering duplicate of it shone out upon the white half of the moon globe. I knew that he had trodden upon one of the fortunate steps.

But Cartright, the globe hidden from him, forbidden to turn – Cartright could not know it!

He shot a swift look at Satan, seeking some sign either of triumph or chagrin. The marble face was expressionless, the eyes unchanged. Nor was there any sound from the black seats.

He walked rapidly up the next two steps and again unhesitatingly set his foot on the next print.

And again another glittered out upon the pale field of the globe. Two chances he had won! Gone from him now was the threat of the thousand deaths. At most he would have his choice of merciful extinction or that mysterious slavery I had heard Satan name.

And again he could not know!

Once more he studied the face of his tormentor for some betraying expression, some hint of how his score stood. Immobile as before, it stared at him; expressionless too was the face of the monstrosity with the cord.

Slowly Cartright ascended the next two steps. He hesitated before the next devilish print, for minutes – and hours they seemed to me. And now I saw that his mouth had become pinched and that little beads of sweat stood out upon his forehead.

Plainly as though he were speaking, I could follow his thoughts. Had the two prints upon which he had trodden been Satan's? And would the next condemn him to the torture of the cord? Had he trodden upon only one? Had he escaped as yet the traps that gave him over to Satan?

He could not know!

He passed that print and paced upward more slowly. He stood looking down upon the fifth footprint. And then, slowly, his head began to turn!

It was as though a strong hand were forcing it. The tormented brain, wrestling with the panic that urged it to look...to look behind...to see what the marks upon the moon-globe showed.

A groan came from his gray lips. He caught his head between his two hands, held it rigid and leaped upon the footprint before him.

And he stood there, gasping, like a man who has run a long race. His mouth hung open, drawing in sobbing breaths to the laboring lungs. His hair was wet, his face dripping. His haggard eyes searched Satan –

The white field of the globe bore a third shining symbol!

Cartright had won –

And he could not know!

My own hands were shaking; my body drenched with sweat as though it were I myself who stood in his place. Words leaped to my lips – a cry to him that he need fear no more! That his torment was over! That Satan had lost! The gag stifled them.

Upon me burst full realization of all the hellish cruelty, the truly diabolic subtlety and ingenuity of this ordeal.

Cartright stood trembling. His despairing gaze ate into the impassive face now not far above him. Did I see a flicker of evil triumph pass over it, reflected on the black mask of his torturer? If so, it was gone like a swift ripple on a still pond.

Had Cartright seen it? So it must have been, for the despair upon his own face deepened and turned it into a thing of agony.

Once more his head began to turn backward with that slow and dreadful suggestion of unseen compulsion!

He swayed forward, fighting against it. He stumbled up the steps. I knew with what destroying effort he dragged his eyes down to the next shining print. He poised over it a shaking foot –

And slowly, slowly, ever his head turned...back, back to the telltale globe!

He drew back the foot. He thrust it forward again...and again withdrew it. He sobbed. And I strained at my bonds, cursing and sobbing with him...

Now his head was half around, his face turned directly to me...

He recoiled from the print. His body swung about with the snap of a breaking spring. He looked at the globe and saw.

The three prints upon the fortunate field!

A vast sighing went up from the black amphitheater.

"The tool again betrays its weakness!" It was Satan's voice. "Lo, deliverance was in your hands, Cartright. And like Lot's wife, you turned to look! And now you must descend...and all is to do again. But wait. Let us see if you may not have lost something far greater than deliverance. That footprint upon which you could not summon the courage to tread. What was it? I am curious to know."

He spoke in some strange tongue to the guard at the right of the print. The man came forward and pressed his foot upon the mark.

Out upon the pale semi-disk of the globe flashed out another shimmering print!

Crown and scepter! Empire of Earth! Not only free from Satan – but his master!

All this Cartright might have won.

And he had turned to look – and lost.

A groan went up from the darkness, murmurings. They were stilled by the dreadful laughter that rolled from Satan's still lips.

"Lost! Lost!" he mocked. "Go back, Cartright, And climb again. And not twice, I think, will such luck as this come to you. Go back, traitor. And climb!" He pressed the lever and the hidden mechanism whirred and the seven prints flashed out.

Cartright tottered down the steps. He walked like a puppet whose legs are pulled by strings.

He stopped at the base of the steps. He turned, and again, like some marionette, began to climb, putting his foot automatically on each mark as he came to it. His eyes were fixed upon the scepter and the crown. His arms were stretched out to them. His mouth was drawn at the corners like a heartbroken child, and as he climbed he wept.

One – and a shining print sprang out on the black field of the globe.

Two – another.

Three – a print on the white side.

Four – a print on the black I

A roar of hellish laughter shook Satan. For an instant I seemed to see his black robe melt, become vaporous and change into an enveloping shadow. A blacker shadow seemed to hover over him.

And still his laughter roared and still Cartright climbed the steps, his eyes streaming, face contorted, gaze fixed upon the glittering baubles in the golden throne, arms reaching out for them...

There was a swishing sound. The black horror had leaned forward and cast his cord. It circled over Cartright's head and tightened about his shoulders.

A tug, and he had fallen.

Then hand over hand, unresisting, the torturer pulled him up the steps and to him like a fish:

The light went out. It left a blackness made darker by the rolling, demonic laughter.

The laughter ceased. I heard a thin, wailing cry.

The light came on.

The black throne was empty. Empty too was the dais. Empty of Satan, of the torturer and of – Cartright!

Only the orb of the scepter and the crown glittered mockingly on the golden throne between the two lines of watching, white-robed men.

CHAPTER SEVEN

I felt a touch upon my arm, sprang back and faced Consardine. On his face was a shadow of that horror I knew was on my own.

The bands around my arms and legs sprang back, veil and gag were lifted from me. I leaped from the chair. And again blackness fell.

The amber glow returned, slowly. I looked toward the back of the temple. Empty now was the amphitheater of all that hidden audience whose sighing and murmuring had come to me. I stared back at the steps.

Golden throne and its burden had vanished. Gone were all but two of the white-robed figures. These stood guarding the black throne.

The blue eyes of the stone Satan blazed out at me. The seven shining prints of a child's foot sparkled.

"They opened his way into Paradise, and he weakened, and they led him straight into Hell."

Consardine stared at the seven shining footsteps, and on his face was that avid look I had seen on faces bent over the rouge-et-noir tables at Monte Carlo; faces molded by the scorching fingers of the gambler's passion which is a lust exceeding that for women; faces that glare hungrily at the wheel just before it begins to spin and that see not the wheel but the golden booty its spinning may draw for them from Fortune's heaped hands. Like them, Consardine was seeing not the gleaming prints but that enchanted land to which they led where all desire was fulfilled.

The web of Satan's lure had him!

Well, despite what I had just beheld, so had it me. I was conscious of an impatience, a straining desire to put my own luck to the test. But in it, stronger far than the desire to gain the treasures he had promised was the desire to make that mocking, cold and merciless devil do my bidding as he had made me do his.

Consardine broke the spell that held him and turned to me.

"It's been rather an evening for you, Kirkham," he said. "Do you want to go to your room now, or will you stop in my quarters and have a night-cap with me?"

I hesitated. I had a thousand questions to ask. And yet I felt even more the necessity of being by myself and digesting what I had heard and seen since I had been brought to this place. Besides – of my thousand questions how many would he answer? Reasoning from my recent experiences, few. He, himself, ended the uncertainty.

"You'd better go to bed," he said. "Satan desires you to think over what he has proposed to you. And, after all, I am not permitted" – he caught himself hastily – "I mean I can add nothing to what he did say. He will want your answer tomorrow – or rather" – he glanced at his watch – "today, since it is nearly two o'clock."

"What time shall I see him?" I asked.

"Oh, not till afternoon, surely," he answered. "He" – a slight shudder passed over him – "he will be occupied for hours still. You may sleep till noon if you wish."

"Very well," I said, "I'll go to my room."

Without further comment he led me back toward the amphitheater, and up to the rear wall. He pressed, and one of the inevitable panels slid away revealing another of the little elevators. He looked back at the footprints before closing the panel. They glimmered, alertly. The two white-robed guards stood at the sides of the black throne, their strange eyes intent upon us.

Again he shivered, then sighed and closed the slide. We stepped out into a long, vaulted corridor sheathed with slabs of marble. It was doorless. He pressed upon one of the slabs and we entered a second lift. It stopped and I passed out of it into the chamber where I had changed into evening clothes.

Pajamas had been laid out for me on the bed, slippers and a bathrobe were on an easy chair. On a table were decanters of Scotch, rye and brandy, soda, a bowl of ice, some fruit and cakes, several boxes of my favorite cigarettes – and my missing wallet.

I opened the latter. There were my cards and letters and my money all intact. Making no comment, I poured myself out a drink and invited Consardine to join me.

"To the fortunate steps," he raised his glass. "May you have the luck to pick them!"

"May you," I answered. His face twitched, a haggard shadow dimmed his eyes, he looked at me strangely, and half set down his drink.

"The toast is to you, not to me," he said at last and drained his glass. He walked across the room. At the panel he paused.

"Kirkham," he spoke softly, "sleep without fear. But – keep away from these walls. If you should want anything, ring the bell there" – he pointed to a button on the table – "and Thomas will answer it. I repeat – do not try to open any of these panels. And if I were you I would go to sleep and do no more thinking until you awaken. Would you like, by the way, a sleeping draught? I am really a doctor, you know," he smiled.

"Thanks," I said, "I'll need nothing to make me sleep."

"Good night," he bade me, and the panel closed.

I poured myself another drink and began to undress. I was not sleepy – far from it. Despite Consardine's warning I went over the walls both of the bed chamber and bathroom, touching them cautiously here and there. They seemed solid, of heavy wood, beautifully grained and polished. As I had thought, there were no windows or doors. My room was, in truth, a luxurious cell.

I switched off the lights, one by one and, getting into the bed, turned off the last light upon the side table.

How long I had lain there in the darkness, thinking, before I sensed some one in the room besides myself I do not know. Perhaps half an hour at most. I had heard not the slightest sound, but I knew with absolute certainty that I was no longer alone. I slipped out of the light covering, and twisted silently to the foot of the bed. There I crouched upon one knee, ready to leap when my stealthy visitor had reached its side. To have turned on the light would have put me completely at his mercy. Whoever it was, he evidently thought me asleep and his attack, if attack there was to be, would be made where he would naturally suppose my body to lie. Well, my body was in an entirely different place, and it was I who would provide the surprise.

Instead of an attack came a whisper:

"It's me, Cap'n Kirkham – 'Arry Barker. For God's sake, sir, don't myke no noise!"

I seemed to know that voice. And then I remembered. Barker, the little cockney Tommy that I had run across, bled almost white, in a shell-torn thicket of the Marne. I had given first aid to the little man and had managed to carry him to a field hospital. I had happened to be for some days in the town where was the base hospital to which he had finally been taken and had dropped in regularly to talk to him, bringing him cigarettes and other luxuries. His gratitude to me had been dog-like and touching; he was a sentimental little beggar. Then I had seen him no more. How in the name of Heaven had he come to this place?

"You remember me, Captain?" the whispering voice was anxious. "Wyte a bit. I'll show you..."

There was the flash of a small light held in a cupped hand so that it illuminated for a second only the speaker's face. But in that second I recognized it as Barker's – shrewd and narrow, sandy hair bristling, the short upper lip and buck teeth.

"Barker – well, I'll be damned!" I swore softly, but did not add that the sight of him was so welcome that had he been close enough I would have embraced him.

"S-sh!" he cautioned. "I'm fair sure there ain't nobody watchin'. You can't always tell in this Gord awful plyce, though. Tyke me 'and, sir. There's a chair over there just beside where I come through the wall. Sit in it an' light a cigar. If I 'ear anything I can slip right back – an' all you're doin' is sittin' up smokin'."

His hand caught mine. He seemed to be able to see in the dark for he led me unerringly across the floor and pressed me into the cushioned seat.

"Light up, sir," he said.

I struck a match and lighted a cigar. The flare showed the room, but no Barker. I flicked it out and after a moment I heard his whisper close to my ear.

"First thing I want to say, sir, is don't let 'im scare you with that bunk about bein' the devil. 'E's a devil right enough, a bloody, blinkin' one, but 'e ain't the devil. 'E's pullin' your leg, sir. 'E's a man just like me an' you. A knife in 'is black 'eart or a bullet through 'is guts an' you'd see."

"How did you know I was here?" I whispered.

"Seen you in the chair," he answered. "'Ere's my 'and. When you want to sye anything, squeeze it an' I'll lean my ear close. It's syfer. Yes, seen you in the chair – out there. Fact is, sir, I'm the one that looks after that chair. Look after a lot of such damned things 'ere. That's why 'e lets me live. Satan, I mean."

He went back to his first theme, bitterly.

"But 'e ain't the devil, sir. Always remember 'e ain't. I was brought up Gord-fearin'. Pentecosters, my people was. Taught me Satan was in 'ell, they did. An' won't 'e just give this bloody swine particular 'ell for tykin' 'is nyme in vyne when 'e gets 'im in 'ell! Christ, 'ow I'd like to see it.

"From h'outside lookin' in," he added hastily.

I pressed his hand and felt his ear close to my lips.

"How did you get here, Harry?" I murmured. "And who is this – Satan, and what's his real game?"

"I'll tell you the 'ole tale, Captain," he answered. "It'll tyke a little time, but Gord knows when I'll get the chance again. That's why I beat it to you quick as I could. The bloody beast is gloatin' over that poor devil Cartright. Watchin' 'im die! The rest is either sleepin' or drinkin' themselves blind. Still, as I said, we'll tyke no chances. You let me talk an' ask your questions afterwards."

"Go on," I said.

"I was an electrician before the war," came the whisper in the dark. "None better. Master at it. 'E knows I am. It's why 'e let me live, as I told you. Satan – augh-h-h!

"Things was different after the war. Jobs 'ard to get an' livin' 'igh. Got lookin' at things different, too. Seen lots of muckers what hadn't done a thing in the war but live cushy and pile up loot. What right 'ad they to 'ave all they 'ad when them as 'ad fought an' their families was cold an' 'ungry?

"'Andy with my 'ands I always was. An' light on my feet.

Climb! Climb like a cat. Climb like a bloody centipede. An' quiet! A spook in galoshes was a parade compared to me. I ain't praisin' myself, sir. I'm just tellin' you.

"Syes I to myself, "Arry, it's all wrong. 'Arry, it's time to turn your talents to account. Time to settle down to real work, 'Arry.'

"I was good from the very start at the new trade. I kept goin' 'igher an' 'igher. From villas to apartment 'ouses, apartment 'ouses to mansions. Never once caught. King Cat 'Arry they called me. Swarm up a water pipe as easy as porch pillar, up an apartment 'ouse wall as easy as a water pipe. Master at my new trade just like my old.

"Then I met Maggie. They only myke one like Maggie once, sir. Quick with 'er fingers! She made 'Oudini an' 'Errman look like slow movies. An' a lydy. Regular Clare Vere de Vere when she wanted to be!

"Lot's of swell mobsmen wanted to myke Maggie. She'd 'ave none of them. All wrapped up in 'er work she was. "Ell!' she'd sye, just like a duchess, 'what do I want with a 'usband? 'Ell,' she'd sye, 'A 'usband is about as much use as a 'eadache!' Sort of discouragin', was Maggie.

"Captain, we was crazy h'about each other right off. Married we was, quick. Took a nice 'ouse down in Maida Vale. Was I 'appy? Was she? Gord!

"'Now, Maggie,' I syes after we come back from the 'oneymoon, 'there ain't no reason for you workin' no more. I'm a good provider. I'm a 'ard an' conscientious worker. All you 'ave to do is enjoy yourself an' make our 'ome comfortable an' 'appy.'

"An' Maggie said, 'Righto, 'Arry.'

"I was wearin' I remember a stick pin she'd give me for a weddin' present. Big ruby in it. An' a watch she'd give me, an' a nifty ring with pearls. Admired 'em I 'ad when I see 'em on a couple of toffs at the 'otel we stopped at. An' that night when we went to our room she 'anded 'em to me as a present! That was the kind of a worker Maggie was."

I suppressed a chuckle with difficulty. This whispered-in-the-dark romance of the conscientious soldier and able electrician turned into just as able and conscientious a burglar was the one touch needed to make the night complete. It washed away the film of horror in my mind and brought me back to normal.

"Night or two lyter I was takin' a dye off an' we went to the theayter. 'Ow do you like that pin, 'Arry?' whispers Maggie an' shoots a look at a sparkler in the toff's tie next me. 'Ain't it pretty,' syes I, 'eedlessly.' 'Ere it is!' syes Maggie when we get 'ome.

"'Now, Maggie,' I syes, 'I told you I don't want you to work no more. Ain't I the good provider I promised? Can't I get all the pins I want, myself? All I want, Maggie, is a snug, comfortable, 'appy 'ome when I come back from a 'ard night's work an' my wife to welcome me. I won't 'ave you workin', Maggie!"

"'Righto, 'Arry,' syes she.

"But, Captain, it wasn't all right. It got so that when we went out together I didn't dare to look at a man's tie or 'is watch or nothin'. I couldn't even stand an' admire things in shops. Sure's I did, there when we got 'ome or the next dye would be the things I'd admired. An' Maggie so proud like an' pleased she'd got 'em for me that I 'adn't the 'eart – Oh, it was love all right, but – Oh, 'ell!

"She'd be waitin' for me when I got 'ome. But if I'd wyke up from sleep before my time, she was out. An' when I'd wyke up after she got back, first thing I'd see was laces, or a fur coat, or a ring or two lyde out on the tyble.

"She'd been workin' again!

"'Maggie, I'd sye, 'it ain't right. It 'urts my pride. An' ow'll it be when kiddies come? With their daddy out workin' all night an' sleepin' while their mother's out workin' all dye an' sleepin' while their daddy's workin' – 'ell, Maggie, they might as well be h'orphants!'

"But 'twas no good, Captain. She loved 'er work more than she did me, or maybe she just couldn't tell us apart.

"An' at last I 'ad to leave 'er. Fair broke my 'eart, it did. I loved 'er an' my 'ome. But I just couldn't stand it.

"So I come to America. Me, King Cat 'Arry, an exile because my wife couldn't stop workin'.

"Did well, too. But I wasn't 'appy. One dye I was out in the country an' I ran across a big wall. Fair built to tempt me, it was. After while I come to a pair of gates, iron and a guard house behind 'em. Gates not barred. Solid.

"'Goramighty!' syes I to myself. 'It must be the Duke of New York lives 'ere.' I reconnoitered. That wall must 'ave been five miles long. I 'id around an' that night I climbed on top of it. Nothin' but trees an' far-off lights shinin' as though it was a big castle.

"First thing I look for is wires. There was a wire just at the h'inner edge of the wall. Careful I was not to touch it. Charged, I guessed it. I looked over an' took a chance at shootin' my flash. There was two more wires down at the base just where any one would land on 'em if they shinned down the wall. An' it was a twelve-foot drop.

"Anybody else would have been discouraged. But they didn't nyme me King Cat for nothin'. Took a leap, I did. Landed soft as a cat. Sneaked through the trees like a weasel. Came up to the big 'ouse.

"Saw a 'ole lot of queer people goin' in an' around. After while most of the lights went out. Swarmed up a place I'd spotted an' found myself in a big room. An' Cripes, the stuff in that room! It fair myde my 'ed swim. I picked up a few tysty bits, an' then I noticed something funny. There wasn't no doors to that room! ''Ow the 'ell do they get in?' I asked myself. An' then I looked around at the windows I'd come through."

"Goramighty, Captain, I fair fell out of my shirt! There wasn't no windows. They'd disappeared. There wasn't nothin' but wall!"

"An' then a big light blazed up an' out of the walls come about a dozen men with ropes an' a big man after them. I shriveled when he turned them h'eyes of 'is on me. Scared! If I'd nearly fell out of my shirt before, now I was slippin' from my pants.

"Well, it was this bloody bloke Satan, y'understand. 'E just stood scorchin' me. Then 'e started to ask me questions.

"Captain, I told 'im everythin'. Just like 'e was Gord. 'E 'ad me fair kippered. Told 'im all about bein' an electrician, an' my new work, an' about Maggie. Just as I been tellin' you, only more so. 'Strewth, sir, 'e 'ad my life from the time I was out of swaddles.

"'E laughed. That awful laugh. You've 'eard it. 'Ow, 'e

laughed 1 An' next thing I knows I'm standin' at 'is table an' tellin' it all over to Consardine.

"An' 'ere I've been ever since, Cap'n Kirkham. 'E put me under sentence of death, sir, an' sooner or later 'e'll do for me. Unless 'e's done for first. But 'e finds me very useful, 'e does, an' 'e won't do for me as long as I'm that to 'im. Also 'e syes I entertain 'em. Fair prize 'og for entertainment 'e is! Gets me in there with Consardine an' others and mykes me tell 'em about my work, an' ambitions an' my sacredest sentiments. All about Maggie, too. Everything about 'er, sir.

"Gord, 'ow I 'ate 'im! The muckin', bloody, blue-eyed son of a mangy she-dog! But 'e's got me! 'E's got me! Like 'e's got you!"

The little man's voice had risen dangerously high. The shrill edge of hysteria was beginning to creep into it. All along I had sensed the tension under which he was laboring. But aside from the welcome diversion of his unintentionally droll story, I had realized the necessity of letting him run along and pour out his heart to me. Mine was perhaps the first sympathetic ear he had encountered since his imprisonment in this place. Certainly I was the only friend, and it must have seemed to him that I had dropped down from Heaven. I was deeply touched by the swiftness with which he had flown to me as soon as he had recognized me. That he had run grave risks to do this seemed sure.

"Quiet, Harry! Quiet!" I whispered, patting his hand. "You're not alone now. Between the two of us, we ought to find some way to get you free."

"No!" I could almost see the despairing shake of his head. "You don't know 'im, sir. There wouldn't be a bit of use in my gettin' away. 'E'd 'ave me in no time. No. I can't get away while 'e's alive."

"How did you know where I was? How did you find me?" I asked.

"Come through the walls," he said. "There ain't an honest stairs or door in this 'ole place. Nothin' but passages in the walls, an' panels that slide, an' lifts all over, thick as the seeds in a pumpkin. Satan, 'e's the only one that knows the 'ole combination. Consardine, 'e's 'is right 'and man 'ere, knows some of 'em. But I know more than

Consardine. I ought to. Been 'ere nigh on two years now, I 'ave. Never once been out. 'E's warned me. If I go outside 'e does for me. Been creepin', creepin', creepin', round like a rat in the walls whenever I got the chance. A lot of wires to look after, too, an' that learned me. I don't know all – but I know a 'ell of a lot. I was close behind you and Consardine all the time."

"What is Satan?" I asked. "I mean, where does he come from – admitting it's not from Hell?"

"I think he's part Rooshian and part Chink. 'E's got Chink in 'im, sure. Where 'e was before 'e come 'ere, I don't know. I don't dare ask questions. But I found out 'e took this plyce about ten years ago. An' the people who tore it apart inside an' fixed up the panels an' passages were all Chinks."

"But you can't look after a place like this all by yourself, Harry," I considered. "And I can't see Satan giving many the chance to learn the combination."

"'E lets me use the kehjt slyves," he answered astonishingly.

"That's twice tonight I've heard their name," I said. "What are they?"

"Them?" there was loathing and horror in his voice. "They fair give you the creeps. 'E feeds 'em with the kehjt. Opium, coke, 'asheesh – they're mother's milk compared to it. Gives each one of 'em 'is or 'er particular Paradise – till they wake up. Murder's the least of what they'll do to get another shot. Them fellows in the white nightgowns that stood on the steps with their ropes, was some of 'em. You've 'eard of the Old Man of the Mountains who used to send out the assassins. Feller told me about 'em in the war.

"Satan's gyme's the syme. One drink of it an' they can't do without it. Then he gets 'em believin' if they get killed for 'im 'e can stick their souls where they get forever the 'appiness the kehjt gives 'em 'ere only occasionally. Then! They'll do anything for Satan! Anything!"

I broached the question I had long been waiting to ask.

"Do you know a girl named Eve? Big brown eyes and–"

"Eve Demerest," he answered. "Poor kid! 'E's got 'er all right. Gord, what a shyme! 'E'll drag 'er down to 'ell, an' she's an angel, a –

Careful! Smoke up!"

His hand jerked from mine. I heard a faint sound from the opposite wall. I drew upon my cigar, and stretched and sighed. Again the sound, the veriest ghost of one.

"Who's there?" I called, sharply.

A light flashed up and by the wall, beside an opened panel, stood Thomas, the valet.

"Did you call, sir?" he asked. His eyes glanced swiftly around the room, then came to rest on mine, and there was suspicion in them.

"No," I said, indifferently.

"I am sure the bell rang, sir. I was half asleep–" he hesitated.

"Then you were dreaming," I told him.

"I'll just fix your bed for you, sir, while I'm here."

"Do," I said. "When I've finished my cigar I'll turn in."

He made it up and drew a handkerchief from his pocket. A coin dropped upon the floor at his feet. As he stooped to pick it up it slipped from his fingers and rolled beneath the bed. He got down upon his knees and felt about. It was very neatly done. I had been wondering whether he would boldly look under the bed or devise some such polite stratagem.

"Will you have a drink, Thomas?" I asked him, cordially, as he stood up, once more searching the room with his eyes.

"Thank you, sir, I will," he poured himself a rather stiff one. "If you don't mind I'll get some plain water."

"Go ahead," I bade him. He walked into the bathroom and turned on the light. I continued to smoke serenely. He emerged, satisfied apparently that there was no one there. He took his drink and went to the panel.

"I hope you will sleep, sir."

"I shall," I answered cheerfully. "Turn out the light as you go."

He vanished, but I was certain that he was still behind the wall, listening. And after a little while I yawned loudly, arose, walked over to the bed and making what noise I could naturally, turned in.

For a little while I lay awake, turning over the situation in the light of what Barker had told me. A castle with no stairs or "honest doors."...A labyrinth of secret passages and sliding panels. And the little thief creeping, creeping through the walls, denied the open, patiently marking down one by one their secrets. Well, there was a rare ally, indeed, if I should need one.

And Satan 1 Dealing out Paradise by retail to these mysterious slaves of his potent drug. Promising Paradise to those others by his seven shining footsteps. What was his aim? What did he get out of it?

Well, I would probably know more this afternoon after I had obeyed his second summons.

And Eve? Damn that prying Thomas for interrupting just as I was finding out something about her.

Well, I would play Satan's game – with a few reservations.

I went to sleep.

CHAPTER EIGHT

When I woke up, Thomas was at the closet selecting a suit. I heard the taps running in the bath. How long he had been in the room I could not tell. No doubt he had made a thorough search of it. Lazily I wondered what it had been that had aroused his suspicions. I looked at my watch. It had stopped.

"Hello, Thomas," I hailed him. "What's the time?"

He popped out of the wardrobe like a startled rabbit.

"It's one o'clock. I wouldn't have disturbed you, sir, but the Master is expecting you to breakfast with him at two."

"Good." I made for the bath. As I splashed around, the half-formed plan upon which I had gone to sleep suddenly crystallized. I would try my luck at the footprints at once. But – I would not go the distance. Not this time. I would step upon two of them and no more. There was much I wanted to know before running the risk of delivering myself over to Satan body and soul.

What I hoped was that only one of the two would be his. At the worst I would incur a year's bondage. Well, I did not mind that so much either.

I had, in fact, determined to match my wits against Satan rather than my luck.

I did not want to escape him. My keenest desire was to be incorporated among his entourage, infernal or not. Barker gave me a unique advantage. Out of it might well come the opportunity to tumble this slanting blue-eyed devil off his black throne, break his power and – well, why mince words – loot him.

Or, to put it more politely, recover from him a thousand fold what he had so casually stripped me of.

That had been twenty thousand dollars. To wipe off the debt at that rate I must strip Satan of twenty millions –

That would be a good game indeed. I laughed.

"You seem quite gay, sir," said Thomas.

"The birds, Thomas," I said, "are singing everywhere.

Everywhere, Thomas. Even here."

"Yes, sir," he answered, looking at me dubiously.

It was a quarter of two when I had finished. The valet walked me into the hall and out again, stopping the lift this time at a much higher level. Again I emerged into a small antechamber whose one door was guarded by two tall slaves.

Passing through it, I was dazzled by a flood of sunshine. Then the sunshine seemed to gather itself and center upon the girl who had half risen from her seat at the table as I entered. It was Eve, but a far different Eve than she who had so ably aided in my kidnaping the night before. Then I had thought her extraordinarily pretty; now I realized how inadequate was the adjective.

The girl was beautiful. Her clear brown eyes regarded me gravely, studying me with a curious intentness. Her proud little head had the poise of a princess, and the sunlight playing in her hair traced a ruddy golden coronet within it; her mouth was sweeter even than I had found it.

And as I looked at the lips I had kissed so ruthlessly, a quick rose tinted her face.

"Eve – this is Mr. Kirkham," it was Consardine's voice, faintly amused. "Miss Demerest and you have met, I think."

"I think," I answered, slowly, "that I am seeing Miss Demerest for the first time. I am hoping that she – will consider it so."

It was as near to an apology as I could come. Would she take the proffered olive branch? Her eyes widened as though with reproachful surprise.

"To think," mused Eve, mournfully, "that a man could so soon forget having kissed me! It seems hardly a compliment, does it, Dr. Consardine?"

"It seems," said Consardine, truthfully, "impossible."

"Ah, no," sighed Eve. "No, Mr. Kirkham. I can't think it is our first meeting. You have, you know, such a forceful way of impressing one with your personality. And a woman cannot forget kisses so easily."

I flushed. That Eve was a consummate little actress she had

given me plenty of convincing proof. But what did this bit of by-play mean? I could not believe that she was so bitterly offended by my actions in the Subway; she was too intelligent for that. Yet if she distrusted me, disliked me, how could I help her?

"My remark," I said, "was prompted wholly by politeness. The truth is, Miss Demerest, that I consider those kisses generous payment for any inconveniences of my interesting journey here."

"Well, then," she said coldly, "you have made your trade and the slate is clean. And do not trouble to be polite with me, Mr. Kirkham. Just be yourself. You are much more amusing."

I choked back an angry retort and bowed.

"Quite right," I returned, as coldly as she. "After all there seems to be no reason why I should be polite to you."

"None at all," she answered indifferently. "And, frankly, the less I come into contact with even your natural self, Mr. Kirkham, the better it will be for both of us."

That was an oddly turned phrase, it flashed upon me. And there was an enigmatic something deep in the brown eyes. What did she mean? Was she trying to convey to me some message that Consardine would not suspect? I heard a chuckle and turned to face – Satan.

I could not know how long he had been listening. As his gaze rested on the girl I saw a momentary flashing of the brilliant eyes, and a flicker passed over his face. It was as though the hidden devil within him had licked its lips.

"Quarreling! Oh fie!" he said unctuously.

"Quarreling? Not at all," Eve answered coolly. "It happens that I dislike Mr. Kirkham. I am sorry – but it is so. It seemed to me better to tell him, that we may avoid each other in the future except, of course, when you find it necessary for us to be together, Satan."

It was disconcerting, to say the least. I made no effort to hide my chagrin. Satan looked at me and chuckled again. I had a curious conviction that he was pleased.

"Well," he purred, "even I have no power over personal prejudices. All that I can do is to make use of them. In the meantime –

I am hungry."

He seated himself at the table's head; Eve at his right hand, I at his left and Consardine beside me. The Manchu butler and another Chinese served us.

We were in a tower room, clearly. The windows were set high above the floor and through them I could see only the blue sky. The walls were covered with Fragonard and Boucher panels, and I had no doubt that they had been acquired by the "eloquence" of Satan's messengers. The rest of the chamber was in keeping; furnished with that same amazing eclecticism and perception of the beautiful that I had noted in the great hall and in the room where I had first met the blue-eyed devil.

Eve, having defined my place – or lack of place – in her regard, was coolly aloof to me but courteous, and sparkling and witty with Satan and Consardine. The drama of the temple and Cartright's punishment seemed to be forgotten by the three of them. Satan was in the best of humors, but in his diabolic benignity – it is the only way I can describe it – was, to me, the sinister suggestion of a wild beast playful because its appetite has been appeased, an addict of cruelty mellowed by the ultimate anguish to which he has subjected a sacrifice. I had a vivid and unpleasant picture of him wallowing like a tiger upon the torn carcass of the man whom he had sent out of life a few hours before through the gateways of hell.

Yet the sunlight stripped him of much of his vague terror. And if he was, as Barker had put it, "an 'og for entertainment" he was himself a masterly entertainer. Something had shifted the conversation toward Jenghis Khan and for half an hour Satan told us stories of that Ruler of the Golden Horde and his black palace in his lost city of Khara-Khoto in the Gobi that wiped all the present out of my mind and set me back, seeing and hearing, into a world ten centuries gone; stories tragic and comic. Rabelaisian and tender – and all as though he had himself been a witness to what he described. Indeed, listening, it seemed to me that he could have been nothing else. Devil or not, the man had magic.

And at the end he signaled the two servants to go, and when

they had gone he said to me, abruptly: "Well, James Kirkham, is it yes or no?" I feigned to hesitate. I leaned my head upon my hand and under its cover shot a glance at Eve. She was patting her mouth with slim fingers, suppressing a yawn – but there was a pallor upon her face that had not been there a moment before. I felt Satan's will beating down upon me, tangibly.

"Yes – or no?" he repeated.

"Yes," I said, "if, Satan, you will answer one question."

"It is always permitted to ask," he replied. "Well, then," I said, "I want to know what kind of an – employer you are before I make a play that may mean life service to me. A man is his aims plus the way he works to attain them. As to your methods, I have had at least an illuminative inkling. But what are your aims? In the olden days, Satan, the question would have been unnecessary. Everybody who dealt with you knew that what you were after were souls to keep your furnaces busy. But Hell, I understand, has been modernized with its Master. Furnaces are out of date and fuel therefore nothing like so valuable. Yet still, as of old, you take your prospective customers up a high mountain and offer them the kingdoms of Earth. Very well, the question. What, Satan, do you get out of it now?"

"There you have one reason for my aversion to Mr. Kirkham," murmured Eve. "He admits nothing that cannot be balanced in a set of books. He has the shopkeeper outlook."

I ignored this thrust. But once more Satan chuckled from still lips.

"A proper question, Eve," he told her. "You forget that even I always keep my accounts balanced – and present them when the time comes for payment."

He spoke the last words slowly, contemplatively, staring at her – and again I saw the devil's gloating flicker over his face. And she saw it too, for she caught her lip between her teeth to check its trembling.

"Then answer," I spoke abruptly to draw his attention from her back to me. He studied me as though picking the words to reply.

"Call it," he said at last, "amusement. It is for amusement that I exist. It is for that alone that I remain upon a world in which, when all is said and done, amusement in some form or guise is the one great aim of all, the only thing that makes life upon it tolerable. My aim is, therefore, you perceive, a simple one. But what is it that amuses me?

"Three things. I am a great playwright, the greatest that has ever lived, since my plays are real. I set the scenes for my little single acts, my farces and comedies, dramas and tragedies, my epics. I direct the actors. I am the sole audience that can see every action, hear every line, of my plays from beginning to end. Sometimes what began as a farce turns into high tragedy, tragedies become farces, a one-act diversion develops into an epic, governments fall, the mighty topple from their pedestals, the lowly are exalted. Some people live their lives for chess. I play my chess with living chessmen and I play a score of games at once in all corners of the world. All this amuses me. Furthermore, in my character as Prince of Darkness, which I perceive, James Kirkham, that you do not wholly admit, my art puts me on a par with that other super-dramatist, my ancient and Celestial adversary known according to the dominant local creed as Jehovah. Nay, it places me higher – since I rewrite his script. This also amuses me."

Under the suave, sardonic mockery I read truth. To this cold, monstrous intellect, men and women were only puppets moving over a worldwide stage. Suffering, sorrow, anguish of mind or body were to it nothing but entertaining reactions to situations which it had conceived. Like the dark Power whose name Satan had taken, souls were his playthings. Their antics amused him. In that he found sufficient reward for labor.

"That," he said, "is one of the three. The second? I am a lover of beauty. It is, indeed, the one thing that can arouse in me what may be called – emotion. It happens now and then that man with his mind and eyes and heart and hands makes visible and manifest some thing which bears that stamp of creative perfection the monopoly of which tradition ascribes to the same Celestial adversary I have named. It may be a painting, a statue, a carved bit of wood, a crystal, a vase, a fabric – any one of ten thousand things. But in it is that essence of beauty humanity calls divine and for which, in its blundering way, it is always seeking – as it is amusement. The best of these things I make from time to time my own. But – I will not have them come to me except by my own way. Here enters the third element – the gamble, the game.

"For example. I decided, after mature reflection, that the Mona Lisa of da Vinci, in the Louvre, had the quality I desired. It could not, of course, be bought; nor did I desire to buy it. Yet it is here. In this house. I allowed France to recover an excellent duplicate in which my experts reproduced perfectly even the microscopic cracks in the paint. Only now have they begun to suspect. They can never be sure – and that amuses me more than if they knew.

"James Kirkham, men risk their lives over the globe in search of treasure. I tell you that never, never since mankind began, was there ever such a treasure trove as this house of mine. The fortunes of the ten richest men in all the world could not buy it. It is more precious than all the gold in the Bank of England.

"Its values in dollars and pounds is nothing to me. But to possess this pure essence of beauty, to dwell with it, that is – much! And to know that the best of my ancient adversary's choicest inspirations are mine, Satan's – that is amusing! Ho! Ho!" he roared.

"Third and last," he checked his laughter, "is the game. Collector of souls and beauty I am. Gambler am I, too, and as supreme in that as in my collecting. It is the unknown quantity, the risk, that sharpens the edge of my enjoyment of my plays. It is what gives the final zest to my – acquirements. And I am a generous opponent. The stakes those who play with me may win are immeasurably higher than any I could win from them. But play with me – they must!"

For a moment he stared at me, huge head thrust forward.

"As for the rest," he said, "I have, as you surmised, no further interest in stoking my traditional furnaces. What happens to any man after he leaves this earth concerns me no longer. I have given up my ancient domain for this where I am amused so well. But, James Kirkham" – his blue eyes blazed out at me – "those who cross me find that I have lost none of my old skill as a Hell maker. Now are you answered?"

"Fully, sir," I bowed. "I will gamble with you. And, win or lose, you shall have no occasion to find fault with me. But, by your leave, one more question. You have said that he who mounts the four fortunate steps can have anything that he desires. Very well, if I do so can I have" – I pointed to Eve – "her?"

I heard a gasp from Eve, watched Satan bend toward me, scrutinizing me with eyes in which a menacing coldness had appeared. Consardine spoke:

"Oh, come, now, Kirkham, be reasonable. Eve's been honest with you. She's made it pretty plain you're not an acceptable candidate for bridegroom."

I sensed a certain anxiety in his voice; the desire to placate. Placate whom – me or Satan? It interested me, hugely. Perhaps Consardine –

"Marry – you? Not for anything in this world, not to save my life, not to save myself torture!"

Eve's voice was shrill with anger. She had sprung to her feet and stood, eyes flashing wrath, red danger signals on her cheeks. I met Satan's gaze, squarely.

"Have I mentioned – marriage?" I asked him, blandly.

He took, as I had thought he would, the worst interpretation out of that. I saw the menace and suspicion fade away as swiftly as it had come. Yes, he took the worst interpretation, but – so did Eve.

"Satan," she stamped her foot and thrust her chair from her with such force that it went careening over on its side, "Satan, I have a question, too. If I take the steps will you give me this man to do with as it pleases me?"

Satan looked from one to the other of us. Very evidently the situation gave him much gratification. The blue eyes sparkled and there was a benignant purr in his voice when he spoke.

"To both of you I must answer – no. No, to you, Eve, because James Kirkham has accepted my challenge to the gamble of the steps. That being so, I could not withdraw if I would. He must have his chance. Also, if he should lose to me for one undertaking or enter my service for a year, I am bound to protect him. I am bound also to give him his other chances, should he claim them. But, Eve – if he should decide to gamble no more – why, then, ask me again."

He paused and stared at me. I had no doubt as to his meaning.

"And no to you, James Kirkham," he said, "because all that I have said to Eve as to your position applies equally to hers. She too has her right to her chances. But" – his voice lost its benignity and grew heavy – "there is another reason. I have decreed for Eve a high destiny. Should she fulfill it – she will be far above the reach of any man. Should she shirk it–"

He did not finish the sentence; only brooded upon her with unwinking, blazing eyes. I watched the blood slowly drain from her cheeks, saw her own eyes falter and drop. There was a sharp snap and a tinkle of glass. Consardine's hand had been playing with a heavy goblet of thick crystal and now, tightening around it, had crushed it as though it had been made of paper. He thrust the hand into his pocket, but not before I had seen blood upon it. Satan's eyes dwelt upon him inscrutably.

"Strength like yours, Consardine," he said, "is often dangerous – to its owner."

"Faith, Satan," Consardine answered, ruefully, "I was dreaming, and thought it was a neck I held in my hand."

"A warning, I should say," said Satan, grimly, "to leave that particular neck alone."

"I've no choice," laughed Consardine, "since the throat I had in mind was of an old enemy these ten years dead."

For another moment or two Satan studied him, but made no further comment. He turned to me.

"You have decided," he said. "When will you mount the steps?"

"Any time," I answered. "The sooner the better. Now, if it's possible. I'm feeling lucky."

"Consardine," he said, "have the temple prepared. Bid those who are here assemble in half an hour, Eve."

He watched them go, the girl through a panel with never a look at me, Consardine by way of the door that led into the tiny anteroom. For long minutes Satan sat silent, regarding me. I smoked calmly, waiting for him to speak.

"James Kirkham," he said at last, "I have told you before that you please me. Everything I have seen of you since then pleases me even more. But I must warn you of one thing. Do not let whatever chagrin or feeling of dislike that you have toward Eve Demerest be the cause of the slightest harm coming to her. You are not one that I have to threaten, but – heed this warning."

"I put her out of my mind, Satan," I answered. "Yet I confess I'm a bit curious about that high destiny you've promised her."

"The highest destiny," again there was the fateful heaviness in his voice. "The highest honor that could come to any woman. I will tell you, James Kirkham, so you may know how urgent is my warning. Sooner or later I shall be compelled to visit other of my worlds. When that time comes I shall turn this one over to my son and heir, and his mother shall be – Eve!"

CHAPTER NINE

I consider it one of my few enough major victories that I took the shock of that infernal enunciation with perfect outward composure. Of course, in a way, I had been prepared. In spite of the rage and hatred that seethed up in me, I managed to raise my glass with a steady hand and my voice held nothing but the proper surprise and interest. "That is an honor, sir, indeed," I said. "You will pardon me if I express a certain wonder as to your choice. For you, I would have thought, some empress, at least one of royal blood–"

"No, no," he interrupted me, but I knew that he swallowed with relish my flattery, "you do not know the girl. You let your prejudice blind you. Eve is as perfect as any of the masterpieces I have gathered around me. To her beauty she adds brains. She has daring and spirit. Whatever – to me – otherwise desirable qualities may be lacking in her to pass on to my son, I can supply. He will be – my son. His training will be in my hands. He will be what I make him."

"The son of Satan!" I said.

"Satan's own son!" a flame leaped from his eyes. "My true son, James Kirkham."

"You will understand," he went on, "that there is in this nothing of what is called – love. Something of emotion, yes – but only that emotion which any truly beautiful thing calls up in me. It is intrinsically, solely, a matter of selective breeding: I have had the same idea before, but – I was not fortunate in my selections."

"You mean–"

"They were girl children," he said somberly. "They were disappointments. Therefore, they ceased to be."

And now behind the imperturbable, heavy mask of his face I glimpsed the Chinese. Perceptibly the slant of the eyes had accentuated, the high cheek bones became more prominent. I nodded, thoughtfully.

"But if again you are–" I had meant to add "disappointed."

He caught me up with a touch of that demonic fury he had shown at the ordeal of Cartright.

"Do not dare say it! Do not dare think it! Her first-born shall be a son! A son, I say!"

What I might have answered, what have done, I do not know. His sudden deadliness, his arrogance, had set my smoldering wrath ablaze again. Consardine saved me. I heard the door open and the menacing gaze turned from me for a moment. It gave me my chance to recover myself.

"All is prepared, Satan," Consardine announced. I arose eagerly, nor was that eagerness feigned. I was conscious of the beginning of a curious excitement, a heady exaltation.

"It is your moment, James Kirkham." Satan's voice was again expressionless, his face marble, his eyes sparkling. "But a few minutes – and I may be your servant. The world your plaything! Who knows! Who knows!"

He stepped to the farther wall and opened one of the panels.

"Dr. Consardine," he said, "you will escort the neophyte to the temple."

He brooded upon me, almost caressingly – I saw the hidden devil lick its lips.

"Master of the world!" he repeated. "And Satan your loyal slave! who knows!"

He was gone. Consardine drew a deep breath. He spoke, in carefully matter-of-fact fashion.

"Want a drink before you try it, Kirkham?"

I shook my head, the tingling excitement increasing.

"You know the rules," he said briskly. "You step on any four of the seven footprints. You can stop at any one of them you choose, and abide by the consequences. One of Satan's gives you to him for one – service; two give you to him for a year; three – and you are his forever. No more chances for you then, Kirkham. Hit the four fortunate ones and you sit on the top of the world, just as he promised you. Look back while you're on the climb, and you have to begin all over again. All clear?"

"Let's go," I said, somewhat huskily – my throat felt oddly dry.

He led me to the wall and through it into one of the marble-lined corridors. From that we passed into a lift. It dropped. A panel slid aside. Consardine leading, I stepped out into the webbed temple.

I was close to the base of the steps, just within the half-circle of brilliant light that masked the amphitheater. From it came a faint rustling and murmuring. Foolishly, I hoped that Eve had picked out a good seat. I realized that I was trembling. Cursing myself silently, I mastered the tremor, praying that it had been too slight to be noticed.

I looked up at the black throne, met Satan's mocking eyes and my nerves steadied, my control clicked into place. He sat there in his black robe, just as I had seen him the night before. The blue jeweled eyes of his stone counterpart glittered behind him. Instead of the fourteen white-robed, pallid-faced men with the noosed ropes there were but two, midway up the steps. And something else was missing. The black-visaged fiend of an executioner!

What did that mean? Was it Satan's way of telling me that even if I trod upon his three prints he would not have me killed? Or at least that I need not fear death until I had finished the work for which he had picked me?

Or was it a trap?

That was the more likely. Somehow I could not conceive Satan thus solicitously though subtly reassuring me of a suspended sentence. Was it not, rather, that by cutting down his guards and eliminating his torturer he had schemed to plant that very thought? Lure me on to make the full gamble and go the limit of the four steps in the belief that if I lost I was sure of a reprieve that might give me time to escape him?

Or, admitting that his present purpose was benevolent, if I did lose, might it not suddenly occur to him that he would derive greater amusement from evoking his hellish servant with the cord of woman's hair and giving me to him – like Cartright.

As Cartright had, I studied his face. It was inscrutable, nothing in it to guide me. And now, far more vividly than when I had watched that despairing wretch being hauled in to his torment, did I realize the infernal ingenuity of this game. For now it was I who had to play it.

I dropped my eyes from Satan's. They fell upon the seven

shining footprints and followed them up to the golden throne. Crown and scepter glittered upon it. Their gem fires beckoned and called to me. Again the excitement seized me, tingling along every nerve.

If I could win them! Win them and what they stood for!

Satan pressed down the lever between the two thrones. I heard the whirring of the controlling mechanism and saw the seven marks of the childish foot shine with intenser light.

"The steps are ready," he intoned, and thrust his hands beneath his black robe. "They await their conqueror, the chosen one of fortune! Are you he? Ascend – and learn!" I walked to the steps, mounted and set my foot unhesitatingly upon the first of the prints. Behind me, I knew, its symbol glimmered on the telltale of the luminous globe –

On Satan's side – or mine?

Again I ascended, more slowly, and paused at the next print. But it was not to weigh its probabilities of good or evil that I halted. The truth is that the gambler's fever was rising high within me, crazily high, undermining my determination to limit this first game of mine with Satan to only two of the footsteps.

Common sense bade me go slow and get back my grip upon my judgment. Common sense, fighting for time, moved me past that mark and slowly on to the next.

I trod upon it. There was another symbol on the telltale – mine – or Satan's?

Now the fever had me wholly. My eyes were bright with it as Satan's own. My heart was thumping like a drum, my fingers cold, a dry electric heat beating about my head. The little feet of fire seemed to quiver and dance with eagerness to lead me on.

"Take me!" beckoned one.

"Take me!" signaled another.

The jeweled crown and scepter summoned. On the golden throne I saw a phantom – myself, triumphant, with crown upon my head, scepter in my hand, Satan at my beck and the world at my knees!

It may be true that thoughts have form, and that intense emotion or desire leave behind something of themselves that persists, lives on in the place where it was called forth and wakes, ravening, when some one moved by the same impulses that created it appears in that place. At any rate, it was as though the ghosts of desire of all those who had ascended those steps before me had rushed to me and, hungering for fulfillment, were clamoring to me to go on.

But their will was also my will. I needed no urging. I wanted to go on. After all, the two prints upon which I had trodden might well be fortunate ones. At the worst, by all the laws of chance, I should have broken even. And if so then there would be no more risk in making one more throw than I had already resolved to incur.

What did the telltale show?

Ah, if I could but know! If I could but know!

And suddenly a chill went through me, as though the ghosts of despair of all those who had mounted before me and lost had pressed back the hungry wraiths of desire.

Glitter of crown and scepter tarnished and grew sinister.

For an instant I saw the seven shining prints not as those of a child's foot, but as of a cloven hoof!

I drew back up and looked up at Satan. He sat head bent forward, glaring at me, and with distinct shock I realized that with full force of his will he was commanding me to proceed. Instantly after that apperception came another. It was as though a hand touched my shoulder, drawing me still further back, and clearly as though lips were close to my ear I heard a counter-command, imperative –

"Stop! Stop now!"

The voice of – Eve!

For another minute I stood, shaken by the two contending impulses. Then abruptly a shadow lifted from my mind, all fever fled, the spell of the shining prints and lure of crown and orb broke. I turned my face, reeking with sweat, once more to Satan.

"I've had enough...for this...time!" I panted.

He stared at me silently. I thought that behind the cold sparkle of his gaze I read anger, thwarted purpose, a certain evil puzzlement. If so, it was fleeing. He spoke.

"You have claimed the player's right. It was yours to stop

when you willed. Look behind you."

I swung around and sought the telltale globe.

Both of the prints upon which I had trodden had been – Satan's!

CHAPTER TEN

I was Satan's bond servant for a year, bound to do whatsoever he commanded me.

The balance of that afternoon I had spent in my room, alternating between intensive thought and hope of Barker cat-footing it out of the wall. It was plain that my liberty was still limited. Not yet might I run with the pack. Tentative overtures to Consardine following my retreat from the steps, a hint that perhaps I ought to make a tour of this citadel of the Prince of Darkness now I was enlisted among his legionaries, had met courteous but firm rebuff. He had gravely prescribed, as a doctor, the quietness of my chamber as a sedative for the nervous strain I had just undergone.

What I had hoped for, of course, had been a chance to run across Eve. Reflection assured me that it was much more important at the moment to get in touch with the little cockney burglar.

As I waited I tried to analyze the fever that had so swept me off my feet. I had thought myself cooler headed, better balanced. The fact is that I was both ashamed of myself and uneasily puzzled. If I admitted that the intensity of the passion I had felt had been due to Satan's will, an actual compelling force pouring down upon me as I climbed the steps – well, at least that was an explanation to soothe my smarting pride.

But if it left me with the comforting thought that my will was quite as strong as I had deemed it, it involved the humiliating alternative that it was far weaker than Satan's. I took no credit for abstaining from that next step which might have given me to him forever. It had been the warning whisper, whether from Eve's mind or my own subconscious one, that had pulled me back.

And Satan's attitude puzzled me. Why had he been so bent on forcing me upward? Had it been simply the natural instinct of the gambler? The urge to win? Had the sight of those two symbols flashing out one after the other on his side of the telltale aroused the blood-lust in him? If one or both of them had been on my side of the globe would he have shown the same eagerness?

Or had he from the beginning willed me to go the limit and lose?

And if so – why?

I could find no answer to the questions, nor did Barker appear. And at last, Thomas aiding, I dressed and was escorted by way of walls and lifts to still another immense and vaulted chamber that in size and trappings might have been a feast hall of the Medicis in the golden prime of that magnificent clan. There were a score or more men and women at a great oval table with Satan at the head, his flawless evening dress giving him an oddly accentuated sardonic note. Plainly I was late, but as plainly informality was the custom.

"Our newest recruit – James Kirkham."

With no more introduction than this, Satan waved me to my appointed place. The others smiled and nodded and went on talking.

As I seated myself I saw with secret amazement that my right-hand neighbor was a certain famous actress whose name was seldom missing from Broadway's electrics. My rapid glance around the table showed me a polo player of enviable American lineage and international reputation, and a brilliant attorney high in the councils of Tammany Hall. The others were unknown to me, but one and all bore the stamp of unusual intelligence. If this were a representative slice of Satan's court, then indeed his organization must be quite as extraordinary as he had boasted. Eve was not there. Cobham was.

Walter sat at the actress's right. As the dinner went on I exerted myself to be pleasant to him. For my own reasons, I wanted no lurking enemies just then. He was a bit stiffish at first, then mellowed. He drank freely, but, I noted with interest, not so freely as he would have liked. Very clearly Walter loved to look upon the wine when it was not only red, but all along the rainbow. I thought at first that it was the restraint he had placed upon himself as to the rate of his consumption that stirred up in him antagonism against other inhibitions, and particularly that of discretion in expression of opinion. Then I realized it was the drink itself that bred in Cobham a stern passion for truth, a contempt for euphemisms and circumlocutions.

What he wanted was the plain fact unadorned, and no evasions. As he put it, "no tampering with the formula." He was in fact an in-vino-veritas drinker of Fundamentalist fervor. Also he was amusing, and the actress was vastly entertained by our cross-conversation.

Some day or other soon, I resolved, I would usefully irrigate Walter into such condition that he could not bear to leave even a shred of covering on the clear-eyed goddess of the verities. I was astonished to find that he was a chemist and spent much time in his laboratory in the chateau. That explained his remark about the formula. He was very explicit in telling me what an amazing chemist he was. I was to learn later that he had not exaggerated. That is why I have lingered over his picture.

It was a wonderful dinner, with a high note of sophistication and delicately reckless gayety that had a constantly ringing undertone as of fine steel. The only hints as to our peculiar position were when the distinguished attorney, glancing at me, proposed a toast to "the happy near damned," and when Satan sent for a casket and displayed some of the most magnificent jewels I had ever seen.

He told their histories. This emerald set in turquoise was the seal which Cleopatra had pressed upon the letters she wrote to Anthony; this necklace of diamonds was the one with which the Cardinal de Rohan had thought to buy the favors of Marie Antoinette, and so had set in motion that trial which had been one of the midwives of the Revolution, and finally cost the unhappy queen her head; this coronet had shone among the curls of Nell Gwynne, set there by Charles, her royal lover; this ring with its regal rubies had been given by Montespan to the poisoner La Voiture for a love philter to warm the cooling heart of the Roi du Soleil.

At last he gave the flashing little Frenchwoman who sat at his right a bracelet of sapphires that had been, he said, Lucrezia Borgia's. I wondered what she had done to deserve it, and if there were ironic significance in his naming of its old owner. If so, it made no difference in her delight.

And it gave me an enormously increased respect for Satan's power that in this gathering there was no melodramatic secrecy, no masking, no stale concealment of names by numbers. His people met face to face. Evidently any thought of mutual betrayal was incredible, their faith in Satan's protection absolute. That all of them, or many of them, had witnessed my ordeal of the steps I had no doubt – nor that they had watched the tragedy of Cartright. There was nothing to show it in their behavior.

They bade good night to Satan. I arose and would have gone with them, but his eyes caught mine and he shook his head.

"Remain with me, James Kirkham," he commanded.

And soon we were alone, the table cleared, the servants gone.

"And so," his lashless eyes glittered at me over the edge of his great goblet, "and so – you have lost!"

"Yet not as much as I might have, Satan," I smiled, "since had I gone but a bit higher my fall might have been like that ancient one of yours – straight into Hell."

"A journey," he said blandly, "never devoid of interest. But a year soon passes, and then you shall have your chance again."

"To fall, you mean?" I laughed.

"You gamble against Satan," he reminded me, then shook his head. "No, you are wrong. My plans for you require your presence on earth. I commend, however, your prudence in climbing. And I admit you – surprised me."

"I have then," I arose and bowed, "begun my bondage with a most notable achievement."

"May we both find your year a profitable one," he said. "And now, James Kirkham – I claim my first service from you!"

I seated myself, waiting, with a little heightening of the pulse, for him to go on.

"The Yunnan jades," he said. "It is true that I arranged matters so that you might retain them, if you were clever enough. It is also true that it would have amused me to have possessed the plaques. I was forced to choose between two interests. Obviously whichever way the cards fell I was bound to experience a half-disappointment."

"In other words, you observed, sir," I remarked, solemnly, "that even you cannot have your cake and eat it, too."

"Exactly," he said. "Another blunder of a bunglingly devised world. The museum has the jades; well, they shall keep them. But they must pay me for my half-disappointment. I have decided to accept something else that the museum owns which has long interested me. You shall – persuade – them to let me have it, James Kirkham."

He raised his glass to me, ceremoniously, and drank; I followed suit, with no illusion as to the word he had used.

"What is it," I asked, "and what is to be my method of – persuasion?"

"The task," he said, "will not be a difficult one. It is, in truth, in the nature of the initial deed all knights of old were compelled to perform before they could receive the accolade. I follow the custom."

"I bow to the rules, sir," I told him.

"Many centuries ago," he continued, "a Pharaoh summoned his greatest goldsmith, the Benvenuto Cellini of that day, and commanded him to make a necklace for his daughter.. Whether it was for her birthday or her bridal, none knows. The goldsmith wrought it of finest gold and carnelian and lapis lazuli and that green feldspar called aquamarine. At one side of the golden cartouche that bore in hieroglyphs the Pharaoh's name, he set a falcon crowned with the sun's disk – Horus the son of Osiris, God, in a fashion, of Love, and guardian of happiness. On the other the winged serpent, the uraeus, bearing the looped cross, the crux ansata, the symbol of life. Below it he made a squatting god grasping sheaves of years and set upon his elbow the tadpole symbol of eternity. Thus did the Pharaoh by amulets and symbols invoke an eternity of love and life for his daughter.

"Alas for love and human hope and faith! The princess died, and the Pharaoh died and in time Horus and Osiris and all the gods of ancient Egypt died.

"But the beauty which that forgotten Cellini wrought in that necklace did not die. It could not. It was deathless. It lay for centuries with the mummy of that princess in her hidden coffin of stone. It has outlived her gods. It will outlive the gods of today and the gods of a thousand tomorrows. Undimmed, its beauty shines from it as it did three thousand years ago when the withered breast on which it was found throbbed with life and sobbed with love and had, it may be, its fleeting shadow of that same beauty which in the necklace is immortal."

"The necklace of Senusert the Second!" I exclaimed. "I know that lovely thing, Satan."

"I must have that necklace, James Kirkham!"

I looked at him, disconcerted. If this was what he thought an easy service, what would he consider a difficult one?

"It seems to me, Satan," I hazarded, "that you could hardly have picked an object less likely to be yielded up by any – persuasion. It is guarded day and night. It lies in a cabinet in the center of a comparatively small room, in fact, and designedly, in the most conspicuous part of that room – constantly under observation–"

"I must have it," he silenced me. "You shall get it for me. I answer now your second question. How? By obeying to the minute, to the second, without deviation, the instructions I am about to give you. Take your pencil, put down these o'clocks, fix them unalterably in your memory."

He waited until I had obeyed the first part of his command.

"You will leave here," he said, "at 10:30 tomorrow morning. Your journey will be so timed that you may drop out of the car and enter the museum at precisely one o'clock. You will be wearing a certain suit which your valet will give you. He will also pick out your overcoat, hat and other articles of dress. You must, as is the rule, check your coat at the cloak room.

"From there you must go straight to the Yunnan jades, the ostensible object of your visit. You may talk to whom you please, the more the better, in fact. But you must so manage that at precisely 1:45 you enter alone the north corridor of the Egyptian wing. You will interest yourself in its collections until 2:05, when you will enter, upon the minute, the room of the necklace. It has a guard for each of its two entrances. Do they know you?"

"I'm not sure," I answered. "Probably so. At any rate, they know of me."

"You will find an excuse to introduce yourself to one of the guards in the north corridor," he continued, "provided he does not know you by sight. You will do the same with one of the guards in the necklace room. You will then go to one of the four corners of that room, it does not matter which, and become absorbed in whatever is in the case before you. Your object will be to keep as far from you as possible either of the two attendants who, conceivably, might think it his duty to remain close to such," he raised his goblet to me, "a distinguished visitor.

"And, James Kirkham, at precisely 2:15 you will walk to the cabinet containing the necklace, open it with an instrument which will be provided for you, take out the necklace, drop it into the ingenious pocket which you will find in the inside left of your coat, close the case noiselessly and walk out."

I looked at him, incredulously.

"Did you say – walk out?" I asked.

"Walk out," he repeated.

"Carrying with me, I suppose," I suggested satirically, "the two guards."

"You will pay no attention to the guards," he said.

"No?" I questioned. "But they will certainly be paying attention to me, Satan!"

"Do not interrupt me again," he ordered, sternly enough. "You will do exactly as I am telling you. You will pay no attention to the guards. You will pay no attention to anything that may be happening around you. Remember, James Kirkham, this is vital. You will have but one thought – to open the case at exactly 2:15 and walk out of that room with Senusert's necklace in your possession. You will see nothing, hear nothing, do nothing but that. It will take you two minutes to reach the cloak room. You will go from there straight to the outer doors. As you pass through them you will step to the right, bend down and tie a shoe. You will then walk down the steps to the street, still giving no attention to whatever may be occurring around you. You will see at the curb a blue limousine whose chauffeur will be polishing the right-hand headlight.

"You will enter that car and give the person you find inside it the necklace. The time should then be 2:20. It must not be later. You will drive with that person for one hour. At 3:20 you will find the car close to the obelisk behind the museum. You will descend from it there, walk to the Avenue, take a taxi and return to the Discoverers' Club."

"The Discoverers' Club, you said?" I honestly thought in my astonishment that it had been a slip of his tongue.

"I repeat – the Discoverers' Club," he answered. "You will upon arriving there go straight to the desk and tell the clerk on duty that you have work to do that demands absolute concentration. You will instruct him not to disturb you with either telephone calls or visitors. You will say to him that it is more than likely reporters from the newspapers will try to get in touch with you. He will tell them that you left word that you would receive them at eight o'clock. You will impress it upon him that the work which you have to do is most important and that you must not be disturbed. You will further instruct him to send up to your room at seven o'clock all the late editions and extra editions of the afternoon newspapers."

He paused.

"Is all clear?" he demanded.

"All except what I am to say to the reporters," I said.

"You will know that," he replied enigmatically, "after you have read the newspapers."

He sipped from his goblet, regarding me appraisingly.

"Repeat my instructions," he ordered.

Soberly, I did so.

"Good," he nodded. "You understand, of course, that this small adventure is not the one that prompted my decision to acquire you. That will be a real adventure. This is in the nature of a test. And you must pass it. For your own sake, James Kirkham – you must pass it."

His jewel-hard eyes held a snake-like glitter. Mad as the performance he had outlined seemed, he was in deadly earnest, no doubt about that. I did not answer him. He had left me nothing to say.

"And now," he touched a bell, "no more excitement for you tonight. I am solicitous for the welfare of my subjects, even those on –

probation. Go to your room and sleep well."

A panel opened and Thomas stepped from the lift and stood waiting for me.

"Good night, Satan," I said.

"Good night," he answered, "and however good it be, may your night tomorrow be a better one."

It was close to eleven o'clock. The dinner had lasted longer than I had realized. I found everything comfortable in my bedroom, told Thomas so and dismissed him. In about half an hour and two brandies and sodas I turned out the lights and went to bed hoping for Barker.

Waiting wide-eyed in the darkness I went over my amazing instructions. I was, it was plain, part of a more or less intricate jig-saw puzzle. I saw myself as a number of pieces that I must fit in at the exact moments to click the whole design. Or better, I was a living chessman in one of those games in which Satan delighted. I must make my moves at the designated times. But what would his other chessmen be doing? And suppose one of them moved a bit too soon or too late? Then where would I be in this unknown game?

The picture of the glittering-eyed, bald devil on the malachite slabs behind the two thrones came to me – Satan's double directing the hands of the Fates. Oddly enough, it reassured me. The ethics of the matter did not bother me greatly. After all, the bulk of the treasures in any museum is loot; loot of graves, of tombs, of lost cities – and what is not, has been stolen, the most of it, time and again.

But aside from all that – there was nothing else for me to do except obey Satan. If I did not, well – that was an end to me. I had no doubt of it. And Satan would go on. As for betraying him – why, I did not even know the place of my polite imprisonment.

No, if it was in the cards that I might beat Satan, I must play the game with him. There was no other way.

And what was any necklace beside – Eve!

I turned my mind to memorizing my instructions. It put me to sleep. Nor did Barker awaken me.

CHAPTER ELEVEN

Before the faithful Thomas could arrive next morning, I was up and in the bath. I accepted without question the suit he laid out for me. It was one I had never known I possessed. On the inner side of the coat, the left, was a wide pocket. It was deep and across the top ran a line of tiny, blunt-edged hooks. I examined them, carefully. The pendent fringes of Senusert's necklace were about six inches long. Its upper strand could be dropped upon the hooks and the whole ornament would then hang from them freely without causing any betraying protuberance through the cloth. It was, as Satan had indicated, ingeniously made for holding that particular treasure.

He handed me, too, a superbly fitting gray overcoat entirely new to me, but I was interested to note, with my name on the inside pocket, my own soft hat and Malacca cane.

And at last he gave me a curiously shaped little instrument of dull gray steel and – a wrist watch!

"I have a watch, Thomas," I said, studying the odd small instrument.

"Yes," he answered, "but this keeps the Master's time, sir."

"Oh, I see." Admiringly I reflected that Satan was taking no chances upon his pawns' timepieces; all, evidently, were synchronized; I liked that. "But this other affair. How does it work?"

"I meant to show you, sir."

He went to a wall and opened a closet. He carried out what appeared to be a section of a strong cabinet with a sash of glass covering it.

"Try to open it, sir," he said.

I tried to lift the top. It resisted all my efforts. He took the steel tool from me. It was shaped like a chisel, its edge razor sharp, its length about four inches, broadening abruptly from the edge to an inch and a half wide handle. In this handle was a screw.

He thrust the razor edge between the top sash and bottom support and rapidly turned the screw. The tool seemed to melt into the almost invisible crack. There was a muffled snap, and he lifted the lid. He handed me back the instrument, smiling. I saw that the edge had opened like a pair of jaws and that through them had been thrust another blade like a tongue. The jaws had been raised and the tongue pushed forward by incredibly powerful levers. The combination had snapped the lock as though it had been made of brittle wood.

"Very easy to manage, sir," said Thomas.

"Very," I replied, drily. And again I felt a wave of admiration for Satan.

I breakfasted in my room and, escorted by Thomas, entered the waiting car at exactly 10:30. The curtains were down and fastened. I thought of using that irresistible little instrument in my pocket. It was an impulse my better judgment warned me not to obey.

At precisely one o'clock I walked through the doors of the museum, keenly conscious both of the empty pocket designed to hold old Senusert's pectoral, and the tool that was to put it there.

I checked my overcoat and hat and cane, nodding to the attendant who had recognized me. I went straight to the jades and spent half an hour, looking them and some rare similar objects over in company with an assistant curator who had happened along. I rid myself of him and at 1:45 to the second strolled into the north corridor of the Egyptian wing. I did not have to introduce myself to the guards there. They knew me. By two o'clock I was close to the entrance of the necklace room.

At 2:05 by Satan's watch I entered it. If my heart was beating somewhat more quickly, I did not show it. I looked casually about the room. A guard stood close to the opposite entrance, the second guard halfway between me and the central case that was my goal. Both of them scanned me carefully. Neither of them knew me.

I walked over to the second guard, gave him my card and asked him a few questions about a collection of scarabs I knew were to be exhibited. I saw his official suspicion drop away from him as he read my name, and his replies were in the tone that he would have taken to an official of the museum. I walked over to the southeast comer of the room and apparently lost myself in a study of the amulets there. Out of the corner of my eye I saw the two guards meet, whisper and look at me respectfully. They separated and resumed their places.

Satan's watch showed 2:10. Five minutes to go!

Swift glances about the room revealed a dozen or more sightseers. There were three couples of manifest respectability, middle-aged outlanders. A girl who might have been an artist, a scholarly looking, white-haired man, a man with German professor written plain upon him, two well-dressed Englishmen discussing learnedly the mutations of the Tet hieroglyphic in well-bred, low, but carrying voices, and an untidy-looking woman who seemed to be uncertain what it was all about, and two or three others. The Englishmen and the girl were standing beside the cabinet that held the necklace. The others were scattered about the room.

Satan's watch registered 2:14.

There was a scurrying of feet in the north corridor. A woman screamed, terrifyingly. I heard a shout:

"Stop him! Stop him!"

A figure flashed by the door. A woman running. Close after her darted another, a man. I caught the glint of steel in his hand.

The watch marked 2:15. I walked over to the cabinet of the necklace, my right hand clutching the opening tool.

The turmoil in the corridor was growing louder. Again the woman screamed. The people in the room were rushing toward the door. The guard from the far entrance ran past me.

I stood before the cabinet. I thrust the razor edge of the little chisel between the flange of the top and the side. I turned the screw. There was a click, and the lock had snapped.

The screaming ended in a dreadful gasping wail. There was another rush of feet by the door. I heard an oath and the fall of a heavy body.

I withdrew my hand from the cabinet, the necklace in it. I dropped it into my pocket, running its upper strand over the line of tiny hooks.

I walked to the entrance through which I had come. One of the guards was lying upon the threshold. The German was bending over him. The girl I had taken for an artist was crouched beside him, hands over her eyes, crying hysterically. From the armor room across the corridor came an agonized shrieking – a man's voice this time.

I went on, between the two black sarcophagi at the entrance to the wing, out into the great hall where the Gobelin tapestries hang, and passed through the turnstile. The guard had his back turned, listening to the sounds which, both because of distance and the arrangement of rooms and corridors, were here barely audible.

I took my coat from the attendant, who, it was clear, had heard nothing.

Walking to the entrance, I stepped to the right as Satan had bade and, leaning over, fumbled with a shoe lace. Some one brushed past me, into the museum.

Straightening, I proceeded to the steps. Down on the sidewalk two men were fighting. A group had gathered around them, I saw a policeman running up. Those upon the steps beside myself were absorbed in watching the combatants.

I passed down. A dozen yards to my left was a blue limousine, the chauffeur paying no attention to the fighters, but polishing with a piece of chamois the right headlight of his car.

Strolling to it, I saw the chauffeur jump from his polishing, throw open the door and stand at attention beside it, his alert gaze upon me.

Satan's watch registered 2:19.

I stepped into the car. The curtains were drawn and it was dark. The door closed behind me and it was darker still.

The car started. Some one moved. Some one spoke softly, tremulously eager.

"Are you all right, Mr. Kirkham?"

Eve's voice!

CHAPTER TWELVE

I struck a match. Eve turned her head quickly away, but not before I had seen the tears in her eyes and how pale was her face.

"I'm quite all right, thank you," I said. "And everything, so far as I know, has gone exactly according to Satan's schedule. I know that I have. The necklace is in my pocket."

"I w-wasn't worrying about th-that," said Eve in a shaky little voice.

Her nerve was badly shattered, there was no mistaking that. Not for a moment did I think that any anxiety about me was the cause of it. That she had thoroughly understood Satan's sinister implications the night before was certain. Probably she had had forebodings. But now she knew.

Nevertheless, for one reason or another, she had felt anxiety for me. I moved closer.

"Satan made it perfectly clear to me that my continued health and getting the necklace were closely tied up together," I told her. "I am obeying his instructions to the letter, naturally. My next move is to give the necklace to you."

I slipped it off the hooks in my pocket.

"How do you turn on the lights?" I asked her. "I want you to be sure that what I give you is what our Master is expecting to get."

"D-don't turn them on," whispered Eve. "Give me the – d-damned thing!"

I laughed. Sorry for her as I was, I couldn't help it. Her hands crept out and touched me. I caught them in mine and she did not withdraw them. And after a time she drew closer, pressing against me like a frightened child. She was crying, I knew, but I said nothing, only slipped an arm around her and let her cry. Yes, very much like a little frightened child was Eve, weeping there in the darkness and clutching my hands so tightly. And in my heart I cursed Satan in seven tongues, a cold, implacable hatred growing within me.

At last she gave a little laugh and moved away.

"Thank you, Mr. Kirkham," she said tranquilly. "You make always a most dependable audience."

"Miss Demerest," I told her bluntly, "I'm done with fencing. You're panic-stricken. You know why – and so do I."

"Why should I be frightened?" she asked.

"At the destiny Satan promised you," I answered. "You know what it is. If you have any doubts at all about it, let me tell you that he left me with none after you had gone from the room last night."

There was a silence, and then out of the darkness came her voice, small and despairing.

"He means to – take me! He will – take me! No matter what I do! I'd kill myself – but I can't! I can't! Oh, God, what can I do? Oh, God, who can help me!"

"I can make a damned good try at it," I told her, "if you'll only let me."

She did not answer immediately, sitting silently, fighting for self-control. Suddenly she snapped on the light and leaned toward me, tear-washed eyes searching mine, and voice firm as though she had come to some momentous decision.

"Tell me, Mr. Kirkham, what made you stop after the second footprint? You wanted to go on. Satan was urging you on. Why did you stop?"

"Because," I said, "I heard your voice telling me to go no farther."

She drew a sharp breath that was like a sob.

"Is that the truth, Mr. Kirkham?"

"It is God's own truth. It was as though you stood beside me, touching my shoulder and whispered to me to stop where I was. To climb no higher. Those devilish jewels on the crown and scepter were calling me out of a thousand mouths. But when I heard you – or thought I did – I heard them no longer."

"Oh!" Eve's eyes were rapt, her cheeks no longer pale, her exclamation a song.

"You did call!" I whispered.

"I watched you from back there beyond the light, with the –

others," she said. "And when the second foot shone out on Satan's side I tried with all my strength of will to send my thought out to you, tried so desperately to warn you. Over and over I prayed as you stood there hesitating – 'Oh, kind God, wherever you are, let him hear me! Please let him hear me, dear God!' and you did hear–"

She stopped and stared at me with widening eyes and swiftly the color deepened in her cheeks.

"And you knew it was my voice!" whispered Eve. "But you would not have heard, or, hearing, would not have heeded, unless – unless–"

"Unless?" I prompted.

"Unless there were something outside our two selves ready to help us," said Eve, a bit breathlessly.

She was blushing now up to her eyes; and I was quite sure that the reason she had given was not exactly that which caused the blush, not the one that had been on the tip of her tongue a moment before.

My own theory of what had happened was more materialistic. Something within me had sensitized my mind, not something without. I've never run across any particularly convincing evidence of disembodied energies acting as spiritual springs to soften the bumps in a bad piece of road on this earthly tour of ours. I much preferred a good tangible Providence like the little cockney burglar with his knowledge of Satan's trick walls. However, such things may be; and if it gave Eve any comfort to believe it, then let her. So I nodded solemnly and assured her it must be true.

"But," I asked, "is there no one among all Satan's people with whom you have come in contact who might be persuaded to work against him?"

"Not one," she said. "Consardine likes me – I think he would go far to protect me. But he is tied to Satan. So are all of them. Not only by fear – you saw what happened to Cartright – but by other reasons as well. Satan does pay highly, Mr. Kirkham. Not only in money, but in other things – he has dreadful power...unholy power. Oh, it's not just money that people want! Nor all that he gives them! You can't even dream as yet..."

"Drugs?" I suggested, unimaginatively.

"You're being stupid – deliberately," she said. "You know very well what Lucifer was supposed to be able to give. And he can...and he does...and even those who have lost to him still have the hope that they may do something that will give them another chance – or that his caprice will."

"Has such a thing ever happened?"

"Yes," she replied, "it has. But don't think it was because he was capable of mercy."

"You mean it was simply a play to hold them tighter by dangling the hope of freedom under their noses?"

"Yes," she said. "So their usefulness would not be weakened by despair."

"Miss Demerest," I asked her bluntly, "why should you think I am any different from these others?"

"You did not come to him of your own will," she said. "And you are no slave to his seven shining prints."

"I came pretty close to being so last night," I said, somewhat ruefully.

"They haven't – got you," she whispered. "Not like the others. And they won't. They mustn't get you, Mr. Kirkham."

"I don't intend to let them," I told her, grimly. She gave me her other hand at that. I glanced at my watch and jumped. "There's only a little more than ten minutes left to us," I said. "We've not even spoken of any plan. We've got to meet again – quickly. And we've got to keep right on hoodwinking Satan."

"That will be the great difficulty, of course," she nodded. "But I'll take care of that. And you understand now, don't you, that it was that necessity that made me treat you so outrageously?"

"Even before Satan's confession to me, I suspected something of the sort," I grinned. "And of course you understand that my equally outrageously sounding proposition to him to turn you over to me was just a following of your lead."

"Better than that," she answered softly. "I knew what you really did mean."

Again I shot a glance at my watch. Six minutes – just about time.

"Look here," I said abruptly. "Answer me truly. When did it first occur to you that I might be the one to get you out of this trap?"

"Wh-when you kissed me," she whispered.

"And when did you get the idea of camouflaging what you thought about me?"

"R-right after you began kissing me."

"Eve," I said, "do you see any necessity for camouflage at this moment?"

"No," answered Eve, ingenuously. "Why?"

"This is why!" I dropped her hands, drew her to me and kissed her. And Eve put her arms around my neck tightly and kissed me quite as whole-heartedly. And that was that uniquely satisfactorily that.

"It's a coincidence," I murmured against her ear a moment or two later, "but the exact second you had that idea was the precise second I decided to stick the game out."

"Oh – Jim!" sighed Eve. This time she kissed me.

The car was going more slowly. I cursed helplessly Satan's inflexible schedule.

"Eve," I said swiftly, and thrust the necklace of Senusert in her hands, "do you know a little Englishman named Barker? The electrician? He seems to know you."

"Yes," she answered, eyes wide with wonder. "I know him. But how–"

"Get in touch with him as soon as you can," I bade her, "I haven't time to explain. But Barker's to be trusted. Tell him he must get to me in my room the first night I return. By hook or crook, he's got to. You understand?"

She nodded, eyes wider.

"Arrange it," I said, "so that you'll be there that night, too."

"All right – Jim," said Eve.

I looked at my watch. I had one and three-quarters minutes more. We put it to excellent use.

The car stopped.

"Remember Barker," I whispered.

I opened the door and stepped out. It closed behind me and the car rolled off. The obelisk was near by. I walked around it obediently. As I started for Fifth Avenue I saw a man on another path about a hundred feet from me. His overcoat and hat were the same as mine. He swung a Malacca cane. A vast curiosity struck me? Was it my double? I started toward him, and halted. If I followed him I was disobeying Satan's instructions. Less than at any time did I want to do that. Reluctantly I turned and let him go.

I hailed a taxi and started to the Club. There was a rosy light outside the windows; I felt like singing; the walkers on the Avenue seemed to skip gaily. Eve had gone a bit to my head.

Suddenly the rosiness dimmed, the song died. Reason began to function. No doubt the absence of the necklace had been soon discovered. The doors of the museum would have been closed, and none allowed to depart without being searched. Perhaps the alarm had been sounded even as I had gone down the steps. It might be that I had been the only one who had gotten out.

If that were so, then, obviously, I must be suspected. I had deliberately drawn the attention of the guards to me, not only in the corridor, but in the treasure room. They would remember me. Why had I slipped away, ignoring the disturbances, if I had not had some strong reason? What reason could I have had except making away with the necklace?

Or supposing the theft had not been discovered until after the museum had been emptied. Still, I would find it difficult to explain why I had so rapidly made my exit; been the only one to take no interest in the happenings.

Had Satan missed a move in his complicated game, made an error in his deliberate calculations? Or had he coldly planned to have suspicion rest upon me? Whether he had or not, it must.

In no easy frame of mind I dismissed the taxi and entered the Club.

"Back early, Mr. Kirkham," smiled the clerk at the desk as he handed me my keys. Quite evidently he had no suspicion that the

Kirkham who had gone out a few hours before and the one who had just returned were two distinct persons. My double, I reflected, must be good indeed.

"I'm going to be almighty busy for the next few hours," I told him. "I've some writing to do that will demand my entire concentration. There's nothing, absolutely nothing, of sufficient importance to break in on me. It's very likely that there will be telephone calls and visitors. Tell everybody that I'm out. If it's reporters, tell them I'll see them at eight o'clock. Slip copies of all the afternoon papers up to me at seven o'clock. Not before. Get me the latest editions. And no matter who calls, don't let me be bothered."

"I'll put an extra key in your box," he said. "It always looks better."

I went to my room. Locking the door, I made a minute inspection. On my desk was my three-day accumulation of mail. There were not many letters, none was important; all had been opened. Two were invitations to speak at dinners. Carbon copies of notes of regret were attached to them. My signature upon them was perfect. My double's powers of imitation were clearly not limited to voice and appearance. My reason for declining, I was much interested in learning, was that I would not be in the city on the dates of the dinners. So? Where the devil, I wondered, was I to be?

Beside my typewriter was a bulky document. Riffling its pages I discovered that it was a report upon the possibilities of certain mineralized lands in China. It was addressed to that same brilliant attorney who had toasted the "near-damned" at Satan's feast of the night before. It was corrected and annotated in my own handwriting. I had, of course, no knowledge of its purpose, but I was sure that the lawyer would be able to discuss it with easy familiarity if circumstances forced it to his attention. My confidence in Satan revived. I felt much more comfortable.

I looked through the pockets of my clothes, hanging in the closet. There was not even a scrap of paper.

Seven o'clock came, and with it a discreet knock at my door. It was Robert, the night clerk, with a bundle of the evening papers. His eyes were rather wide, and I could see questions sticking out all over him. Well, he couldn't be more curious about what I had to say regarding what was in those papers than I was to know what was in them. Nor would it do to let him suspect the extent of my ignorance.

So I took them from him with a discouragingly faraway air, and absent-mindedly closed the door in his face.

The headlines leaped out at me from the first I opened:

TRIPLE TRAGEDY AT THE METROPOLITAN MUSEUM; PRICELESS RELIC MISSING.

WOMAN MURDERED BEFORE EYES OF GUARDS AND VISITORS, HER SLAYER KILLED BY ANOTHER WHO COMMITS SUICIDE WHEN HE IS CAPTURED.

EXPLORER KIRKHAM BALKS THIEVES, GIVES THE ALARM THAT CLOSES DOORS WHEN MYSTERIOUS SERIES OF FATAL STABBINGS THROWS TREASURE HOUSE INTO CHAOS – ROBBER HIDES OLD EGYPTIAN PRINCESS'S NECKLACE AND MAKES ESCAPE – METROPOLITAN TO BE CLOSED UNTIL SEARCH REVEALS IT.

In different words, all the rest of the headlines said about the same thing. I read the stories. Now and then I had the feeling that somebody was shooting a fine spray of ice-water between my shoulder blades. I quote from the most complete account.

An unknown woman was stabbed to death this afternoon in the Metropolitan Museum of Art before the eyes of half a dozen guards and some twenty or more visitors.

Her murderer tried to escape, but before he could get far was attacked by the companion of the woman, tripped, and a knife thrust through his heart.

The second slayer was caught after a chase. As he was being taken to the Curator's office to await the police, he collapsed. He died within a few seconds, the victim, apparently, of some swift poison which he had managed to slip into his mouth.

Both the murders and the suicide occurred close to the Egyptian room where are kept some of the choicest treasures of the museum. Taking advantage of the confusion, some one forced open the case containing the ancient necklace given to his daughter by the Pharaoh Senusert II. The necklace, a priceless relic of the past, and long the admiration of thousands of visitors, was taken. Its removal from the building was frustrated, however, by the alertness of Mr. James Kirkham, the noted explorer, who caused the doors to be locked before any one could leave the museum.

Search of everyone within the walls failed to reveal the stolen treasure. It is supposed that the thief became panic-stricken when he found that no one could get out, and tucked the necklace away in some hidden corner. Whether he did it thinking to return and recover it, or merely to get rid of it cannot, of course, be known. The museum will be closed to visitors until it is found, which, thanks to Mr. Kirkham's quick thinking, is only a matter of time.

Neither the museum authorities nor the police believe that there is any connection between the tragedy and the theft, the latter having obviously been a sudden temptation born from the opportunity-giving confusion.

Well, I reflected, I could tell them better than that. And if the museum remained closed until they found the necklace there, the door hinges would have a chance to become rusty.

But three lives the price of the bauble! I resumed the reading with cold horror at my heart.

It was shortly after two o'clock when one of the guards in the Egyptian wing first took special notice of the woman and the two men. They were talking together earnestly, discussing seemingly an exhibit of ushabtiu figures, toy-like wooden models from a tomb. The woman was about thirty, attractive, blonde and apparently English. The men were older and the guard took them to be Syrians. What had particularly drawn his attention to them was the curious pallor of their faces and the out-of-the-ordinary largeness of their eyes.

"Looked like dopes," he says, "and then again they didn't. Their faces weren't a sick white, more of a transparent. They didn't behave like dopes, either. They seemed to be talking sensible enough. Dressed top-notch, too."

He put them down finally as foreigners, and relaxed his attention. In a few minutes he noticed one of the men walking by him. It was later ascertained that this man had accompanied the woman when she entered the museum about 1:30. The cloak room attendant's attention had also been attracted by their pallor and their curious eyes. This man passed the entrance to the small room where the Senusert necklace was on display with other ancient jewels. He turned into the next corridor and disappeared.

The woman had continued talking to the second man, who, it appears, came into the museum a little before two o'clock.

Suddenly the guard heard a scream. He swung around and saw the two struggling together, the woman trying to ward off blows from a long knife with which the man was stabbing at her. The guard, William Barton, shouted and ran for them. At the same time, visitors came running in from all directions, drawn by the cries.

They got in Barton's way, and he could not shoot for fear of hitting the woman or some of the excited spectators.

The whole affair was a matter of seconds. The knife plunged into the woman's throat!

The murderer, brandishing his red blade, burst through the horror-stricken onlookers and ran in the direction the first man had gone. As he was close to the door of the necklace room the people who had been in it came rushing out. With them was one of the two guards who keep watch there. They piled back, falling over each other in their haste to get out of reach of the knife. There was a panic-stricken scramble, which the second guard tried to quiet. In the meantime, the murderer had come face to face with the woman's companion at the turn of the next corridor. He struck at the latter and missed, and fled into the armor room with the other close behind him, a knife now in his own hand.

The pair gripped and fell, rolling over the tiled floor, and each striving to plunge his dagger into the other. Guards and visitors were piling in from every side, and the place was in pandemonium.

Then they saw the hand of the pursuer flash up and down. The under man shrieked – and the knife was buried in his heart!

The killer leaped to his feet, and began to run blindly. With the guards and others after him he darted out into the Egyptian wing corridor.

There they cornered him and brought him down.

He was beaten half into insensibility. As he was being carried to the Curator's office, his body went limp, and heavy. They put him down.

He was dead!

Either shock or some quick and powerful poison which he had taken when he had realized escape was impossible had killed him. The autopsy will decide which.

The whole tragedy had occurred in an almost incredibly brief time. Less than five minutes had elapsed between the first scream of the woman and the third death.

But it was time enough to give the necklace thief his opportunity.

Among the visitors at the museum was Mr. James Kirkham, the noted explorer, who recently brought to America the famous Yunnan jades which Mr. Rockbilt presented to the Metropolitan. Mr. Kirkham had been preparing an exhaustive report upon mining possibilities in China for a certain powerful American syndicate. He had been working on it for the last two days with intense concentration, and felt the need this afternoon of a little relaxation. He decided to spend a couple of hours at the museum.

He had strolled into the Egyptian room where the necklace was kept and was studying some amulets in a case in a far corner when he heard the woman's scream. He saw those who were in the room running and followed them. He did not see the killings, but was a witness to the capture of the second man.

Preoccupied by the necessity of completing his report, and deciding that he had had enough "relaxation," Mr. Kirkham started to leave. He had just reached the doors of the museum when a suspicion seized him. Trained by the necessities of his occupation to keenest observation, he recalled that while he was hastening to the entrance of the necklace room, following the others, some one had brushed past him going into the room. He recalled also hearing immediately afterward a sharp click, like the forcing of a lock. With his attention focused upon what was going on without, the impressions then carried with them no significance.

But now it seemed that they might be important.

Mr. Kirkham turned back instantly, and ordered the alarm to be sounded which at once closes the doors of the museum. As he is well known at the Metropolitan, he was as instantly obeyed.

And it was that trained observation of his and quick thinking which beyond all doubt foiled the thief of the necklace.

There followed an account of the discovery of the raped cabinet, the verification of the fact that no one had gone out of the museum either during or after the disturbances, the searching of everybody in the Curator's offices, and the careful shepherding of them out one by one so no one could stop and pick up the necklace from wherever it had been hidden. It interested me to find that I had demanded to be searched with the rest, despite the Curator's protests!

I came to my interview, substantially the same in all the papers.

"The truth is," so I was quoted as having said, "I feel a bit guilty that I did not at once realize the importance of those impressions and turn back into the room. I could probably have caught the thief red-handed. The fact is that my mind was about nine-tenths taken up with that infernal report which must be finished and mailed tonight. I have a vague idea that there were about a dozen people in the room, but not the slightest recollection of what they looked like.

"When I heard the woman scream, it was like being jarred out of sleep. My progress to the door was half-automatic. It was only when I was about to go out of the museum that memory began to function, and I recalled that furtive brushing past me of some one and the clicking noise.

"Then, of course, there was only one thing to be done. Make sure that nobody got out until it was determined whether or not anything had been stolen. The entrance guard deserves great credit for the promptness with which he sounded that alarm.

"I agree with the Curator that there can be no connection between the theft and the killings. How could there possibly be? Some one, and he can be no professional because any professional would know that there was no way of selling such a thing, had a sudden crazy impulse. His probable next thought was one of sincere repentance and an intense desire to get rid of the necklace instantly. The only problem is finding where he slipped it.

"You say it was a lucky thing for the museum that I turned back when I did," smiled Mr. Kirkham. "Well, I think it was a mighty lucky thing for me. I wouldn't like being in the position that having been the first one out of the museum – and maybe the only one, for the theft would soon have been discovered – would have put me."

At this the Curator, despite his anxiety, laughed heartily.

There was more to the story, much more; but that was all I was quoted as saying. The guard whom I had seen lying across the threshold told how he had been knocked down in the backward rush, and somebody "had kicked me in the ear, or something." The second guard had joined in the chase. One paper had a grisly "special" about the possibility of the thief having crawled into one of the suits of armor and dying within it, of thirst and hunger. The writer evidently thought of armor as an iron box in which one could hide like a closet.

All the accounts agreed that there was little chance of identifying the three dead. There was not a thing in their clothing or about them to give a single clew.

Well, there it all was. There was my alibi, complete. There were Satan's chessmen now all properly clicked into place, including the three who would never be moved again. It wasn't nice reading for me, not at all. Particularly did I wince at the Curator's amusement that my honesty could come into question.

But again my double had done a good job. It had been he, of course, who had slipped by me as I had bent to tie my shoe, smoothly taking up my trail without apparent break. And it had been he whom I had passed at the obelisk as I had slipped as smoothly back into his.

No one had noticed me come down the museum's steps and enter the automobile that held Eve. The diversion on the sidewalk had made sure of that. There were no gaps in the alibi.

And the three dead people who had furnished the diversion in the museum that had enabled me to steal the necklace? Slaves of Satan's mysterious drug, the kehjt. The description of their strange eyes and their pallor proved that – if I had needed proof. Satan's slaves, playing faithfully the parts he had given them, in blissful confidence of a perpetual Paradise for their immediate reward.

I read the stories over again. At eight o'clock the reporters were sent up to my room. I restrained myself severely to the lines of my early interview. Their visit was largely perfunctory. After all, there was not much that I could say. I left the report that had "preoccupied" me so greatly lying where they could see it.

I went even further. Taking the hint from my double's remarks, I sealed and addressed it and asked one of them to drop it into the Post Office for me on his way back to his paper.

When they had gone, I had dinner sent up to my room.

But when I went to bed, hours later, it was with a cold little sick feeling at the pit of my stomach. More than at any time, I was inclined to credit Satan's version of his identity.

For the first time I was afraid of him.

CHAPTER THIRTEEN

Early next morning, the telephone rang, awakening me. The clerk at the desk was on the other end. There was an urgent message for me, and the bearer had instructions to wait until I had read it. I told him to send it up. It was a letter. I opened it and read:

"You have done well, James Kirkham. I am pleased with you. Visit your friends at the museum this afternoon. You will receive further instructions from me tomorrow. S."

I phoned the desk to dismiss the messenger, and to send me up breakfast and the morning papers.

It was a good story, and they had spread upon it. It surprised me, at first, that they had given so much more space to the theft of the necklace than they had to the murders and suicide. Then I realized, inasmuch as there was no suspicion of any connection between them, that this was sound newspaper judgment. After all, the lost lives were only three among millions. They had been – and they were not. There were many more.

But the necklace was unique.

That, I reflected, was undoubtedly the way Satan felt about it. Certainly those three lives had seemed to him nothing like so important as had the necklace. And quite plainly the newspapers agreed with him.

The three bodies remained in the morgue, unidentified. The museum, after an all-night search, had been unable to find the necklace. That was all there was new, if new it could be called.

I went downstairs, and carried on the inevitable discussions of the affair with various members of the Club. At one o'clock a messenger brought me another letter. The name on the envelope was that of an important legal firm of which the brilliant attorney was the head.

In it was a check for ten thousand dollars.

The accompanying note complimented me upon my report. The check, it said, was for that and further possible services. For the latter only, of course, in the nature of a retainer. Other work which I might be asked to do would be paid for commensurately.

Again Satan had spoken the truth. He did pay well. But the "other work"?

At three o'clock I went to the museum. I had no difficulty in passing the barricade. In a fashion, I was a hero. The Curator was unhappy, but hopeful. I, when I departed, was much more unhappy than he, and, so far as the recovery of the necklace was concerned, with no hopes whatever. Obviously, I was at pains to conceal both of these states of mind from him.

The day went by without further word from Satan, or from any of his servitors. As the hours passed, I became more and more uneasy. Suppose that this one thing was all that he had wanted of me? That, now I had carried it out, I was to be cast aside! Hell might be his realm, but with Eve therein it was Paradise to me. I did not want his gates closed against me. Nor, cast out, could I storm them. I did not know where they were. What sleep I had that night was troubled indeed, swinging between bitter rage and a nightmarish sense of irretrievable loss.

When I opened Satan's letter next morning it was with the feeling that the angel with the flaming sword had stood aside from the barred doors of Eden and was beckoning me in.

"I am having a house party, and you will find congenial company. You can have your mail called for at the Club, daily. On second thought, I won't take no for an answer. A car will come for you at four o'clock. S."

On the surface, nothing but a cordial, insistent invitation to have a little holiday. Actually, a command. Even had I wanted to, I would have known better than to refuse.

My conscience abruptly ceased to trouble me. With a light heart I packed a traveling bag, gave my instructions at the desk, and waited impatiently for the hour to roll around. Precisely at four, a smart limousine stopped in front of the Club, as smartly a liveried chauffeur entered, saluted me respectfully and, in the manner of one who knew me well, took my bag and ushered me into the car.

Here I had immediate proof that I had passed my novitiate and had been accepted by Satan. The curtains were up. I was to be allowed to see where I was going.

We went up Fifth Avenue and turned to the Queensborough Bridge. We went over it into Long Island. In about forty minutes we had struck the entrance of the Vanderbilt Speedway. We did its forty-five miles to Lake Ronkonkoma in a flat fifty minutes. We turned north toward the Sound, passed through Smithtown and out the North Shore road, A little after six we swung toward the Sound again, and in a few minutes came to a narrow private road penetrating a thick growth of pine and oak. We took it. A couple of hundred yards farther on we paused at a cottage where my driver gave a slip of some sort to a man who had walked out to stop us. He carried a high-powered rifle, and was plainly a guard. A mile or so farther on we came to another cottage and the process was repeated.

The road began to skirt a strong high wall. I knew it was the one Barker had told me about, and I wondered how he had managed to evade these outer guards. At 6:30 we stopped at a pair of massive steel gates. At a signal from the chauffeur they opened. We rolled through, and they clanged behind us.

Under the high wall, on each side of the road, was a low, domed structure of heavy concrete. They were distinctly warlike defenses. They looked as though they might house machine guns. Several men came out of them, questioned my driver, inspected me through the windows, and waved us on.

My respect for Satan was steadily mounting.

Fifteen minutes more and we were at the doors of the chateau. It lay, I figured, about ten miles on the New York side of Port Jefferson, in the densely wooded section between it and Oyster Bay. It was built in a small valley, and probably little if any of it could be seen from the Sound which, I estimated, must be about three-quarters of a mile away. So extensive were the grounds through which we had come and so thickly wooded, that I doubted if the house could be seen even from the public roads.

Consardine welcomed me. I had the impression that he was curiously glad to see me. I had been shifted to new quarters, he told me, and he would stay with me, if I didn't mind, while I dressed for dinner. I told him that nothing would delight me more. I meant it. I liked Consardine.

The new quarters were fresh evidence of my promotion. There was a big bedroom, a bigger sitting-room and a bath. They were rather more than wonderfully furnished, and they had windows. I appreciated the subtlety of this assurance that I was no longer a prisoner. The efficient Thomas was awaiting me. He grinned openly at my bag. My clothes had been already laid on the bed. Consardine chatted as I bathed and dressed.

Satan, he said, would not be with us this night. He had ordered Consardine, however, to tell me that I had fulfilled his every expectation of me. Some time tomorrow he would have a talk with me. I would find an engaging lot of people at dinner. Afterwards there would be a bridge game which I could join or not, as I pleased. We did not discuss the affair of the necklace, although Thomas must have known all about it.

I wanted rather badly to ask if Eve would be at the table, but decided not to risk it. When we had reached the dining room, by three of the wall passages and two of the lifts, she was not there.

We were eighteen, all told. My companions were all that Consardine had promised, interesting, witty, entertaining. Among them a remarkably beautiful Polish woman, an Italian count and a Japanese baron, the three frequently featured in the news. Satan's webs spread wide.

It was an excellent dinner among excellent company – no need to go into detail. There was no discussion of our absent host, nor of our activities. Back of my mind throughout it was a strong impatience to get to my rooms and await Barker. Did he know of my change of quarters? Could he get to me? Was Eve in the chateau?

The dinner ended, and we passed into another room where were the bridge tables. There were enough partners for four, and two persons left over. It gave me my chance to avoid playing. Unfortunately for my plans, it gave Consardine the same opportunity. He suggested that he show me some of the wonders of the place. I could not refuse, of course.

We had looked over half a dozen rooms and galleries before I was able decently to plead weariness. Of what I saw I will not write, it is not essential. But the rareness and beauty of their contents stirred me profoundly. Satan, so Consardine told me, had an enormous suite in which he kept the treasures dearest to him. What I had seen had only been a fraction of what the chateau contained, he said.

We looked in on the bridge game on our way back. Others had drifted in during our absence, and several more tables were going.

At one of them, with Cobham for her partner, sat Eve.

She glanced up at me as I passed and nodded indifferently. Cobham got up and shook hands with great friendliness. It was plain that all his resentment was gone. While I was acknowledging introductions, Eve leaned back, humming. I recognized the air as one of the new jazzy songs:

"Meet me, darling, when the clocks are chiming twelve – At midnight, When the moonlight Makes our hearts bright–"

I needed no moonlight to make my own heart bright. It was a message. She had seen Barker.

After a moment or two, I pressed Consardine's foot. Eve was being deliberately impolite, yawning and riffling the cards impatiently. Cobham gave her an irritated glance.

"Well," she said, rudely, "are we playing bridge or aren't we? I'm serving notice – twelve o'clock sees me in bed."

Again I understood; she was underscoring the message.

I bade them good night, and turned away with Consardine. Another little group came in, and called to us to stay.

"Not tonight," I whispered to him. "I'm jumpy. Get me out."

He looked at Eve, and smiled faintly.

"Mr. Kirkham has work to do," he told them. "I'll be back in a few minutes."

He, took me to my rooms, showing me, as we went, how to manipulate the panels through which we passed and the lifts.

"In the event of your changing your mind," he said, "and wanting to come back."

"I won't," I told him. "I'll read a while and go to bed. Truth is, Consardine, I don't feel as though I could stand much of Miss Demerest tonight."

"I'm going to speak to Eve," he answered. "There's no reason for your being made uncomfortable."

"I wish you wouldn't," I said. "I'd rather handle the situation myself."

"Have it your own way," he replied, and went on to tell me that Thomas would awaken me in the morning. Satan would probably send a message by him. If I wanted the valet I could call him by the room 'phone. The 'phone gave me an impression of privacy that the bell had not. Thomas, I inferred, was no longer on duty as my guard. I was very glad of that.

Consardine bade me good night. At last I was alone.

I walked to the windows. They were not barred, but they were covered with a fine steel mesh quite as efficient. I turned out all the lights but one, and began to read. My watch showed 10:30.

It was very still. The time went slowly. It was close to eleven when there came a hoarse whisper from the bedroom:

"'Ere I am, Cap'n, an' bloody glad to see you!"

Despite my absolute certainty that Barker would appear, my heart gave a great leap, and a load seemed to slip from me. I jumped into the bedroom and shook him by the shoulders.

"And, by God, Barker, but I'm glad to see you!" I said.

"Got your message," he grinned, his little eyes snapping. "Ain't no need to 'ide in 'ere, though. Nobody's goin' to come bargin' in on you now, they ain't. Ace 'igh, you are with Satan. A reg'ler one of 'em. Tysty bit o' work, Cap'n, you done. Tyke it from me what knows what good work is."

He took a cigar, lighted it and sat down, eyeing me admiringly.

"A tysty bit o' work," he repeated. "An' you with no trainin'! I couldn't 'ave done better myself."

I bowed, and pushed the decanter over to him.

"Not me," he waved back. "It's all right if you're goin' to sleep an' got a 'oliday. But old John Barleycorn ain't no use in our line o' work, sir."

"I'm just a beginner, Harry," I said apologetically, and set the decanter down untouched. He watched me approvingly.

"When Miss Demerest told me," he resumed, "you could fair 'ave wyved me over with a feather. Bring 'im to me, syes she, the minute you can. If I'm sleepin' or wykin' it mykes no difference, I want 'im she syes. Any hour it's syfe, she syes, but don't you let 'im run no risks. 'Ell on seein' you she is, sir."

"She just let me know she'd be back in her room by twelve," I said.

"All right, we'll be there," he nodded. "Got any plans? To squash 'im, I mean."

I hesitated. The thought in my mind was too nebulous as yet even to be called an idea. Certainly too flimsy to be brought out for inspection.

"No, Harry, I haven't," I answered him. "I don't know enough about the game. I've got to have a chance to look around. I know this though – I'm going to get Miss Demerest free of Satan or go out doing my damnedest."

He cocked an ear at me, like a startled terrier.

"And if that's the only way, I'll pick the time and place to make sure that I take Satan with me," I added.

He hitched his chair close up to mine.

"Cap'n Kirkham," he said earnestly, "that's the last plye to make. The very last plye, sir. I'd be 'ot for it if we could get anybody else to do it. An' if nobody knew we was behind it. But there ain't nobody 'ere who'd do for 'im, sir. Nobody. It's like pryin' for a mountain to fall on 'im, or the h'earth to swaller 'im, sir."

He paused for a moment.

"It's just this, Cap'n. If you do for 'im, or I do for 'im, we got to do for 'im knowin' there ain't no out for us. Not h'even a bloody 'arf-chance of us gettin' awye. The kehjt slyves'd see to that if nobody else did. What! Us tykin' their 'Eaven from 'em? Suicide it'll be, Cap'n, no less. An' if they suspect Miss Demerest knows anything about it – Gord, I 'ates to think of it! No, we got to find some other wye, Cap'n."

"I meant – only if there was no other way," I said. "And if it comes to that I don't expect you to figure in it. I'll go it alone."

"Now, Cap'n, now, Cap'n!" he said, short upper lip quivering over buck teeth and face contorted as though on the edge of tears. "You ain't got no call to talk like that, sir. I'm with you whatever you do. 'Ell, ain't we partners?"

"Sure we are, Harry," I answered quickly, honestly touched. "But when it comes to killing, well – I do my own. There's no reason why you should run any suicidal risks for us."

"Ow!" he snarled. "There ain't, ain't there? Ow, the 'ell there ain't 1 Maybe you think I'm 'avin' a 'appy 'oliday runnin' around these walls like a bloody rat? A decent, Gord-fearin' jail I wouldn't 'ave a word to sye against. But this – what is it? Just plain 'ell! An' you an' Miss Demerest like my own family! No reason, ain't there! Christ, don't talk like that, Cap'n!"

"There, there, Harry, I didn't mean it quite that way," I said, and patted his shoulder. "What I mean is to leave Satan to me, and, if the worst does come about, try to get Miss Demerest away."

"We stand together, Cap'n," he answered stubbornly. "If it comes to killin' I'll be in it" – he hesitated, then muttered, "but I wish to Gord I could be sure any honest bullet would do for 'im."

That touched me on the raw. It came too close to some damnably disconcerting doubts of my own.

"Snap out of it, Harry," I said sharply. "Why, the first thing you told me was that Satan's only a man like you and me. And that a bullet or a knife would do for him. Why the change of heart?"

"I was braggin'," he muttered. "I was talkin' loud to keep my pecker up. 'E ain't exactly what you'd call human, sir, now is he? I said 'e wasn't the devil. I never said 'e wasn't a devil. An' – an' – Oh, Gord, 'e's so bloody 'uge!" he ended helplessly.

My uneasiness increased. I had thought I had an anchor in Barker's lack of superstition about Satan. And now it apparently had him by the throat. I tried ridicule.

"Well, I'll be damned!" I sneered. "I thought you were hard-boiled, Harry. Satan tells you he comes from Hell. Sure, where else could he come from, you tell yourself. I suppose if somebody told you the story of Little Red Riding Hood you'd think every old woman with a shawl was a wolf. Go hide under the bed, little man."

He looked at me somberly.

"'Ell's behind 'im," he said. "An' 'e's got all the passwords."

I began to get angry. One reason was that in arguing against him I had also to argue against myself. After all, he was only voicing my thoughts that I was reluctant to admit were my own.

"Well," I told him, "if he's made you think that, he's got you licked. You're no use to me, Harry. Go back to your walls and creep. Creep around them and stay alive. Devil or no devil, I fight him."

I had thought to prick him. To my surprise, he showed no resentment.

"An' devil or no devil, so do I," he said quietly. "Tryin' to pull my leg, ain't you, Cap'n? You don't 'ave to. I told you I was with you, and I am. I'm through bein' a rat in the walls. That's all, Cap'n Kirkham."

There was a curious dignity about Barker. I felt my face grow hot. I was ashamed of myself. After all, he was showing the highest kind of courage. And surely it was better for him to spread out his fears in front of me than to let them ride him in secret. I thrust my hand out to him.

"I'm damned sorry, Harry–" I began.

"No need to be, sir," he checked me. "Only there's lots about this plyce an' – 'im – that you don't know about yet. I do, though. Maybe there wouldn't be no 'arm in showin' you a bit. Maybe you'd be seein' a wolf or two yourself. What time is it?"

There was a hint of grimness in his voice. I grinned to myself, well pleased. There was good hard metal in the little man. It was a challenge he was throwing down to me, of course. I looked at my watch.

"Twenty after eleven," I said. "So that you keep a certain appointment at midnight – lead on, Macduff."

"Your shirt," he said, "would look like a light'ouse in the dark. Put on another suit."

I changed rapidly into the most unobtrusive of the wardrobe's contents.

"Got a gun?" he asked.

I nodded, pointing to my left armpit. I had replenished my personal arsenal, of which Consardine had deprived me, while at the Club.

"Throw it in a drawer," he bade me, surprisingly.

"What's the idea?" I asked.

"No good," he said, "you might be tempted to use it, Cap'n."

"Well, for God's sake," I said, "if I was, there would be good reason."

"Might just as well carry along an alarm clock," said Barker. "Do you just as much good, Or 'arm. Mostly 'arm. We don't exactly want no h'advertisin' on this trip, Cap'n."

My respect for Harry took an abrupt upward swing. I dropped my gun into the casual mouth of a nearby vase. I unslung my armpit holster, and poked it under a pillow.

"Get thee behind me, Temptation," I said. "And now what?"

He dipped into a pocket.

"Sneakers," said Barker, and handed me a pair of thick rubber soles. I slipped them over my shoes. He fumbled in another pocket.

"Knucks," he dropped a beautiful pair of brass knuckles in my hand. I thrust my fingers through them.

"Good," said Barker. "They ain't got the range of a gun, but if we 'ave to get violent we'll 'ave to see it's quiet like. Get up close an' 'it 'ard an' quick."

"Let's go," I said.

He snapped off the lights in the outer room. He returned, moving with absolute silence, and took my hand. He led me to the bedroom wall.

"Put your 'and on my shoulder, an' step right be'ind me," he ordered. I had heard no sound of a panel, and could distinguish no opening in the blackness. But a panel had opened, for I walked through what a moment before had been solid wall. He halted, no doubt closing the aperture. He swung off at a right-angle, I following. I had counted fifty paces before he stopped again. The corridor was a long one. He flashed a light, brief as the blink of a firefly. Before me was one of the little lifts. He pressed my arm, and guided me in. The lift began to drop. He drew a faint sigh, as of relief.

"There was dynger along there," he whispered. "Now it'll be fair clear goin'!"

The descent of the elevator seemed very slow. When it stopped, I was sure that we must be well below the floor of the great hall, somewhere down among the foundations.

"What we're goin' into is one of 'is private wyes," again he whispered. "I don't think even Consardine knows it. An' we won't meet Satan on it. 'Cause why? I'm goin' to show you."

We slipped out of the lift, and crossed what was apparently a ten-foot-wide corridor, black as a windowless dungeon. We passed, I conjectured, through its opposite wall, and along another passage of eighteen short paces. Here Barker paused, listening.

Then in front of me a hair line of faint light appeared. Slowly, ever so slowly, it widened. Barker's head became silhouetted against it. Cautiously he advanced, peering out. Then he nodded, reassuringly. He moved forward.

We were in a dimly lighted, narrow corridor. It was hardly wide enough for two men to walk side by side. It was lined and paved with some polished black stone into which the light, from some hidden source, seemed to sink and drown. We were at one end of it. The floor fell in a gradual ramp for a hundred yards or more, and there the way either ceased or curved, the light was so faint and the effect of the polished stone so confusing I could not tell which.

"Looks like a h'alley into 'Ell, don't it?" muttered Harry. "Well, in a minute or two try to sye it ain't."

He set grimly forth down it, I at his heels. We came to the part that had perplexed me, and I saw that it was a curve, a sharp one. The curve was unlighted, its darkness relieved only by faint reflections from behind. I could not see its end. We moved on into the thickening gloom. The floor had become level.

Suddenly Barker halted, his mouth close to my ear.

"Lay down. Not a sound now when you look in. On your life! Don't 'ardly breathe!"

I looked through the crack. I felt a cold prickling along my spine and in the roots of my hair.

A little below me and not more than fifty feet away sat Satan. And he was opening the gates of his Black Paradise to the dying souls of his kehjt slaves!

The meaning of the scene struck clear with my first glimpse of it. Satan was leaning forward from a massive throne of heavy black stone cushioned in scarlet and standing on a low broad dais. His robes were scarlet. At his side squatted the ape-faced monstrosity of an executioner, Sanchal. At his left hand stood two figures with veiled faces. One of them held a deep ewer, and the other a golden goblet.

At Satan's feet was a woman, rising from her knees. She was not old, fair haired, and must once have been very beautiful. Her body, seen through the one white robe that was her only covering, was still so. Her wide eyes were fixed with a dreadful avidness upon another golden goblet in Satan's hand. Her mouth was half open, her lips drawn tight against her teeth. Her body quivered and strained as though she were about to leap upon him.

The executioner whirred the loop of his cord, and grinned. She shrank back. Satan lifted the goblet high. His voice rolled out, sonorous and toneless.

"You, woman who was Greta von Bohnheim, who am I?"

She answered as tonelessly.

"You are Satan."

"And what am I, Satan?"

She replied:

"You are my God!"

I felt Barker shudder. Well, I was doing a little shivering myself. The infernal litany went on.

"You shall have no God but me!"

"I have no God but you, Satan!"

"What is it, woman, that is your desire?"

Her hands were clenched, and she drew them up to her heart.

Her voice was tremulous, and so low that barely could I hear it.

"A man and a child who are dead!"

"Through me they shall live again for you! Drink!"

There was faint mockery in his voice, and derision in his eyes, as he handed the goblet to the woman. She clutched it in both hands, and drained it. She bowed low, and walked away. She passed out of the narrow range of my vision, stepping ever more firmly, face rapt, lips moving as though she talked with one unseen who walked beside her.

Again I felt the cold creep down my back. In what I had beheld there had been something diabolic, something that truly savored of the Prince of the Damned. It betrayed itself in Satan's cold arrogance and pride during the blasphemous litany. It was in his face, his glittering eyes, and in the poise of his huge body. Something truly of Hell that possessed him, emanated from him, hovered around him. As though, as once before I have tried to describe it, as though he were a mechanism of flesh and blood in which a demon had housed itself.

My gaze followed the woman until I could see her no more. The chamber was immense. What I could see of it through the crack must have been less than a third of it. The walls were of rose marble, without hangings or ornamentation of any kind. There were pierced openings like the mouths of deep niches over which silvery curtains fell. There was a great fountain that sent up tinkling jets of water out of a blood-red bowl. Couches of the rosy stone were scattered about. They were richly covered and on them lay, as though sleeping, men and women. There must have been dozens of these, for there were a score of them within my limited vision alone. I could not see the roof.

I thought that these curtained apertures might be cubicles or cells in which the slaves dwelt.

A gong sounded. The curtains were plucked aside. In each of the openings stood a slave, their eyes fastened upon Satan with a horrid eagerness. I shivered. It was like an eruption of the damned.

Satan beckoned. A man stepped forward toward the dais. I took him for an American, a Westerner. He was tall and lanky, and in his gait something of the rocking habit of the range rider. His face was the hawk-like type that the mountain country breeds, and, curiously, it made the peculiar pallor and dilated eyes mask-like and grotesque. His mouth was thin and bitter.

Like the woman, he prostrated himself before Satan. The veiled figure with the goblet held it out to the ewer bearer who poured into it a green liquid. The cup bearer handed the goblet to Satan.

"Rise," he commanded. The suppliant sprang to his feet, burning gaze upon the cup. The unholy ritual began again!

"You, man who was Robert Taylor, who am I?"

"You are Satan!"

"And what am I, Satan?" Again the blasphemous avowal: "You are my God!"

"You shall have no God but me!"

"I have no God but you, Satan!"

"What is it, man, that is your desire?" The slave straightened, his voice lost its lifelessness. His face grew cruel as that of the executioner's own.

"To kill the man I hate...to find him...to ruin him...to kill him slowly in many ways!"

"As you killed him once – too swiftly," said Satan maliciously, and then, again tonelessly:

"Through me you shall find him whom you hate, and slay him as you desire! Drink!"

He drank and passed. Twice more I heard the clang of the summoning gong, and twice I watched the white faces of these doomed ones with their avid eyes appear through the silver curtains and disappear behind them. I heard one man ask for dominance over a kingdom of beasts. Another for a Paradise of women.

And Satan promised, and gave them the green draught. The kehjt!

The subtle, devilish drug that gave to its drinkers the illusion of fulfilled desire. That turned the mind upon itself, to eat itself. And that by some hellish alchemy dissolved the very soul.

I stared on, fascinated, Eve forgotten. But if I had forgotten, Barker had not. The crack through which I was looking closed. He touched me, and we arose. Soundlessly we slipped up the ramp through the dim, black passage. I felt a bit sick.

It had been no nice picture, that of Satan wallowing in the worship of those slaves of his, dealing them out love and hate, dark power and lust, sardonically and impartially giving each what he or she most desired.

Illusions, yes. But more real than life to the drinkers when the drug had them. But, God, their awakening!

And after that awakening the burning craving to escape reality! To return to that place of illusion to which the kehjt was the only key!

No wonder that the three of the museum affair had gone to their deaths with such blind obedience!

And, if Satan was not what he pretended, very surely he was not disgracing that power whose name he had taken.

I had paid little attention to where we were going, blindly following Barker's lead.

"Well," he whispered, suddenly, "was I right? Wasn't it a h'alley into 'Ell? What price Satan now, Cap'n?"

I came back to myself with nerves jumping.

"A drug dealer," I answered him. "A dope den à la Ritz. That's all. I've seen opium joints in China that would make it look like a trench dugout. And the pipe hitters there would cut your throat for a pill just as quick as these would for Satan."

Neither of which assertions was at all true, but it gave me comfort to say them.

"Yes?" he said, cynically. "Well, it's a good wye to think. I 'opes you keep on thinkin' that wye, Cap'n."

I hoped that I might begin to think so.

"Soft along 'ere," he whispered. We were moving like ghosts in the darkness of a passage. I had an indistinct memory of having entered several lifts. Of even the probable location of my room I had not the slightest idea.

"'Ere we are," he muttered, and stood for an instant listening. I thrust my hand into the pocket where I had slipped my wrist watch, that its illuminated dial might not betray us. I took a swift look. It was almost half past midnight.

    Barker drew me forward. There was a faint scent in the air, a delicate fragrance.

    Eve's! We were in her room.

CHAPTER FOURTEEN

"Beat her to it," I whispered incautiously.

There was a rustle, as of some one sitting hastily up in bed.

"Who's there?" came Eve's voice, softly. "I've got my finger on the alarm!"

"It's me – Jim," I answered, as softly as she, but mighty hastily.

"Jim!" A subdued light gleamed suddenly. "Where have you been? I've been worried to death about you!"

Eve was leaning forward from her pillows, brown eyes wide and luminous, silken mop of hair a bit tousled. She looked like a wakeful little girl who had been exasperatedly pulling it. She was, also, the prettiest thing I had ever seen. Every time I looked at Eve she seemed prettier. I wondered where she was going to stop. She had on some sort of a lacy pink negligee. All the rest of my life, I knew, my heart would beat faster whenever I saw a lacy pink negligee, even when it was only in a shop window.

She slipped out of bed, ran straight to me, and kissed me. It was so pleasant that I entirely forgot everything else.

I became aware of a queer noise behind me. Harry was teetering from side to side, his hands clasped, his eyes half closed and moist, his face ecstatic, and he was crooning like an affectionate parrot. He was a sentimental little burglar, Harry.

Eve looked, and laughed.

"If you want to say 'Bless you, my children,' go ahead, Harry," she said mischievously.

He blinked, snapped out of it, and grinned at her.

"Made me think of me an' Maggie," he said. "Just like when we was courtin'. Fair warmed my 'eart, it did."

"Well," I said, "I move that this meeting comes to order. We've got a lot of ground to cover, and not much time to do it. What's the chance of us being interrupted, Eve?"

"Hardly any," she answered. "Frankly, everybody does as they like about having room parties. So everybody is extraordinarily discreet about visiting without an invitation. On the other hand, Jim, you're the one person it wouldn't do to have found here. Our aversion to each other has been so marked, darling, you know. Satan would be bound to hear about it. And the second he did–"

She didn't have to finish the sentence. I had a very clear idea of what Satan would do.

"It would be hard to explain Barker, too," she added.

"How about it, Harry?" I asked him. "Likely to be any calls for you? Any awkward searching parties?"

"Not unless something big goes wrong," he said. "If they look for me in my room, I can say I was workin' somewhere else. Satan won't be 'untin' me, that's certain."

"Well," I said, "we have to take some chances. But we'll talk low and in the dark."

Eve stepped over, and put out the lamp. She drew aside the heavy curtains from one of the windows. A faint light flickered in from the moon hidden behind a hazy sky. Barker and I moved the chaise longue to a shadowed corner. The three of us sat down upon it.

We talked. Not the slightest use of setting down a word of it. We got nowhere. A few schemes gleamed brightly for an instant, and then went glimmering like will-o'-the-wisps. The spell of what I had beheld in Satan's unholy shrine was heavy on me, try as I would to throw it off. I had to fight a sense of futility. We were like three flies in a web of the Temple of the Footsteps. If we got out of one, it was only to find ourselves in another. But steadily Eve's warm, soft body pressing against mine, her courage, her trust, armed me against the devastating sapping of my confidence. There was a way. There must be a way.

More than an hour had passed, and we had found not a solitary clew to it.

And Barker had been growing fidgety, nervously abstracted.

"What's the matter, Harry?" I asked him at last.

"I'm h'uneasy, sir," he said. "I don't know why. But I 'ave a feelin' somethin's wrong somewhere."

It struck me as funny.

"You're devilish well right there is," I couldn't help chuckling. "It's what we've been giving all this time trying to right."

"No," he said soberly. "I'm bl – I'm h'unusually h'uneasy. An' I'm never that wye h'unless somethin's bl – 'orrible wrong. Cap'n, I think we'd better call it a night an' get back."

I hesitated. As I say, we had gotten nowhere. At any moment one of us might get a flash that would open up a way out. Truth was, of course, I didn't want to leave Eve. But there was no denying the little man's distress. And if he should go and not be able to return – well, then I would be in a pretty fix. I hadn't the slightest idea of where my room was, or how to get to it.

"We've decided a lot of things won't do," said Eve. "It sounds Pollyanna-ish, I know, but it really is some progress. The day may bring some new ideas. We'll meet again tonight."

"All right," I said. "We'll go, Harry."

By the involuntary breath of relief he drew, I realized how troubled he was. Eve slipped to the windows, and let drop the curtains. The room resumed its original darkness. I felt her hand touch mine, and then her arms were around my neck.

"It's going to seem a long, long time till tonight, Jim, darling," whispered Eve.

"'Urry!" came Harry's whisper. "'Urry up, Cap'n!"

I cautiously began to make my way toward where he stood by the wall.

"Gord!" I heard him gasp.

The word was thick with terror. I leaped forward.

The ray of the flashlight struck Barker full in the face. A hand shot out with the quickness of a snake, and caught his throat. I saw his face distorted with agony as his own two hands flew up to break that merciless grip.

The light struck me in the eyes, dazzling me. I ducked, and dived in. Before I could touch whoever it was that held it, the flash dropped to the rug and Barker's body hit me like a bag of sand hurled by an elephant. I staggered back with a grunt. The lights in the room flashed up.

Just in front of me, menacing me with his automatic, stood Consardine!

And Consardine's eyes were cold and deadly. There was death in them. They flashed from me to Eve. His face softened, as though with relief from some fear. Swiftly it gave way to bewilderment, incredulity. It grew hard and deadly again. The muzzle of the gun pointing at me never wavered. At my feet Harry gasped, and staggered up dizzily. I put an arm out and steadied him.

"What are these men doing here, Eve?"

Consardine's voice was still and flat, as though he were holding himself in check by enormous effort. I had read the thought behind those swiftly changing expressions. First, that we had crept into Eve's room for some sinister purpose. Then – suspicion of Eve herself. I must wipe that out. Keep Eve out of it. Play on Consardine's first card. I answered before she could speak.

"You're rather – impetuous, Consardine," I said in a voice as hard as his own. "But your gun makes that safe, I suppose, when you let loose on an unarmed man. I was restless, and decided to go back to the bridge game. I got lost in your cursed rabbit warren. I ran across this man here who told me that he was working around the place. I asked him to guide me back to my room. By some damned irony, he managed to make the mistake of all mistakes of getting me into Miss Demerest's. Believe me, I was quite as anxious to get away as she was for me to go. Miss Demerest, I think you will confirm what I say?"

I turned to her. It was an open lead, and it sounded plausible enough. Consardine paid no attention to me whatever.

"I asked you, Eve, what these men are doing here?" he repeated.

Eve looked at him steadily for a moment, and then walked over and stood beside me.

"Dr. Consardine," she said, "Mr. Kirkham is lying like a gentleman, to save me. The truth is that I asked him to come and see me. And I asked Barker to guide him to me. Both of them are entirely innocent of anything except courteously doing as I asked. The whole responsibility is mine."

The veins suddenly stood out on Consardine's temples, and the gun in his hand wavered. His face flushed. The cold fury had given way to hot anger. He might be just as dangerous, but I had a flash that Eve knew what she was doing, that her instinct had been truer than mine.

"So!" said Consardine thickly. "You thought you could make a fool out of me! Dupe me! I don't enjoy being fooled, and I don't enjoy being a dupe. How long have you two known each other?"

"We never set eyes on each other until you brought us together," said Eve.

"And why did you send for him?"

"To get me away from Satan," answered Eve, steadily. "What else?"

He regarded her with smoldering eyes.

"And why did you think he could do that?" he asked her.

"Because I love him! And because he loves me!" said Eve quietly.

He stared at us. Then abruptly all anger fled, his eyes softened.

"Good God," said Consardine. "You Babes in the Wood!"

Eve put her hand out to him. He took it, patting it gently. He looked us over carefully again, as though we were some new and puzzling specimens. He turned out all the lights except the shaded one beside Eve's bed, strode over to the window, and peeped out the curtains. He came back to us.

"Let's talk this over," he said. "Barker, I'm sorry I choked you. Kirkham, I'm sorry I bowled you over. I'm sorry, too, that I misjudged you. And glad I did. Eve, I wasn't spying on you from out there. You were on my mind. You have been, child, for some time. I could see how restless and disturbed you were at the game. I thought – it was something else. You were on my mind, I say. I thought that perhaps you had not gone to bed. And that a talk with me, who am more than old enough to be your father, might help. There were – some things I had to say. I stood out there for minutes, hesitating. I thought I might slip the panel a mite and see if you were up – or awake. I thought you might be crying. And just as I was about to do it, it opened and I heard Barker curse. Then the rest happened. That's all."

I gave him my hand. Barker grinned widely, and saluted.

"Had I better be goin', sir?" he asked.

"Not yet," said Consardine. "Kirkham, how long have you known Barker?"

"'E syved my life, 'e did," broke in Harry. "'E pulled me out o' 'Ell. An' while we're all tellin' the truth, Dr. Consardine, I'll sye I'm fair set on doin' the syme by 'im an' 'is young lydy."

I gave Consardine a brief account of my acquaintance with Barker. He nodded, approvingly.

"First," he said, "it will be well to clarify the situation by stating my own position. I am Satan's servant. I am bound by a certain oath to him. I took that oath with open eyes, fully realizing all that it entailed. I came to him voluntarily, not like you, Kirkham. I recognize that your oath was under duress, and that therefore you are entitled to act in ways that I am not. I do not break my voluntary oath nor my word. Besides that I am convinced that if I did I would not live long. I have a foolish partiality for living. I could cheat Satan of his pleasure in my torture, but – I do not believe in any existence beyond the grave, and I find life, at times, vastly interesting. Furthermore, I have certain standards of living, appetites, desires and likings which my contact with Satan insures of satisfaction. Away from him they certainly would not be satisfied. Also I was an outlaw when I came to him. Outlaw I am, but hunted outlaw I would be without his protection. First and last – there is my oath.

"Let it be understood, then, that any assistance that I can promise you will be largely negative. It will consist of warning you of pitfalls to avoid, and of closing my eyes and ears to what I may see or hear. Like this affair tonight, for instance."

"It is all we could ask, sir," I said. "And a great deal more than I had any right to expect."

"And now I say to you, Kirkham," he went on, "that I think you have little chance to win against Satan. I think that the road you have picked has death at its end. I tell you so because I know you have courage, and you should be told what is in my mind. And I say it before you, Eve, because you too have courage. And you must consider, child, whether you should allow your lover to take this almost certain risk of death, or whether you should do – something else."

I looked into Eve's face. Her mouth was quivering, and her eyes were tortured.

"What – what is the something else, Dr. Consardine?" she whispered.

"Become Mme. Satan, I suppose!" I answered for him. "Not while I'm alive."

"That," he acquiesced quietly, "of course. But it is not what I had in mind–" He hesitated, shot a glance at Harry and quickly switched to another thought, or back, rather, to his old one.

"Understand," he said, "I want you to win, Kirkham. In any way that does not break my oath to Satan, or threaten my prejudice for remaining alive, I will help you. At least – I will keep my hands off. But realize this – I am Satan's servant. If he orders me to take you, I shall take you. If he orders me to kill you, I shall – kill you."

"If Jim dies, I die. If you kill him, you kill me," said Eve tranquilly. She meant it. He knew she meant it, and he winced.

"Nevertheless, child, I would do it," he told her. And I knew he meant that. So did Eve.

"You – you started to – you were about to speak of another way–" she faltered.

"I do not want you to tell me your plans, Kirkham," he interrupted her, quickly. "Only this. Do any of them involve your trying to kill Satan?"

I hesitated. It was a dangerous question to answer. After all, Consardine had warned me he could be trusted only so far. What did he consider the limits of his oath?

"I perceive they do," he had interpreted my silence. "Well, it is the one thing you must not attempt. It is the one thing that is impossible. You may think you can kill him while you and he are alone. Kirkham, I tell you Satan is never alone. Always there are guards hidden about – in the walls, in secret places. Before you could fire, they would have you winged. And there is Satan's abnormal quickness of mind. He would perceive your thought before it could be transformed into action. If you tried it while others were about, they would have you down before you could fire a second shot – assuming that you managed to get in a first one. And Satan has an unhuman vitality. I do not believe one bullet or two could kill him any more than they could an elephant. The real point is, however, that you would never get the chance."

Well, Consardine did not know everything – that was clear. With that stone in the wall of the slavers' hall up half an inch instead of a quarter, and a rifle poking through the crack, I would not have given much for Satan's survival. Assuming, of course, that basically he was human.

"Furthermore," he went on, almost as in answer to my thought, "suppose you did perform what I believe the impossible – kill him. Still there could be no escape for you. Better to be slain at once. There is not a place on earth where you could hide from the vengeance of his people. For it is not only by fear that Satan rules. Far from it. As he has told you, he pays his servants well. His continuance means ease, luxury, safety, power – most of the things of life for which man commonly strives – to more people than you can imagine. Satan has his splendid side as well as his dark one. And his people are scattered over all the globe. Many of them are more highly placed than you, as yet, can dream. Is it not so, Eve?"

"It is so," she said, and the trouble in her eyes grew.

"Satan's throne does not rest upon the backs of cringing slaves," he said. "As always, he has his princes and his legions. To sum up. I do not believe you can kill him. If you try and fail, you die – horribly. And Eve is not saved. If you did kill him, you die as inevitably. Eve would be saved from him – yes. But will she have her freedom at such a price?"

"No! No!" cried Eve, and stood in front of me, arms outstretched, despair in her face.

"Consardine," I said abruptly, "why does Satan hide his hands when the climbers go up the steps?"

"What's that? What do you mean?" He stared at me.

"I've seen him on the black throne three times," I said. "Twice with Cartright, once with myself. He pulls the lever, and then he hides his hands under the robe. What does he do with them, Consardine?"

"Are you hinting that the steps are a crooked game? That's absurd, Kirkham!" His voice was amused, but I saw his strong hands clench.

"I'm hinting nothing," I answered. "I – wonder. You must have seen many go up those steps. Have you ever seen Satan's hands in the open while they were mounting? Think back, Consardine."

He was silent. I could see him marshaling in his memory those he had beheld beckoned by the shining footprints. And his face had whitened.

"I – can't tell," he said at last. "I didn't notice. But – I don't think so."

He jumped to his feet.

"Nonsense!" he said. "Even so – it means nothing!"

I was shooting in the dark. No, not quite. I was giving substance to that shadowy thought, that nebulous suspicion, I had feared to bring out before Barker.

"No?" I said. "Do you believe, then, that Satan, with all his genius for details, his setting up of the cards, his discounting of every chance – do you believe that Satan would leave any door open through which one could come and rule him? Has crown and scepter ever been won?"

"Yes," he replied, disconcertingly. "Unfortunately for the doubt with which you nearly netted me, Kirkham, they have. I have been with Satan eight years. Three times I have seen the steps conquered!"

That was like a slap in the face. For the moment it silenced me. Not so Eve.

"What became of them?" she asked.

"Well," he looked at her, uneasily, "one of them wanted something – something rather peculiar. He died of it in six months."

"Yes," drawled Eve, "so he died of it. What about the others?"

"One of them died in an aeroplane accident between London

and Paris," he said. "She was on her way to – what she wanted. Not even Satan could have helped that. Everybody was burned."

"Rather unlucky, weren't they?" asked Eve, innocently. "Both of them. But the third?"

"I don't know," said Consardine, half angrily. "I suppose he's all right. He went to Asia. I've never heard of him since then. He wanted a sort of a hidden little pocket kingdom where he could do as he pleased. Satan gave it to him."

"Two dead, and one – disappeared," mused Eve. "But don't you think that you ought to have heard something about that third one, Dr. Consardine? Couldn't you find out what became of him? Maybe – maybe, he died, too, like the others."

"As Eve says, two of them didn't last long," I said. "The third is doubtful. If you were in Satan's place, Consardine, wouldn't it occur to you that it was advisable to keep up hope in the aspirants by showing them now and then that it could be done? It would to me. And, still assuming that we thought like Satan, wouldn't we handpick our successful climbers? I would. But I wouldn't pick the kind that would be likely to live long, would you? Or if they were well and hearty, a little accident might be arranged. Like that Croydon air bus you've mentioned, for instance."

"Gorblyme!" gasped Harry. "The swine! That wouldn't be 'ard to do. An' I'll bet 'e done it!"

"What does Satan do with his hands when he hides them under his robe?" I repeated.

"And what became of that third winner?" murmured Eve.

On Consardine's forehead little beads of sweat stood out. He was trembling.

"See here, Consardine," I said, "you told us you didn't like being a dupe. You didn't like being fooled. Suppose Satan has been making a colossal mock of you – and the others. What happens?"

I saw the effort with which he mastered himself. It frightened me a bit. After all, I hadn't the slightest evidence to back up what I had been hinting. And if Consardine thought that I was deliberately deceiving him –

But I wasn't. The doubts I had raised were entirely legitimate. Satan did hide his hands. The bad after-luck of the step conquerors had been something that Consardine had known, not we.

"Barker," he turned to Harry, "have you ever looked over the mechanism that Satan tells us controls the choice of the shining footprints? Answer me! Is it what he says it is?"

Barker wrung his hands, looking first at him and then at Eve and me, piteously. He swallowed once or twice.

"Answer me," ordered Consardine.

"Gord 'elp me, Cap'n," Harry turned to me desperately, "I never wanted to lie so 'ard in my life. I want to sye I 'aven't seen it. Or that it don't work them bloody prints. But Gord 'elp me, Miss Demerest, I 'ave looked it over. An' it does work 'em, Dr. Consardine. It does, just as 'e syes it does!"

Well, that was that. It knocked, apparently, my theories clean through the vanishing point. For a moment I had hoped that the little man would be diplomatic. Say, at least, that he didn't know. But I could not deny him his right to tell the truth – if he felt like it.

"That's all right, Harry," I said cheerfully. "What we're looking for is the truth. And what you say settles everything, I suppose."

"I'd like to 'ave lied, Cap'n," he half whimpered. "But, 'ell, I couldn't."

Consardine, I suddenly noticed, was behaving rather oddly. He did not seem at all like one whose faith in Satan had been impregnably re-enforced. He seemed, indeed, more disturbed than ever.

"Barker," he said, "you'd better go now. I will see Captain Kirkham back to his room."

Harry slid over to one of the walls. He bowed to us, miserably. A panel opened, and he was gone. Consardine turned to us.

"Now, Eve," he said, "I'll tell you what brought me here tonight. I told you that you'd been on my mind. So you have. Damnably. I wanted to save you from Satan. I had a way to suggest. I stole the idea from Shakespeare. You remember the stratagem by which the honest friar schemed to get Juliet to her Romeo? And cheat their respective warring families? Their Satan, in a sense."

"The draught that would make her appear to be dead," whispered Eve.

"Exactly," nodded Consardine. "It was something like that which I was about to propose to you. To treat you, from my medical knowledge, in such a way that the health and beauty and spirit which makes you so desirable to Satan would fade – temporarily. To put you in such condition as obviously to make impossible, at least in the near future, his personal plans for you. And to keep you in that condition until he had found a substitute for his paternal impulses – or something else happened.

"There was risk to it, certainly. Great risk to you, Eve. The waiting might be too long – I might not be able to restore to you what I had taken from you. Yet you might have preferred that risk to the certainty of – Satan's arms. I was going to let you decide."

"Was going to?" repeated Eve breathlessly. "Of course I'll take the risk. Oh, Dr. Consardine – it seems like the way out!"

"Does it?" asked he grimly. "I think not – now. The original scheme from which I stole my idea came to grief, you remember, because of Romeo. Well, I was reckoning without Romeo. I didn't know there was one."

"I – I don't quite – get that," said Eve.

"Child," he took her hands, "are you willing to give up your lover? Never see him, never meet him, never communicate with him? Not for weeks or months, but for years? Kill your love for him, or live on, starving upon memories?"

"No," answered Eve directly, and shook her curly head.

"And even if you persuaded her to, Consardine, what do you think I would be doing 1" the bare suggestion stirred in me resentment and stubborn anger. "Fold my hands and turn my eyes Heavenward and meekly murmur, 'Thy will be done!' Not me!"

"I'm persuading no one, Kirkham," he replied quietly. "I'm only pointing out that it's the only way the thing could be done. If I did to Eve what I have described, what would happen? Treatment here for a time, of course, so Satan could see her failing. Then her removal somewhere, for other doctors to look after her. Her symptoms could not be feigned. They would have to be real. The medical fraternity is not wholly represented by me in Satan's entourage. He has some highly placed specialists among his dependents. And if he had not, he could call them in. And would, unless at the very outset he was persuaded that her condition would inevitably mean a faulty maternity weakness in offspring. Forgive me, child, for talking so plainly, but it's no time to be beating around the bush.

"The specialists I could take care of. Hoodwink. I could have been a very great" – he hesitated, and sighed – "well, no matter. But Satan has set his will on you, Eve. He will not lightly give up his purpose. If it were only as a woman that he desired you, it would not be so difficult. But you are more than that to him, far more. You are to be the bearer of his child. Not upon my word alone, much as he trusts my judgment, would he relinquish you as unfit. He would have to be convinced beyond all doubt – and therein lies the danger to you and possibly – death."

He paused, looked pityingly into her troubled eyes.

"Too great a risk," I said. "I'll try my way first, Consardine."

"Enter Romeo," he smiled faintly. "You'll have to, Kirkham. You've made the other impossible. You think that life would be worthless without Eve, I take it?"

"I don't think it, I know it," I answered.

"And you feel the same way about – Jim?"

"Yes," she said softly. "But – to save his life–"

"It wouldn't," said Consardine. "I know men and women. No matter what you made up your mind to do, Eve, he would be working and planning to get you away. Nor are you exactly the kind to sit down, as he expresses it, with meekly folded hands. He would be trapped, sooner or later. It might very likely follow that the trick would be discovered. Then I would have to give up my foolish prejudice for living. I won't take the chance of that. But assume that you do escape. Together. You would be two hares running around the world with the hounds constantly at your heels. Satan's hounds, always on the move. Always with his threat hanging over you. Would such a life be worth living? There might be a child. Be sure that Satan's vengeance would not spare it. I repeat – would such a life be worth living?"

"No," I said, and Eve drew a deep breath and shook her head.

"What can we do!" she whispered.

Consardine strode once across the room, and back. He stood before me, and I saw that again the veins in his forehead were standing out like cords, and that his gray eyes were hard and cold as steel. He tapped me thrice on the breast with his clenched fist.

"Find out what Satan does with his hands when he hides them!" he said.

He turned from us, plainly not trusting himself to speak further. Eve was staring at him, wondering, even as I, at the intensity of the rage that was shaking him.

"Come, Kirkham," he had mastered himself. He ran his fingers through Eve's bob, ruffling it caressingly.

"Babes in the Wood," he repeated.

He walked to the panel, slowly. Considerately.

"Tonight," I whispered to Eve.

Her arms were around my neck, her lips pressed to mine.

"Jim – dear!" she whispered, and let me go.

I looked back as I passed through the opening. She was standing as I had left her, hands stretched out to me, eyes wide and wistful. She was like a lonely little child, afraid to go to bed. I felt a deeper twinge at my heart. A strengthening of resolve. The panel closed.

In silence I followed Consardine as he led me to my room. He entered with me and stood for a moment staring at me somberly. Quite suddenly I felt dog-tired.

"I hope you sleep better tonight than I shall," said Consardine, abruptly.

He was gone. I was too tired to wonder what he had meant by that. I managed to get out of my clothes, and was asleep before I could draw the bed covers over me.

CHAPTER FIFTEEN

The ringing of the telephone aroused me. I reached out for it, only half awake, not in the least realizing where I was. Consardine's voice brought me out of my lethargy like a bucket of water.

"Hello, Kirkham," he said. "Don't want to spoil your beauty sleep, but how about having breakfast with me, and then taking a canter? We've some excellent horses, and the morning's too nice to be wasted."

"Fine," I answered. "I'll be down in ten minutes. How will I find you?"

"Ring for Thomas. I'll be waiting." He hung up.

The sun was streaming through the windows. I looked at my watch. It was close to eleven. I had slept soundly about seven hours. I rang for Thomas.

Sleep, a plunge and the brilliant sunshine were charms that sent the shadow of Satan far below the rim of the world. Whistling, I hoped half-guiltily that Eve felt as fit. The valet brought me out what Barker would have called a "real tysty ridin' rig." He convoyed me to a sunny, old-world lovely room looking out on a broad, green terrace. There were a dozen or so nice-looking people breakfasting at small tables. Some of them I had met the night before.

Over in a corner I saw Consardine. I joined him. We had an extremely pleasant meal, at least I did. Consardine did not seem to have a care on earth. His talk had a subtly sardonic flavor that I found most stimulating. So far as the conversation was concerned, our encounter in Eve's room might never have been. He made no slightest reference to it. Nor, following his lead, did I.

We went from there to the stables. He took a powerful black gelding that whinnied to him as he entered. I mounted a trim roan. We rode at a brisk canter along bridle paths that wound through thick woods to scrub pine and oak. Now and then we met a guard who stood at attention, and saluted Consardine as we passed by. It was a silent ride.

We came abruptly out of the woods. Consardine reined in. We were upon the cleared top of a low hillock. Below us and a hundred yards away sparkled the waters of the Sound.

Perhaps a quarter mile out lay a perfect beauty of a yacht. She was about two hundred feet long and not more than thirty in beam. Seagoing and serviceable, and built for speed as well. Her paint and brass shone, dazzling white and golden.

"The Cherub," said Consardine, dryly. "She's Satan's. He named her that because she looks so spotless and innocent. There is a more descriptive word for her, however, but not a polite one. She can do her thirty knots, by the way."

My gaze dropped from the yacht to a strong landing that thrust out from the shore. A little fleet of launches and speed boats were clustered near it. I caught a glimpse of an old-fashioned rambling house nestled among the trees near the water's edge.

My eyes followed the curve of the shore. A few hundred feet from the pier was a pile of great rocks, huge boulders dropped by the glacier that once covered the Island. I started, and looked more closely.

Upon one of them stood Satan, black-cloaked, arms folded, staring out at the gleaming yacht. I touched Consardine's arm.

"Look!" I whispered, "Sat–" I stopped. The rock was bare. I had turned my eyes from it for the barest fraction of a second. Yet in that time Satan had disappeared.

"What did you see?" asked Consardine.

"Satan," I said. "He was standing on that pile of rocks. Where could he have gone!"

"He has a hole there," he answered indifferently. "A tunnel that runs from the big house to the shore."

He swung around to the woods. I followed. We rode along for a quarter of an hour more. We came out into a small meadow through which ran a brook. He dismounted, and dropped the reins over the black's neck.

"I want to talk to you," he said to me.

I gave the roan its freedom, and sat down beside Consardine.

"Kirkham, you've set my world rocking under my feet," he

said curtly. "You've put the black doubt in me. Of the few things that I would have staked my life on, the first was that Satan's gamble of the seven footprints was a straight one. And now – I would not."

"You don't accept Barker's testimony, then?" I asked.

"Talk straight, Kirkham," he warned, coldly. "Your implication was that Satan manipulated the telltale from the Black Throne. With his hidden hands. If so, he has the cunning to do it in a way that Barker, going over the other mechanism, would never suspect. You know that. Talk straight, I tell you."

"The thought that Barker might be wrong occurred to me, Consardine," I said. "I preferred to let it occur to you without my suggesting it. I had said enough."

"Too much – or not enough," he said. "You have put the doubt in me. Well, you've got to rid me of it."

"Just what do you mean by that?" I asked him.

"I mean," he said, "that you must find out the truth. Give me back my faith in Satan, or change my doubt into certainty."

"And if I do the latter–" I began eagerly.

"You will have struck a greater blow at him than any with knife or bullet. You will be no longer alone in your fight. That I promise you."

His voice was thick, and the handle of his riding crop snapped in the sudden clenching of his strong hand.

"Consardine," I said bluntly, "why should the possibility of Satan's play being crooked move you so? You are closest to him here, I gather. His service, so you say, brings you all that you desire. And you tell me he is the shield between you and the law. What difference, then, does it make to you whether his gamble of the seven footprints is on the level or isn't?"

He caught my shoulder, and I winced at the crushing grip.

"Because," he answered, "I am under Satan's sentence of death!"

"You!" I exclaimed, incredulously.

"For eight years," he said, "that threat has been over me. For eight years he has tormented me, as the mood swayed him. Now with hint of the imminent carrying out of that sentence. Now with half-promise of its wiping out, and another trial at the steps. Kirkham, I am no coward – yet death fills me with horror. If I knew it to be inevitable, I would face it calmly. But I believe it to be eternal blackness, oblivion, extinction. There is something in me that recoils from that, something that shrinks from it with a deadly terror, with loathing. Kirkham, I love life.

"Yet if the gamble was straight, he was within his rights. But if it was not straight – then all those eight years he has played with me, made a mock of me, laughed at me. And still laughing, would have watched me go to whatever death he had decreed, unresisting, since I would have believed that by my oath I was so bound.

"And that, Kirkham, is not to be endured. Not by me!

"Nor is that all. I have watched many men and women take the steps, risking all on Satan's word. And I have seen some of them go to death, as calmly as I would have done, their honor, like mine, rooted in dishonor. And others go broken and wailing. Like Cartright. While Satan laughed. And there are more who live like me on Satan's sufferance. And all this on a cast of loaded dice? If so, then I tell you, Kirkham, it is not a thing to be borne! Nor shall it be borne!"

He plucked at his collar, gasping, as though it choked him.

"God!" he whispered. "To pay him back for that! If it is true...I would face death...singing...but I must know if it is true."

I waited until he had regained control.

"Help me find out whether it is or not," I said. "It may well turn out to be an impossible job for me – alone."

He shook his head.

"You have Barker to help you," he replied.

"I don't want to run him into any more risks." I would cover up the little man as much as I could. "There's a certain amount of prowling involved, Consardine. We might run across somebody not so well disposed as you. But the three of us ought to be able to settle matters one way or the other quickly."

"No," he said, stubbornly. "Why should I? It is up to you, Kirkham. It is you who have raised the doubt. It is you who must resolve it. One way or the other. After all, your suspicions are based upon the vaguest evidence. A triviality, and two, or it may be three, perfectly explicable happenings. The chances that you are wrong are enormously greater than those that you are right. Why should I risk my life upon them? I have already gone far. I have promised you neutrality, and somewhat more. I will go no further. Take Barker. I promise neither to see nor hear you should I meet you in your – wanderings. But at this time I will not invite certain death by joining you in them. I have been reasonably content. If you are wrong, I shall still be. If you are right – ah, then, I repeat, you will be no longer alone.

"In the meantime – Michael Consardine holds fast to his place in the sun."

He chirruped to the black gelding, and mounted it. There was no use in further argument, that was plain. We rode away, through the woods, and after a while turned back to the chateau.

I left him at the stable, and went to my rooms to change. There was a note pinned to my pillow. It was from Satan. A casual sort of message. He hoped I was enjoying myself as I deserved, and would see me about nine o'clock that evening.

The rest of the day passed uneventfully. The more I thought over Consardine's talk, the more I sympathized with his viewpoint. Also, oddly enough, the higher rose my spirits. I sat down to dinner in a pleasantly reckless state of mind.

Consardine was at the head of the board as on the previous night. I had Cobham for companion. I saw Eve toward the far end. She ignored me. It was difficult for me to do the same toward her.

Cobham had been drinking. For some reason he seemed to feel a certain responsibility for me. He paid no attention to any one else, nor would he let me. He was vastly interesting, but as the time wore on I began to feel a profound distaste for Cobham. He was expounding his theories of life as a mere electrochemical reaction. He made it clear that neither the individual nor the mass meant anything to him in terms of what is commonly called humanity. He was appallingly callous about it.

He seemed to have no more feeling about men and women

than he would have about his test tubes. Rather less, I fancied. In fact, that was what men and women appeared to him to be, just a lot of animated test tubes with minute curiosity-provoking differences in their contents. And he saw no reason why they should not be broken, or emptied or the contents changed in the way of experimentation. He sketched a few rather awful experiments with gases upon the kehjt slaves. At least, I hoped that the unfortunate subjects had been the slaves. He did not say so.

Listening, I was convinced that of the two, Satan might be the more humane. Cobham kept on drinking steadily. The only effect of the liquor was to make him more coldly, inhumanly scientific.

"You've got too much sentiment in your ferment, Kirkham," he said. "You probably think that life is sacred, to use the cant word, not to be destroyed unless by dire necessity. Bosh! It is no more sacred than the current I turn on or off at will from my lamps, nor the ferments in my tubes that I end at will. Whenever did Nature give a damn about the individual? Neutralize the weakening ingredient in you, Kirkham, and you might become a great man. I can do it for you, if you will let me."

I promised to think it over.

At 8:30 Satan appeared. I had been wondering where I was to see him. Consardine yielded his place, and Satan beckoned me to sit at his left hand.

"To my new follower, James Kirkham," he raised his glass. "I am much pleased with him."

They drank to me, standing. I saw Eve pointedly set down her glass untouched. So, as she had meant him to do, did Satan.

At 8:45, as though at some signal, the company began to drift out of the room. In a few minutes there remained only Satan, Cobham and myself. It rather surprised me to see Consardine leave. Servants cleared the table, and at a nod from Satan withdrew.

"There is a ship," he said abruptly, "that sails from Havre within three days. She is the Astarte. A slow boat. She carries some things of superlative beauty which I feel it time for me to claim. There is a painting by Sir Joshua Reynolds, another by Romney. There is a ewer of rock crystal and twelve rock crystal cups, marvelously engraved and set with great cabochon sapphires and rubies. They were made, it may be, in ancient Crete for Queen Pasiphae. At least, they are immemorially old. And to them an unknown genius gave his best. They were long hidden in the Kremlin. The Communists have sold them. There is a necklace of emeralds upon each of which is graven one of the *Metamorphoses* of Ovid. There is nothing like it in the world."

He paused, then bent his head toward me.

"I must have them, James Kirkham. You and Cobham shall get them for me."

I bowed, awaiting further enlightenment. Cobham, I noticed, had not drunk anything since Satan's entrance. He did not show at all what he had drunk. He sat silent, eyes upon the glass with which his fingers played; cynical, a faint smile upon his full lips. Yet I felt that he was watching me covertly, as though awaiting something. Whatever Satan was about to tell me, I suspected that he had already gone over it with him.

"I have selected you as leader," Satan went on, "not only because the task may demand the exercise of unusual resourcefulness, but also that close obedience to orders which you have proved to me you can exercise. I am merely outlining the venture tonight so you may be turning it over in your mind. You will receive your detailed instructions before you sail."

Sail? That meant leave Eve! I moved restlessly. I suppose my discomfort showed in my face. At any rate, he sensed it.

"Yes," he said. "The transfer will not be made on land after the Astarte arrives. I prefer to make it on the high seas. You are to engage in what the prejudiced would call piracy, James Kirkham. Ah, well, it is a romantic calling."

He eyed me, faint malice in the sparkling gaze.

"And you have your romantic side," he purred. "I admire it. For I, too, have mine. Therefore, I envy you, somewhat, this venture."

"And I am grateful," I smiled, meeting his scrutiny squarely. But the palms of my hands had grown suddenly moist.

"The Astarte," he continued, "will take the southern route.

There is little likelihood of her encountering any serious storms at this time of year in those latitudes. On the day she sails, you and Cobham will set out in my yacht which I perceived you admiring today. Besides her crew, the yacht will carry a dozen of my drinkers of the kehjt. They will be for use in emergency. But it is my hope that none such may arise. The Cherub – is it not a lovely name? – the Cherub will leave ostensibly for a coastwise voyage. On the first day out, the night rather, the Cherub will cease to be her angelic self – yes, I assure you there were girl cherubs as well as boy ones. She will be cunningly changed to the semblance of the Sea Wolf, the yacht of an eminently respectable financier which at that moment will be logging along its unsuspecting way to Havana. This also in case of emergency. And, of course, the name of the Sea Wolf will replace that of the Cherub wherever the name is noticeable.

"You will circle the Astarte two days later at a designated section, keeping out of sight, of course. Her speed is fifteen knots, yours thirty. You will be able, therefore, to stop her, remove what I desire, and get back here – again the innocent, spotless Cherub – at least two days before she can arrive in port."

My heart, which had been growing steadily heavier, lightened. Satan intended no mischief to the ship then, or to its crew. Else he would not speak of her return. Cobham gave a short bark, like a suppressed laugh. The cynicism of his smile had deepened. Satan's blue stare rested upon him for an instant. Cobham moved uneasily.

"You have planned, of course, sir," I said, "how we are to stop the Astarte."

"Naturally," he answered. "I am coming to that. At this time of year, this boat would not carry more than a hundred persons. Some of the passengers she does carry will be my people. But beside that, I have arranged it so that there will be even fewer than usual. A number of staterooms have been reserved for a tourists' club. But, oddly, just before the Astarte is to sail, these reservations will be canceled. There will have been an unavoidable change of plans. The generous representative of the club will waive all claims upon the reservation money, and the line will be guaranteed indemnity. The Astarte, because of the anxiety of the owners of the objects I intend to acquire, will not delay her sailing. I think there will be not more than thirty passengers, of whom ten, at least, will be of my following.

"Very well, James Kirkham. We come now to the night of your adventure. All that afternoon you have been following the Astarte at a distance of ten miles. It is a moonless night. At nine o'clock there is a concert going on in the saloon. The few passengers are a happy little family party. They are probably all there. So are some of the officers. You have put out your lights and have steamed up to within four miles.

"There will be a signal from the Astarte which you will answer. At the moment of that signal, two men assigned to that task will hurl a few bombs into the engine room of the Astarte. The bombs will be filled with a certain gas, the invention of Mr. Cobham. Immediately thereafter the occupants of the engine room will take no further interest in their work. A third man of mine will slip into the engine room and bring the boat to a standstill."

He paused, scrutinizing me; I felt upon me again the covert glance of Cobham. By some miracle I managed to keep from my face the horror I felt in my heart; managed to make my voice indifferent and steady as I spoke:

"Well, that wipes out the engine room crew. Then what?"

For many moments Satan did not answer me. His brilliant eyes searched me. I drove from my mind the swift picture that had come into it of men choking and writhing on the floor of the Astarte's engine room. I bore his gaze, frowning as though puzzled. Whether he had found what he had been hunting I do not know, but suddenly its disconcerting intensity diminished.

"Oh, fie, James Kirkham!" he said unctuously, "it is not necessary to kill. The gas I refer to is not lethal. It is a sleep gas. Its effect is practically instantaneous. At least, it acts within five seconds. But it is harmless. Six hours, and its breathers awaken without even a headache. How bloodthirsty he thinks us, Cobham!"

Something warned me to hide my relief, even as I had hidden my dread.

"We still have the officers and the crew," I said indifferently.

"What happens to them? Frankly, in all you have outlined, Satan, I seem to be nothing but an onlooker. A messenger boy. Where are my piratical thrills?"

"The venture at this point passes into your hands," he answered. "You will by this time have drawn up beside, the Astarte and will board her with Cobham and a sufficient force to take charge. Conditions may now arise which I can foresee, but must trust to your ingenuity and courage to meet. There will be much confusion on board the Astarte. You must see to it that no boats are launched, and that no one escapes from her. Before you board, the captain, and a mate or two, may have suffered some slight accident. Nothing serious. No, no. Merely disabling. Then again – they may not. You may have their resistance to overcome. Without bloodshed, if you can. But with or without – it must be overcome. Then weather conditions may complicate matters. I think you will not find it too tame, James Kirkham."

Nor did I. I had an uneasy feeling that Satan was not presenting me with the full picture.

"In your final instructions you will find definite information as to the location of what you are to bring to me," he said. "The objects are in a strong safe in a steel storeroom. So precious are the jewels that only the captain will know the combination of the safe. You need waste no time trying to persuade him to tell it to you. There will be with you an expert to whom the safe will have no mysteries. After you have recovered the things for me, you will cut loose from the Astarte and make all speed home, taking off from her, before starting, certain of my people on board her who would find it embarrassing to remain. That is all."

I considered for a moment. What he meant was that some of his agents on the Astarte would be questioned and might be recognized for what they were. Well, how about us on the Cherub?

"Have you considered the probability of some one on the Astarte identifying us later, sir?" I began.

"You will all be masked, of course," he interrupted, smoothly. Cobham moved suddenly, impatiently.

"The wireless," I suggested. "I suppose that will be disabled before the engine room attack?"

"It will not be necessary," he answered. "The yacht carries extraordinarily strong batteries. At the moment of the signal, the Astarte's radio will be blanketed, her waves strangled. There will be no message from her that can break through the barrier the able operator of the Cherub will interpose."

I sat for a moment in thought. Everything seemed to be plain. And yet – I felt a cold unease, a boding depression. There was something else, something deadly sinister hiding behind Satan's smooth phrases.

"I trust you were satisfied with the rewards of your necklace venture," he broke the current of my thoughts. "The rewards of this one will be proportionately greater, naturally. The invitation to join me cut your vacation rather short. What would you say to taking, after the affair, a six months' trip? You shall go where you please, and as you please, and do as you please. At my expense, of course. You may also spend what you please, let me add."

"Thank you, sir," I said, "but I feel no need of a vacation. And frankly, I find my contacts with you infinitely more interesting than anything I could hope to experience away from you."

His face was inscrutable as ever, but I felt that I had pleased him.

"Well," he said, "we shall see. Only continue as you have begun, James Kirkham, and you shall have no cause to complain of my generosity."

He arose. I stood up, politely; Cobham, cautiously. Satan for a moment considered us.

"How are you spending the evening?" he asked me.

"Cobham spoke of us joining the bridge game," I answered, "but if you have any other desire–"

Cobham had done nothing of the sort. He had said so much, however, that I hoped he might take it for granted that he had. I particularly did not want to be separated from Cobham just then. If Satan had thought, as I half feared, of asking either of us to accompany him, he changed his mind. He nodded, and walked toward the wall.

"It would be a good idea," he turned beside the opened panel, "to look over the Cherub tomorrow. Familiarize yourself with her. Good night."

Cobham sat silently for a good minute, staring at the point where Satan had disappeared.

"That was damned decent of you, Kirkham," he said at last, slowly. "I don't know how you guessed it, but I couldn't have stood much more of Satan tonight. Damned decent!"

He stretched out a hand to the brandy. I grinned – Cobham had remembered, then, and was aware of my maneuver. He poured his goblet half full of the liquor and drank it neat.

"Damned decent," he repeated, and I saw the brandy take hold of him swiftly. "Have a drink with me."

I poured myself a small one. Again he half filled his glass and tossed it off.

"A damned shame," he muttered, "treating you like a child. Treating a man like you as if you were in swaddles. You're a man, you are, Kirkham. You've got guts, you have, Kirkham. Why should you be coddled? Lied to? God damn it, Kirkham, you deserve the truth!"

So! It was coming, was it! That hidden, sinister something I had sensed was getting ready to crawl from Cobham's lips.

"Have a drink with me," I said, and tipped the decanter. "Who's treating me like a child?"

He glared at me, drunkenly.

"You think that gas is going to put that engine room crew to sleep, eh?" he chuckled. "Nice little lullaby for poor tired sailors? Sweet little chemical sl-slumber song composh-composed by Pa Satan and M-Ma Cobham? Well, Kirkham, you're damned well right it's going put 'em to sh-sleep. Forever!"

I poured myself another brandy, and drank it composedly.

"Well, what of it?" I asked. "A long sleep or a short one – what does it matter?"

"What's it matter? What's it matter!" he stared at me, then brought his fist down with a thump on the table. "By God, I was right!

Told Satan you had the guts! Told him needn't – needn't tamper with the form-florm-formula with you! What's it matter, he asks. Have a drink with me."

I drank with him. He began to shake with laughter.

"Masks!" he said. "You wanted masks so people on Astarte couldn't ren-recognize you later. Later! Ha! Ha! Later! That's good, that is. Hell, man, there's not going to be any later for them!"

The room swam around me. What was Cobham saying now?

"Not exactly accurate. Say – twenty minutes later. Twenty minutes later – Bonk! goes nice bomb. Gentlemanly bomb. Quiet, dignified. But strong. Bonk! Out goes bottom of the Astarte. No boats. Kehjt drinkers have tended to them. Astarte sunk without trace! Bonk! Swoo-oosh! Bubbles! Finish!"

He became drunkenly plaintive.

"Don't – don't believe fooled old Kirkham for a minute. Don't believe he thought Satan would run rish-risk anybody on Astarte running across one of us. Anybody telling police about wicked pirates holding 'em up in midocean. To hell with the witnesses! That's Satan's motto. Make it 'nother unfathomed mish-mystery of the ocean. That's best way. That's Satan's way."

"Well," I said, "I'm damned glad to hear it. It was the one thing that I was uneasy about–"

The drunkenness dropped from Cobham like a cast-off cloak. His face became white and pinched. The glass fell from his hand.

Out of a darkened corner of the room walked Satan!

CHAPTER SIXTEEN

It was a crisis. And a bad one. There was no doubt about that. A time for quick thinking, if ever there was one. I cared nothing about what happened to Cobham. That callous devil could have been whisked to Hell without my turning a hair. But I, myself, was in the gravest danger of sharing his fate. If Satan thought that I had deliberately drawn his confidences he would waste no time asking for explanations. The fact that I had not accepted his word would in itself call for my punishment.

Worst of all, I had caught him lying to me. He might decide that would render me useless to him thereafter. But that was secondary. The paramount thing was that it made him, as the Chinese say, "lose face." If his ancestry was what Barker believed, that was the one unforgivable affront. Whether it was or was not, I knew that Satan's infernal intellect was clothed with as infernal a pride. And that pride had been wounded.

My only chance for escape lay in healing the wound before Satan knew that I had perceived it. I jumped to my feet and walked towards him.

"Well," I laughed, "have I passed the test?"

Instantly he caught it. Whether, at the moment, he believed me as naive as my question implied, I could not know. Still, after all, why not? It was exactly the kind of trap, or rather experiment, he had been teaching me to expect him to conceive.

Nor did I know how long he had been listening. Had he intentionally left Cobham and me together to see what would happen? And heard all? Probably. If so there had been no single word I had spoken upon which his suspicion could feed. At any rate, to follow my lead was the only way he could maintain his pride. Save his face. He followed it.

"Cobham," he said, "you were right."

He turned to me.

"Tell me, James Kirkham, when did you first suspect that you were under test? I am curious to know exactly how keen that perception of yours is."

He waved to me to be seated, and dropped into his own chair. I kept my eyes steadily averted from Cobham.

"The first thing that puzzled me, Satan," I said, "was your attitude toward the Astarte. It would certainly not have been mine. That dead men tell no tales, is a safe and sane old rule. I would have followed your instructions – but," I added, boldly, "I would not have approved of them."

His eyes never left me as I spoke. I felt his will beating against mine like a hammer, endeavoring to strike out the truth.

"When did your suspicion become certainty?" he asked.

"At the moment you appeared here," I told him.

Suddenly I let some of my anger find vent.

"I'll stand for no more such experiments upon me, Satan," I cried, with a cold fury that had none of its roots in the matter in hand, but was real enough nevertheless. "Either I am to be trusted wholly, or I am not to be trusted at all. If you do trust me and I fail you – well, you have the remedy in your hands and I am ready to pay the penalty. But I'll not be the subject of any more laboratory experiments, like a child in a psychological clinic. By God, I won't!"

I thought that I had won. Not only won, but that I had leaped into higher regard than Satan had ever held me. If those gem-hard eyes could be said to soften, they did.

"I agree, James Kirkham," he said, quietly. "Yet I am glad that I put you to this test. Since it has fully revealed to me what dependence I can place upon you."

"I made my decision. I gave my word," I said, a little stiffly. "As long as you play fair with me, I obey your orders, Satan. Let that be understood, and you will find no more loyal servant."

"I do understand, James Kirkham," he answered.

I ventured to look at Cobham. He had regained some of his color. He was watching me, queerly.

"Cobham," I laughed, "you could be as good an actor as you are a chemist."

"Cobham – has been – very valuable to me," said Satan. "And never more than tonight."

I saw a deep shudder shake Cobham. I feigned to observe nothing. Satan arose.

"Come with me, Cobham," he said: "There are matters we must discuss. And you–" he looked at me.

"I'll turn in," I said. "I know the way."

He strode across the room, Cobham following. Once he turned and shot me a strange glance. There was gratitude in it – and there was deadly terror.

I walked over to the panel that was the beginning of the road to my room.

"James Kirkham," I turned, and saw Satan standing by the opposite wall. His bulk almost hid Cobham, now in front of him.

"Sir?" I answered.

James Kirkham," he said, "I was never better pleased with you than I am now. Good night."

"I am glad, sir," I replied. "Good night."

The panel behind him clicked open. I pressed upon a hidden spring, the wall parted. Before me was the tiny elevator. I entered it. Satan and Cobham were passing through that other wall.

I caught a glimpse of two of the kehjt slaves, cords in hands, gliding to Cobham's side.

As my panel closed I thought I saw them pinion his arms!

And now I was in my rooms. Eve would be expecting me, but I had no desire to make further excursion that night. That Satan had taken my bait, I was reasonably sure. But Cobham was in for punishment – how severe I could not tell. The emphasis Satan had put upon that "has been" in speaking of his usefulness was ominous. Cobham had caught the threat. And there had been that swift vision of the slaves closing in on him. I would be on Satan's mind, whatever he believed. It was possible that he might summon me; might even come to me.

It was best to stay where I was. Barker would be along sooner or later. I would send him with a message to Eve.

I snapped out all the lights except a dim one in the living room, undressed, and turned in. I lay there, smoking, I felt more than a little sick, and filled with a hot, helpless rage. The affair of the Astarte would have been bad enough even as Satan had outlined it. Cobham's revelations made it hideous. I would go on with it, of course. There was nothing else to do. If I refused, it would be the end both of Eve and myself. And some one else would take my place. Cobham, in fact, had made it imperative that I should go. I must find some means of averting that ruthless destruction of the treasure ship. Obviously, the chances were that would mean the end for me also. But it had to be done. I knew that if I stood aside and let those helpless people go down, I could never more live at peace with myself. I knew that Eve would feel the same about it.

What I hoped most desperately was that we could find the way to break Satan before the time came for my sailing.

Suddenly I was aware that some one was in the outer room. I slipped noiselessly out of bed and to the curtains. It was Barker.

I beckoned to him.

"Careful, Harry," I whispered. "Come in here, and keep those ears of yours wide open. Things have been happening."

Briefly I sketched the developments of the day, from my conversation with Consardine to Cobham's drunken disclosures and his sinister shepherding by Satan. I could feel the little man shiver at that.

"Gord," he muttered. "Cobham's a proper devil, but I'm sorry for 'im. Satan, 'e'll see 'e don't no more talkin'. We got to work quick, Cap'n."

"I've an unbreakable hunch that my work is to stay right in this room," I told him. "And if you don't think that is going to be the hardest kind of work, with Miss Demerest expecting me, you're wrong."

"No," he said, "you're right, sir. An' I've got to get h'out quick as may be. 'Ere's what I come to tell you. I h'acted like a bloody dummy last night when you 'inted about Satan an' what 'e done when 'e 'id 'is 'ands. Fair took me off my feet, you did, just like Consardine.

I 'adn't been away from you five minutes before I saw 'ow it could be done. 'Ell, I saw a dozen wyes it could be done."

"Right," I whispered, "but cut the explanations. How are we going to find out if he does it?"

"That's what 'as been rackin' my brains all dye," he answered. "'Ow to get in the Temple an' look over the black throne. The gold one sinks down an' under, but the black one's built in. An' there's two of the kehjt slyves watchin' it in there h'every hour of the dye an' night. Four-hour shifts they got, an' you can bloody well wyger 'e picks proper plucked 'uns for that duty, Cap'n."

"No trouble gettin' in, there's 'arf a dozen trick entrances back of them thrones. Ten minutes, an' we'd know what was what. But 'ow the bloody 'ell to get them ten minutes? No good shootin' the paste-faced blighters. That'll bring 'em all down on us. No good killin' 'em nohow. The minute they found 'em Satan'ld know what the gyme was."

He was silent for a moment.

"Cripes!" he said at last, "if we could only get some bloomin' h'angel to drop down an' 'old a glass of the kehjt under their noses ! They'd follow it like a 'ungry lion would a bone! An' see no thin' else!"

I caught his shoulders, heart thumping.

"By God, Harry! You've hit it!" My voice was shaking. "Do you know where he keeps that hell brew? Can you get at it?"

"Sure I know," he said, "An' there ain't none better at my trade than me, Cap'n, as I told you. I'd sye I could get it. But then what?"

"We'll be the angel," I told him. "It works quick, I know that. How long does it keep them under?"

"I don't know," he answered. "Some longer, some shorter. We'd 'ave our ten minutes, though, an' a lot to spare –

"Cripes!" he chuckled. "What a gyme! If they wake up before the relief comes they ain't likely to say nothin'. An' if they don't, they ain't likely to get a chance to say nothin'. An' if they do get a chance either way, who the 'ell would believe 'em?"

"Get the stuff," I said. "Try to get it tomorrow. And now play safe. Get out of here. If you can manage it, tell Miss Demerest not to look for me tonight. Tell her not to worry. But take no chances. Harry, you're a wonder. If you were a girl, I'd kiss you. Scoot!"

Again he chuckled; another moment and I knew he had gone.

I went into the other room and put out the dim light. For the first time since I had fallen into Satan's hands I felt free of that damnable depression – oppression, rather – which had shadowed me. It was as though a door had begun to open. A door of escape.

I slept soundly. I awakened once in the night from a dream that Satan was standing over me, watching me. Whether it was all a dream, I do not know. Perhaps he had really entered to resolve some lingering doubt. If so, my sleep must have reassured him, for it was that of one who had not a care on his mind. I lost no time worrying about it; in another moment I was asleep again.

The next day passed quickly enough. I was up early. As I was dressing, the 'phone rang. It was Consardine. He said that Satan wished me to go out to the yacht after I had breakfasted. He, Consardine, would accompany me.

There had been no change of plans, then. I was still cast for my piratical role.

When I entered the breakfast room, Consardine was waiting for me. We ate together. I was itching with curiosity about Cobham. But I asked no questions, nor did Consardine speak of him. We walked down to the boat landing, talking of this and that. Tacitly, neither of us made any reference to the conversation of the previous day. It must have been uppermost in his mind, as it was in mine. Yet, after all, there was nothing more to say. He had made his position sufficiently plain.

A cutter was waiting for us, and took us out to the Cherub. The yacht was as beautiful inside as out. The captain was a squat, thickset, broad-shouldered Newfoundlander. He was introduced to me as Captain Morrisey. It may or may not have been the name his parents gave him. Probably not. He was a genial pirate. A hundred years back, and he would have been floating the Jolly Roger. The first mate was a clean-cut saturnine chap with the hall mark of Annapolis. The crew were as hard-boiled looking a lot as any the Marine Corps ever produced.

The discipline was military and perfect. It reached its apotheosis in the engine room. The engines, specially designed, oil-burning Diesels, were marvels. So interested was I that lunch time came around before I realized it. I had not been mistaken about Morrisey. He told us tales of smuggling and gun- and rum-running in which he had been active before he had signed with Satan. Born a hundred years too late for the Black Flag, he had done his best with the material at hand. He was a pirate, but I liked him.

When we got back to the chateau, I found a summons from Satan. With many misgivings I obeyed it. The misgivings were all wrong. I spent two of the most fascinating hours I had ever known. I was guided to that part of the great house which was Satan's own intimate domain. I cannot begin to describe what I saw there, nor the atmosphere of those dozen or more chambers, large and small, wherein that dark strange soul took its delight. Each of them was a temple in which the mysterious, indefinable and eternal spirit that humanity calls beauty and has always worshiped and sought to capture had become incarnate. A living thing.

And Satan was different. He was transformed – gentle, no mockery either in word or look. He talked only of the treasures about us. It came to me that he loved beauty even more than he did power; that he considered power only as a means toward beauty. And that, evil though he was, he knew beauty better than any one alive.

When I left him, his spell upon me was strong. I had to fight against the conviction that what I had beheld justified him as to any means he had taken to get it; that the true criminal was he who would try to thwart him. Absurd as it may seem, I felt myself hideously guilty in the plans I was harboring. It was with difficulty that I held myself back from confessing them, throwing myself on his mercy, swearing myself to him. I think that only the thought of Eve kept me from doing so.

That was, perhaps, his object. But I had to tell myself so, over and over again after I had left him, to banish the loathing I felt about going on against him. If this seems deplorable weakness, I can only say that he who thinks so would not if he had been subjected to that same sorcery, and had listened to Satan preaching in the heart of the miracle he had fashioned.

If it was a trap, I escaped it. But to this day – I do not know whether in the greater sense Satan was not right.

The company at dinner helped me to throw off the obsession. A brisk bridge game afterward did more. It was close to midnight when I returned to my rooms. I had not seen Eve all day. Consardine had mentioned, casually, as we were going in to dinner, that she had gone to town, and probably would not return that night. I took it as a hint that it would be useless for me to venture to her room.

I dropped off to sleep hoping for Barker. He did not come.

There were some truly charming people at the breakfast table next morning. Among them an Australian major, a soldierly and engaging scoundrel. We went riding together, following a different road than that which I had covered with Consardine. At one point it ran parallel to the driveway. A smart little roadster hummed by, headed for the chateau. Eve was driving it. She waved. The Australian took the greeting to himself, remarking that there went a damned nice girl. Everything seemed suddenly brighter. It meant that I would see her that night. At least, that was what I thought then.

After we had stabled the horses, I hung about the pleasant terrace. Maybe I would get another glimpse of Eve, maybe even a whispered word. About four o'clock Consardine appeared and dropped down at the table beside me.

Consardine seemed ill at ease. We had a drink or two, and talked of this and that, but it was plain that something was on his mind. I waited for him to speak, not without a certain apprehension. At last he sighed, and shook his great shoulders.

"Well," he said, "unpleasant medicine gets no sweeter while we hesitate over taking it. Come along with me, Kirkham. Satan's orders."

I remembered vividly his declaration that if his master commanded him, he would unhesitatingly take me prisoner. I felt a distinct shock.

"Does that mean that I am under arrest?" I asked.

"Not at all," he answered. "There is something – some one – Satan wishes you to see. Do not ask me his purpose. I do not know it. I might guess, but – ask me no questions. Let us go."

I went with him, wondering. When he finally stopped we were, I thought, in one of the towers, certainly we had gone far above the ground floor. We were in a small, bare room. More a crypt, in fact, than a room. One of its walls was slightly curved, the bulge toward us. Consardine walked over to this wall, and beckoned me beside him. He touched a hidden spring. An aperture about a foot square, like a window, opened at the level of my eyes.

"Look through," he said.

The place into which I peered was filled with a curiously clear and palely purplish light. It was distinctly unpleasant. I became aware of a thin droning sound, faint but continuous, upon one note. I was not enough of a musician to place the note, but it was quite as high as that made by the rapid vibration of a bee's wings. That, too, was unpleasant. Light and droning had a concentration-shattering quality, a blurring effect upon the mind.

At first glance I thought that I was looking into a circular place in which was a crowd of men, all facing a common center. Then I realized that this could not be so, since all the men were in exactly the same attitude, crouching upon one knee. There seemed to be thousands of these crouching men, line after line of them, one behind the other, growing smaller and smaller and vanishing off into immense distances.

I looked to right and to left. There were the kneeling men, but now in profile. I raised my eyes to the ceiling of the place. And there they appeared to hang, heads downward.

I stared again at those facing me. It was strange how the purplish light and the droning clouded one's thought. They held back, like two hands, the understanding from fulfillment.

Then I realized abruptly that all those thousands of faces were – the same.

And that each was the face of Cobham!

They were the face of Cobham, drawn and distorted, reflected over and over again from scores of mirrors with which the place was lined. The circular walls were faceted with mirrors, and so was the globed ceiling, and all these mirrors curved down to a circular mirrored slab about seven feet in diameter which was their focus.

Upon this slab knelt Cobham, glaring at the countless reflections of himself, reflected with sharpest accuracy by that clear and evil purplish light.

As I looked, he jumped to his feet and began to wave his arms, crazily. Like regiments of automatons, the reflections leaped with him, waving. He turned, and they wheeled as one man in diminishing rank upon rank. He threw himself down upon his face, and I knew that unless his eyes were closed his face still stared up at him, buoyed, it must have seemed, upon the backs of the thousands reflected upon the slab from the mirrors in the ceiling. And I knew that no man could keep his eyes closed long in that room, that he must open them, to look and look again.

I shrank back, trembling. This thing was hellish. It was mind-destroying. There could be no sleep. The drone rasped along the nerves and would not permit it. The light was sleep-killing, too, keying up, stretching the tense nerves to the breaking point. And the mimicking hosts of reflections slowly, inexorably, led the mind into the paths of madness.

"For God's sake...for God's sake..." I turned to Consardine half-incoherent, white-lipped. "I've seen...Consardine...a bullet would be mercy..."

He drew me back to the opening.

"Thrust in your head," he said, coldly. "You must see yourself in the mirrors, and Cobham must see you. It is Satan's order."

I tried to struggle away. He gripped my neck and forced my head forward as one does a puppy to make him drink.

The wall at this point was only a couple of inches thick. Held helpless, my head was now beyond that wall. Cobham had staggered to his feet. I saw my face leap out in the mirrors. He saw it, too. His eyes moved from one reflection to another, striving to find the real.

"Kirkham!" he howled. "Kirkham! Get me out!"

Consardine drew me back. He snapped the opening shut.

"You devil! You cold-blooded devil!" I sobbed, and threw myself upon him.

He caught my arms. He held me as easily as though I had been a child, while I kicked and writhed in futile attempt to break the inexorable grip. And at last my fury spent itself. Still sobbing, I went limp.

"There, there, lad," he said, gently. "I am not responsible for what you've seen. I told you it was unpleasant medicine. But Satan ordered it, and I must obey. Come with me. Back to your rooms."

I followed him, all resistance for the moment gone from me. It was not any affection for Cobham that had so stirred me. He had probably watched others in the mirrored cell from that same window. If the necessity had arisen, I would have shot Cobham down without the slightest feeling about it. Nor had the ordeal of Cartright shaken my nerve at all like this. Bad as that had been, it had been in the open, with people around him. And Cartright, so it seemed, had been given some chance.

But this torture of the many-mirrored cell, with its sleep-slaying light and sound, its slow killing, in utter aloneness, of a man's mind – there was something about that, something not to be put in words, that shook me to the soul.

"How long will he – last?" I put the question to Consardine as we passed in to my rooms.

"It is hard to say," he answered, gently again. "He will come out of that room without memory. He will not know his name, nor what he has been, nor anything that he has ever learned. He will know nothing of all these hereafter – ever. Like an animal, he will know when he is hungry and thirsty, cold or warm. That is all. He will forget from minute to minute. He will live only in each moment. And when that moment goes it will be forgotten. Mindless, soulless – empty. I have known men to come to it in a week, others have resisted for three. Never longer."

I shivered.

"I'll not go down for dinner, Consardine," I said.

"I would, if I were you," he said gravely. "It will be wiser. You cannot help Cobham. After all, it is Satan's right. Like me, Cobham had taken the steps and lost. He lived at Satan's will. And Satan will be watching you. He will want to know how you have taken it. Pull yourself together, Kirkham. Come down, and be gay. I shall tell him that you were only interested in his exhibition. What, lad! Will you let him know what he has made you feel? Where is your pride? And to do so would be dangerous – for any plans you may have. I tell you so."

"Stay with me till it's time to go, Consardine," I said. "Can you?"

"I intended to," he answered, "if you asked me. And I think both of us can stand putting ourselves outside of an extra-sized drink."

I caught a glimpse of myself in the mirror as I poured. The glass in my hand shook and spilled.

"I'll never want to look in one again," I told him.

He poured me another drink.

"Enough of that," he said briskly. "You must get it from your mind. Should Satan be at dinner – thank him for a new experience."

Satan was not at dinner. I hoped that he would receive a report, as no doubt he did, of my behavior. I was gay enough to satisfy Consardine. I drank recklessly and often.

Eve was there. I caught her glancing at me, puzzled, now and then.

If she had known how little real gayety there was in my heart, how much of black despair, she would have been more puzzled still.

CHAPTER SEVENTEEN

I sat late at dinner, with a few others who, like me, had declined the bridge game. It was close to twelve when I returned to my room. I had the feeling that I would see Barker this night, whether or not he had been successful in getting hold of the kehjt.

Alone, the memory of Cobham and the mirrored cell swept back on me with full force. Why had Satan willed me to look upon the prisoner? Why to see myself in those cursed glasses? And why had he decreed that Cobham must see me?

To the first two questions there could be but one answer. He meant it as a warning. He was not, then, wholly satisfied with my explanation. And yet, if he were not, would he not have used harsher measures? Satan was not given to taking chances. I decided that he was satisfied, but nevertheless wished to give me a warning of what might happen to me if he should ever become not so.

Why, if Cobham's memory was to be destroyed, he should have wished him to take note of me peering in upon him, I could not tell. There seemed no answer to that, unless it was one of his whims. But, again, Satan's whims, as he called them, were never without reason. I gave it up, reluctantly and uneasily.

It was twelve-thirty when I heard a jubilant whisper from the bedroom.

"Got it, Cap'n!"

I walked into the bedroom. My nerves had suddenly grown taut, and there was a little ache in my throat. The moment had come. There could be no withdrawing now. The hand was ready to be played. And, without doubt, Death in a peculiarly unpleasant mood was the other player.

"'Ere it is!" Barker thrust a half-pint flask into my cold fingers. It was full of that green liquor which I had watched Satan give to the slaves in the marble hall. The kehjt.

It was a clear fluid, with an elusive sparkle as of microscopic particles catching the light. I uncorked the flask and smelled it. It had a faintly acrid odor with an undertaint of musk. I was about to taste it when Barker stopped me.

"Keep awye from it, Cap'n," he said earnestly. "That stuff was brewed in 'Ell, it was. You're close enough."

"All right," I recorked the flask. "When do we go?"

"Right awye," he answered. "They chynged the blighters in the Temple at midnight. Syfe to start now as at anytime. Oh, yes–"

He fished down in a pocket.

"Thought I'd best bring along some of the scenery," he grinned.

He held out a pair of the golden cups into which the veiled figure with the ewer had poured the kehjt.

"Did you have a hard time getting the stuff, Harry?" I asked.

"It was touch an' go," he said soberly. "I 'ate to think of gettin' them cups back. I 'ates to think of it, but it's got to be done. Still," he added, hopefully, "I'm good."

"I'll say you are, Harry," I told him.

He hesitated.

"Cap'n," he said, "I won't 'ide from you; I feel as if we was h'about to slip into a room what's got a 'undred snakes in every corner."

"You've nothing on me, Harry," I answered cheerfully. "I think maybe it's got a snake carpet and scorpion curtains."

"Well," he said, "let's go."

"Sure," I said, "let's go."

I snapped off the lights in the outer room. We passed through the wall of the bedroom into a dimly lighted passage. A little along it and we went into one of the lifts. We dropped. We came out into a long passage, transverse to the first; another short drop, and we were in a pitch dark corridor. Here Harry took my hand and led me. Suddenly he stopped and flashed his light against the wall. He pressed his finger upon a certain spot. I could not see what had guided him, but a small panel slid aside. It revealed an aperture in which were a number of switches.

"Light control," Barker's mouth was close to my ear. "We're

right be'ind the chair you set in. Lie down."

I slipped to the floor. He dropped softly beside me. Another panel about six inches wide and a foot high opened with the noiseless swiftness of a camera shutter.

I looked into the Temple.

The slit through which I was peering was at the level of the floor. It was hidden by the apparatus in which I had been prisoned when Cartright climbed to his doom. By craning my neck, I could see between its legs a horizontal slice of the whole immense chamber.

A brilliant light poured directly upon the black throne. It stood there empty – but menacing. About a dozen feet on each side of it was one of the kehjt slaves. They were tall, strong fellows, white robed, with their noosed cords ready in their hands. Their pallid faces showed dead-white under the glare. The pupilless eyes were not dreaming, but alert.

I caught a glitter of blue eyes behind the black throne. The eyes of the Satan of the pictured stone. They seemed to watch me, malignantly. I turned my gaze abruptly away from them. I saw the back of the Temple.

It, too, was illumined by one strong light. It was larger even than I had sensed it to be. The black seats ranged upward in semicircles, and there were at least three hundred of them.

The slit through which I had been looking closed. Barker touched me, and I arose.

"Give me the dope," he whispered. I handed him the flask of the kehjt; he had kept the golden cups.

Again he flashed his light upon the switches. He took my hands and placed them upon two.

"County sixty," he said. "Then open them switches. It puts out the lights. Keep your 'ands on 'em till I get back. Start now like this – one – two–"

He snapped out the flash. Although I had heard no sound, I knew he was gone. At the sixtieth count I pulled open the switches. It seemed a long time, standing there in the dark. It was probably no more than three or four minutes.

As noiselessly as he had gone, Barker was back. He tapped my hands away, and pressed the switches in place.

"Down," he muttered.

We slid to the floor. Once more the observation panel flew open.

The two guardians of the black throne were standing where I had last seen them. They were blinking, dazed by the swift return of the glaring light. And they were nervous as hunting dogs who had sensed a quarry. They were quivering, twirling their noosed cords, peering here and there.

I saw upon the black throne the two golden cups of the kehjt. The slaves saw them at the same moment.

They stared at them, incredulously. They looked at each other. Like a pair of automatons moved by the same impulse, they took a step forward, and stared again at the glittering lure. And suddenly into their faces came that look of dreadful hunger. The cords dropped. They rushed to the black throne.

They seized the golden cups. And drank.

"Gord!" I heard Barker mutter. He was gasping and shuddering like one who had taken an icy plunge. Well, so was I. There had been something infinitely horrible in that rush of the pair upon the green drink. Something infernal in the irresistible tidal rush of desire that had swept their drugged minds clear of every impulse but that single one. To drink.

They turned from the black throne, the golden cups still clasped in their hands. I watched first one and then the other sink down upon the steps. Their eyes closed. Their bodies relaxed. But still their fingers gripped the cups.

"Now!" said Barker. He shut the slit, and closed the panel that hid the switches. He led me quickly along the dark corridor. We turned a sharp corner. There was the faintest of rustling sounds. Light streamed out in my face from a narrow opening.

"Quick!" muttered Barker, and pushed me through.

We stood on the dais, beside the black throne. Below us sprawled the bodies of the two guardians. The seven shining footprints glimmered up at me, watchfully.

Barker had dropped upon his knees. The lever which Satan had manipulated to set at work the mechanism of the steps lay flat, locked within an indentation in the stone cut out to receive it when at rest. Barker was working swiftly at its base. A thin slab moved aside. Under it was an arrangement of small cogs. He reached under and moved something. The telltale globe swung down from the ceiling.

Barker released the lever, cautiously. He brought it to upright, then pressed it downward, as I had seen Satan do. I heard no whirring, and understood that the little man had in some way silenced it.

"You got to go down and walk up, Cap'n," he whispered. "Make it snappy, sir. Tread on every one of them prints."

I ran down the steps, turned, and came quickly up, treading firmly on each of the shining marks. I turned at the top of the stairs and looked at the telltale globe. From the pale field three symbols shone out, from Satan's darker field gleamed four. My heart sank.

"Cheer up," said Harry. "You look fair crumpled. No need. It's what I expected. Wyte a moment."

He fumbled around among the cogs again, lying flat, his head half hidden in the aperture.

He gave an exclamation, and leaped to his feet, face sharpened, eyes glittering. He ran over to the black throne, pawing at it like an excited terrier.

Suddenly he threw himself into it and began pressing here and there at the edge of the seat.

"'Ere," he beckoned me. "Sit where I am. Put your fingers 'ere and 'ere. When I tell you, press 'em in 'ard."

He jumped aside. I seated myself on the black throne. He took my hands and placed my fingers in a row about five inches long. They rested upon seven indentations along the edge, barely discernible. Nor did what I touched feel like stone. It was softer.

Barker slipped over to the cogs and resumed his manipulation of them.

"Press," he whispered. "Press 'em all together."

I pressed. The indentations yielded slightly under my fingers.

My eyes fell upon the telltale. It had gone blank. All the shining marks upon it had disappeared.

"Press 'em now, one at a time," ordered Barker.

I pressed them one at a time.

"The swine," said Barker. "The bloody double-crossin' swine! Come 'ere, Cap'n, and look."

I dropped beside him and peered down at the cogs. I looked from them up at the telltale. And stared at it, only half believing what I saw.

"Got him!" muttered Harry. "Got him!"

He worked rapidly on the cogs, and closed the slab upon them. The telltale swung back to its resting place in the ceiling.

"The cups," he said. He ran down the steps and took the golden goblets that had held the kehjt from the still resisting fingers of the dreaming guardians.

"Got him!" repeated Harry.

We swung back of the black throne. Barker slid aside the panel through which we had entered. We passed out into the dark passageway.

A wild jubilance possessed me. Yet in it was a shadow of regret, the echo of the afternoon's hours of beauty's sorcery.

For what we had found ended Satan's power over his dupes forever.

Dethroned him!

CHAPTER EIGHTEEN

We had reached the dimly lighted corridor wherein lay the entrance to my rooms. Barker halted with a warning gesture.

"Listen!" he breathed.

I heard a noise, faint and far away; a murmuring. There were men moving somewhere behind the walls, and coming toward us. Could they have found the drugged slaves so soon?

"Get into your room. Quick," whispered Harry.

We started on the run. And halted again. Ten feet ahead of us a man had appeared. He had seemed to melt out of the wall with a magical quickness. He leaned against it for a moment sobbing. He turned his face toward us –

It was Cobham!

His face was gray and lined and shrunken. His eyes were so darkly circled that they looked, in that faint illumination, like the sockets of a skull. They stared vaguely, as though the mind behind them were dimmed. His lips were puffed and bleeding as though he had bitten them through time and time again.

"You're Kirkham!" he staggered forward. "Yes, I remember you! I was coming to you. Hide me."

The murmuring sounds were closer. I saw Barker slip the brass knuckles over his fingers and make ready to leap upon Cobham. I caught his arm.

"No use," I warned him. "They'd find him. The man's more than half mad. But they'd make him tell. I'll take him. Hurry! Get out of sight!"

I seized Cobham's arm, and raced him to the panel that opened into the bedroom. I opened it, and thrust him through. Barker at my heels, I slipped in and closed the slide.

"Get in that closet," I ordered Cobham, and shoved him among my clothes. I shut the doors and moved quickly with Barker into the outer room.

"Good!" he muttered, "but I don't fancy this."

"It's the only way," I said. "I'll have to figure some way to get rid of him later. I don't believe they'll come in here. They won't suspect me. Why should they? Still – there's the chance. If they found you here, then the fat would be in the fire. Is there any way you can dig right out without too much risk?"

"Yes," the little man's voice and eyes were troubled. "I can myke the getawye all right. But, Gord, I don't like leavin' you, Cap'n!"

"Beat it!" I said brusquely. "Get to Consardine. Tell him exactly what we found. Tell Miss Demerest what's happened. If anything does go wrong, it's all up to you, Harry."

He groaned. I heard a faint noise in the bedroom. I walked over to the door and looked in. It was Cobham, stirring in the closet. I tapped upon it.

"Be quiet," I told him. "They may be here any minute."

I snapped all the lights on, full. I went back to the other room. Barker was gone.

I threw off my coat and vest, and piled some books on the reading table. I fixed myself comfortably, lighted my pipe and began to read. The minutes passed slowly. Every nerve was tense, and every sense alert. But I flattered myself I was giving an excellent impersonation of one entirely absorbed in what I was reading.

And suddenly I knew that eyes were upon me. That some one was standing behind me, watching me.

I went on reading. The silent scrutiny became intolerable. I yawned and stretched, arose and turned –

Satan stood there.

He was cloaked from neck to feet in scarlet. At his back were half a dozen of the kehjt slaves. Two more were standing by the open panel in the bedroom.

"Satan!" I exclaimed, and the surprise I put into the words was genuine. Whatever the possibilities I had admitted, that Satan himself would head the manhunt had not been among them.

"You are startled, James Kirkham," there seemed a hint of solicitude in the expressionless voice. "I, too, was startled when, knocking at your wall, you failed to answer."

"I did not hear you," I said, truthfully. Had he really knocked?

"You were, I see, deep in your book," he said. "But you wonder, perhaps, why your silence should have disturbed me? I am in pursuit of a fugitive, a dangerous man, James Kirkham. A desperate man, I fear. The trail led us by here. It occurred to me that he might have attempted to hide in your rooms, and that resisting him you had come to harm."

It sounded reasonable enough. I remembered the extraordinary favor he had shown me that afternoon. My doubts were lulled; I let myself relax.

"I thank you, sir," I told him. "But I have seen no one. Who is the man–"

"The man I seek is Cobham," he interrupted me.

"Cobham!" I stared at him as though I had not understood. "But I thought that Cobham–"

"You thought that Cobham was in the room of the mirrors," he interrupted. "You have wondered, without doubt, why I had put him there. You thought that he was one of my trusted aides. You thought him most valuable to me. So he was. Then suddenly that Cobham whom I trusted and who was valuable – ceased to be. Another spirit entered him, one that I cannot trust and that therefore can never be other than a menace to me."

With a sinking heart I saw the cold mockery in the hard bright eyes, realized that he had raised his voice as though to let it carry throughout the rooms.

"That poor departed Cobham," he intoned, "shall I not avenge him? Yea, verily. I will punish that usurping spirit, torment it until it prays to me to loose it from that body it has stolen. My poor, lost Cobham! He will not care what I do with that body that once was his – so he be avenged."

There was no mistaking the mockery now. I felt my throat contract.

"You say you saw nothing?" he asked me.

"Nothing," I answered. "If anyone had come in the rooms I would have heard them."

Instantly I realized the error of that, and cursed myself.

"Ah, no," said Satan, smoothly. "You forget how immersed you were in your reading. You did not hear me. Either when I knocked or when I entered. I cannot let you run the risk of him being hidden here. We must search."

He gave an order to the slaves attending him. Before they could move, the closet door in the bedroom flew open. Cobham leaped out.

His first jump took him halfway to the opened panel. I caught the gleam of steel in his hand. In an instant he was at the two slaves guarding the opening. One went down gurgling, his throat slit. The other stumbled back, hands holding his side, blood spurting through his fingers.

And Cobham was gone.

Satan gave another curt order. Four of the six behind him raced away and through the panel.

The other two closed in on me, pinioning my arms to my sides with their cords.

Satan considered me, the mockery in his eyes grown devilish.

"I thought he would come here," he said. "It was why, James Kirkham, I let him escape!"

So that, too, had been a web of Satan's weaving! And he had snared me in it!

Suddenly an uncontrollable rage swept me. I would lie no more. I would wear a mask no more. I would never be afraid of him again. He could hurt me, damnably. He could kill me. He was probably planning to do both. But I knew him for what he was. He was stripped of his mystery and – I still had an ace in the hole of which he knew nothing. I drew a deep breath, and laughed at him.

"Maybe!" I said cynically. "But I notice that you couldn't keep him from escaping this time. The pity of it is that he didn't slit your damned black throat as he went, instead of that poor devil's yonder."

"Ah," he answered, with no resentment, "truth begins to pour out of the stricken Kirkham as water poured for Moses from the stricken rock. But you are wrong once more. It is long since I have enjoyed a manhunt. Cobham is an ideal quarry. It was why I left the panel open. He will last, I hope, for days and days."

He spoke to one of the two kehjt drinkers guarding me. I did not understand the tongue. The slave bowed and slipped out.

"Yes," Satan turned to me, "he will probably last for days and days. But you, James Kirkham, equally as probably will not. Cobham cannot escape. Neither can you. I shall consider tonight with what form of amusement you shall furnish me."

The slave who had gone out entered with six others. Again Satan instructed them. They massed about me, and guided me toward the wall. I went, unresisting. I did not look back at Satan.

But as I passed through the wall I could not shut my ears to his laughter!

CHAPTER NINETEEN

A day had gone and another night had come before I saw Satan again. Before, in fact, I saw any one except the pallid-faced drinkers of the kehjt who brought my food.

I had been taken, I conjectured, to one of the underground rooms. It was comfortable enough, but windowless and, of course, doorless. There they had unbound my arms and left me.

And then, my rage swiftly ebbing, hopelessness took possession of me. Barker would make every effort to get to Consardine. I was sure of that. But would he be able to get to him in time? Would Consardine accept his word for what we had discovered? I did not think so. Consardine was of the kind that has to be shown. Or, supposing he did believe, would his own hot wrath lead him to some hasty action that would set him with Cobham and myself? Leave Satan triumphant?

And what of Eve? What might she not do when she heard from Harry what had happened to me? For I had no doubt that the little man would soon find a way of finding out what had occurred.

What deviltries upon me was Satan hatching for his – amusement?

My night had not been an exactly hilarious one. The day had dragged endlessly. When I faced Satan I hoped that I showed no signs of those hours.

He had entered unannounced, Consardine with him. He wore the long black cloak. His eyes glittered over me. I looked from him to Consardine. Had Barker seen him? His face was calm, and he regarded me indifferently. My heart sank.

Satan sat down. Without invitation, I followed suit. I pulled out my cigarette case, and politely offered Satan one; a bit of childish bravado for which I was immediately sorry. He paid no attention to the gesture, studying me.

"I am not angry with you, James Kirkham," Satan spoke. "If I could feel regret, I would feel it for you. But you, yourself, are wholly responsible for your plight."

He paused. I made no answer.

"You would have deceived me," he went on. "You lied to me. You attempted to save from my justice a man I had condemned. You put your will against mine. You dared to try to thwart me. You have endangered my venture regarding the Astarte, if indeed you have not negatived it. You are no more to be trusted. You are useless to me. What is the answer?"

"My elimination, I suppose," I replied, carelessly. "But why waste time justifying one of your murders, Satan? By this time, I should think, murder would be second nature to you, no more to be explained than why you eat when you are hungry."

His eyes flickered.

"You deliberately invited Cobham's confidences, and you would have attempted to prevent the sinking of the Astarte, knowing that I had decreed it," he said.

"Right," I agreed.

"And you lied to me," he repeated. "To me!"

"One good lie deserves another, Satan," I answered. "You began the lying. If you had come clean with me, I'd have told you not to trust me with that job. You didn't. I suspected you hadn't. Very well, the man who lies to me in one thing will lie in another."

I shot a swift glance at Consardine. His face was as indifferent as ever, imperturbable as Satan's own.

"The minute Cogham let the cat out of the bag, I lost all faith in you," I went on. "For all I know, your assassins on the Cherub might have had their orders to do away with me after I had pulled your chestnuts. As I once heard another of your dupes say – blame yourself, Satan. Not me."

Consardine was watching me intently. I was feeling pretty reckless by now.

"Father of Lies," I said, "or to give you another of your ancient titles, Prince of Liars, the whole matter can be summed up in two short sentences. You can't trust me, and I know too much. All right. For both of those conditions you have only yourself to thank.

But I also know you. And if you think I'm going to beg you for any mercy – you don't know me."

"Consardine," he said, tranquilly, "James Kirkham had such good material in him. He could have been so useful to me. It's a pity, Consardine. Yes, it is a pity!"

He regarded me benevolently.

"Although, frankly, I do not see how the knowledge can profit you," he said, "I feel that you should know the error that betrayed you. Yes, I wish to help you, James Kirkham," the great voice purred, "for it may be that there is a land to which we go when this mortal coil is cut. If so, it is probably much like this. You may even find me or my counterpart there. You will not care to repeat your mistakes."

I listened to this sinister jesting silently; after all, I was curious.

"Your first error was your reference to the bridge game. I noted the surprise it caused Cobham. You were too precipitate. You could just as well have waited your time. Remember, then, if you should reach that next world, never to be precipitate.

"Obviously, you had a reason. Equally obviously, it was my cue to discover that reason. Lesson two – in that world to which you may shortly be traveling, be careful to give to your opponent no cue to eavesdrop.

"When I re-entered, you ingenuously forbore to notice Cobham's very apparent consternation. You studiously kept your eyes from him during the ensuing conversation. That was too naive, James Kirkham. It showed you underestimated the intelligence you were seeking to convince. Your proper move was complete and instant indignation. You should have sacrificed Cobham by accusing him to me. In that bright new world in which you may or may not soon find yourself, never underestimate your opponent.

"But I gave you still another chance. Knowing Cobham, I knew that after my careful – ah – treatment – his mind would fasten upon you as a refuge, his only refuge. He was given the treatment, he saw you, and then he was allowed to escape. He came, as I thought he would, straight to you. If, at the moment he entered your rooms, you had caught him, sounded the alarm, again – sacrificed him, perhaps I would still have believed in you. It was weakness, sentimentality. What was Cobham to you? Remember, then, in your new sphere, to eschew all sentimentality."

Out of that cynical harangue two facts apparently shone clear. Satan did not know that I had gone out of my rooms, nor that I had encountered Cobham outside them. I took some comfort from that. But – had Cobham been caught? Would he tell?

"By the way, how is Cobham?" I asked, politely.

"Not so well, not so well, poor fellow," said Satan, "yet he was able to give me an enjoyable afternoon. At present he is lying in the darkness of a crypt near the laboratory, resting. Shortly he will be given an opportunity to leave it. During his carefully guided wanderings thereafter, he will have the chance to snatch a little food and drink. I do not wish him to wear himself out in his efforts to amuse me. Or, to put it another way, it is not my intention to allow him to die of exhaustion or famine. No, no, the excellent Cobham will provide me with many merry hours still. I shall not send him back to my little mirrors. They have drawn his fangs. But at the last I will inform him of your interest, since, I am quite sure, you will be unable."

He arose.

"James Kirkham," said Satan, "in half an hour you shall be judged. Be ready at that time to appear in the Temple. Come, Consardine."

My hope that he would leave Consardine with me went crumbling. Desperately I wanted to talk to him. He followed Satan out. The wall closed behind him. He had not even turned his head.

I remembered Cartright. Consardine had brought him in, stood beside him before he had begun the ordeal of the steps. Probably he would return for me.

But he did not. When the half hour had elapsed four of the kehjt drinkers came for me. Two in front of me, two behind me, they marched me through long corridors and up steep ramps of stone. They halted. I heard the sound of a gong. A panel opened. The slaves would have pushed me in, but I struck aside their hands and stepped through. The panel closed.

I stood within the Temple.

I was within the semidarkness beyond the ring of brilliant light beating down upon the steps. I heard a murmuring. It came from my left where the amphitheater circled. I caught movement there, glimpses of white faces. The seats seemed full. I thought I heard Eve's voice, whispering, vibrant –

"Jim!"

I could not see her.

I looked toward the dais. It was as it had been when I had watched Cartright stumble up toward it. The golden throne gleamed. On it glittered the jeweled scepter and crown.

Upon the black throne sat Satan.

Squatting beside him, fiend's face agrin, twirling his cord of woman's hair, was Sanchal, the executioner.

Again the gong sounded.

"James Kirkham! Approach for judgment!" Satan's voice rolled out.

I walked forward. I paused at the foot of the steps, within the circle of light. The seven glimmering prints of the child's foot stared at me out of the black stone.

Guarding them, seven upon each side, stood the white-robed slaves of the kehjt. Their eyes were fixed upon me.

The thoughts went racing through my brain. Should I cry out the secret of the black throne to those who sat silent, watching me from the circled seats of stone? I knew that before I uttered a dozen words the cords of the kehjt slaves would be strangling me. Could I make one swift dash up the steps and grapple with Satan? They would have me before I had reached halfway.

One thing I might do. Take the steps leisurely. Make my fourth and final one the sixth of the shining prints. Their arrangement was irregular. The sixth was not far from the black throne. Closer than the seventh. I could leap from it upon Satan. Sink fingers and teeth into his throat. Once I had gripped I did not believe it would be easy for any to tear me away, were I alive or dead.

But Barker? Barker might have his plan. It would not be like the little man to lurk hidden, and supinely let me pass. And Consardine? But did Consardine know?

And Eve!

The thoughts jostled. I could not think clearly. I held fast to my last idea, fixing my gaze upon Satan's throat just below the ear. There was where I would sink my teeth.

But was I to be allowed to take the steps?

"James Kirkham," Satan's voice rolled forth, "I have set upon the throne of gold the crown and scepter of worldly power. It is to remind you of that opportunity which your contumacy has lost to you, forever."

I looked at them. For all that I cared they might be bits of colored glass. But I heard a faint sighing from the hidden seats.

"James Kirkham, you would have betrayed me! You are a traitor! It remains now but to decree your punishment!"

He paused again. In all the Temple there was no sound. The silence was smothering. It was broken by a sibilant whirring, the twirling of the noose in the talons of the executioner. Satan raised a hand, and it was stilled.

"Yet I am inclined to be merciful," – only I, perhaps, caught the malicious glint in the jewel-bright eyes. "There are three things which man has to which he clings hardest. In the last analysis, they are all he has. One is contained in the other – yet each is separate. They are his soul, his personality and his life. By his soul I mean that unseen and not yet accurately located essence upon which religion lays such stress, considers immortal, and that may or may not be. By personality I mean the ego, the mind, that which says – I am I, the storehouse of old memories, the seeker of new ones. Life I need not define.

"Now, James Kirkham, I offer you a choice. Upon one side I place your soul, upon the other your life and your mind.

"You may join my drinkers of the kehjt. Drink it, and your life and your ego are safe. From time to time you will be happy, happy with an intensity that normally you would never be. But you lose your soul! You will not miss it – at least not often. Soon the kehjt will be more desirable to you than ever that usually troublesome guest – somewhere within you."

He paused again, scrutinizing me.

"If you do not drink the kehjt," he continued, "you take the steps. If you tread upon my three, you lose your life. Slowly, in agony, at the hands of Sanchal.

"If you tread upon the four fortunate ones, you shall have your life and your soul. But you must leave with me your ego, that which says I am I, all your memories. It will not be dangerous to you, it will not be painful. I will not give you to the mirrors. A sleep – and then a knife, cunningly cutting here and there within your brain. You will awaken as one new-born. Literally so, James Kirkham, since from you will have been taken, and taken forever, all recollection of what you have been. Like a child you will set forth upon your new pilgrimage. But with life – and with your precious soul unharmed."

And now I heard a whispering behind me from the dark amphitheater. Satan raised his hand, and it was stilled.

"Such is my decree!" he intoned. "Such is my will! So shall it be!"

"I take the steps," I said, with no hesitation.

"Your guardian angels," he said unctuously, "applaud without doubt your decision. You remember that they have no power where Satan rules. I thought that would be your choice. And now, to prove how little strained is the quality of my mercy, I offer you, James Kirkham, a door for escape – escape with life and mind and soul, all three of them, intact!"

Now I stared at him, every sense alert. Well I knew that there was no mercy in Satan. Knowing, too, the secret of the steps, the diabolic mockery of that offer of his was an open page to me. But what blacker diabolism was coming? I was soon to learn.

"The roots of this man's offense against me," he turned his gaze toward the amphitheater, "were in sentiment. He placed the welfare of others before mine. Let this be a lesson to all of you. I must be first.

"But I am just. Others he could save, himself he could not save. Yet there may be one who can save him. He gives up, it is probable, his life because he dared to stand between me and the lives of others.

"Is there one who will stand between me and his life?"

Once more there came a murmuring, louder now, from the hidden darkness of the Temple; whisperings.

"Wait!" he raised a hand. "This is what I mean. If there is one among you who will step forth and take but three of the steps in his place, then this is what shall happen. If two of the shining prints are fortunate, both shall go forth free and unharmed! Yes, even with rich reward.

"But if two of the steps are mine – then both shall die and by those same torments which I have promised James Kirkham.

"Such is my decree! Such is my will! So shall it be!

"And now, if such person there be, let him step forth."

I heard a louder murmuring. I believed that he suspected I had not been alone. It might even be that this was a trap for Barker. I did not know to what lengths the little man's devotion might take him. At any rate, it was a line thrown out for the unwary. I walked hastily forward to the very base of the steps.

"I can do my own climbing, Satan," I said. "Set your game."

The murmuring behind me had grown louder.

Satan's immobility dropped from him.

For the first time I watched expression transform the mask of his face. And that transformation was at first utter incredulity, then a rage that leaped up straight from the Pit. Plainly, as though that heavy face had melted away under it, I saw the hidden devil stand forth stark naked. I felt a touch upon my arm.

Eve stood beside me!

"Go back!" I whispered to her, fiercely. "Get back there!"

"Too late!" she said, tranquilly.

She looked up at Satan.

"I will take the steps for him, Satan," she said.

Satan raised himself up from the black throne, hands clenched. He glanced once at the executioner. The black leaned forward, loop whirling. I threw myself in front of Eve.

"Your word, Satan," came a voice from the amphitheater, a voice I did not recognize. "Your decree!"

Satan glared out into the darkness, striving to identify the speaker. He signed to the executioner, and the black dropped the whirling cord. Satan sank into his throne. With dreadful effort he thrust back the freed devil that had snatched away the mask. His face resumed its immobility. But he could not banish that devil from his eyes.

"It was my decree," he intoned monotonously, but there was something strangled in the voice. "So shall it be. You offer, Eve Demerest, to take the steps for him?"

"Yes," she answered.

"Why?"

"Because I love him," said Eve, calmly.

Satan's hands twisted beneath his robe. The heavy lips contorted. Upon the enormous dome of his bald head tiny drops of sweat suddenly sprang out, glistening.

Abruptly, he reached forward, and drew back the lever; the shining prints glimmered out as though touched with fire –

I heard no whirring of the hidden cogs!

What did that mean? I looked at Satan. Either I had been mistaken, or else in the rage that ruled him he had not noticed. I had no time to speculate.

"Eve Demerest," the rolling tones still held their curiously strangled note, "you shall take the steps! And all shall be according to my decree. But this I tell you – none who has ever taken them and lost has died as you shall die. What they went through was Paradise, measured against that which you shall undergo if you lose. And so shall it be with your lover.

"First you shall see him die. Before he passes, he will turn from you with loathing and with hate...that ever he knew you. And then I shall give you to Sanchal. But not for him to slay. No, no! Not yet! When he is through with you the drinkers of the kehjt shall have you. The lowest of them. It shall be after them that Sanchal shall possess you again...for his cords and his knives and his irons...for his sport...and for mine!"

He pulled at the neck of his cloak as though it choked him. He signaled to the slaves who stood on the bottom steps. He gave them some command in the unknown tongue. They slithered toward me. I tensed my muscles, about to make one despairing rush upon the blazing-eyed devil in the black throne.

Eve covered her face with her hands.

"Jim, darling," she whispered swiftly, under their shelter, "go quietly! Barker! Something's going to happen–"

The slaves had me. I let them lead me over to the chair from which I had watched Cartright mount to his doom. They pressed me into it. Arm and leg bands snapped into place. The veil dropped over my head. They marched away.

A whisper came from below and behind me:

"Cap'n! The clamps don't hold! There's a gun right be'ind the slide. It's open. I'm in a 'ell of a 'urry. When you see me next, grab it an' get busy."

"Eve Demerest!" called Satan, "the steps await! Ascend!"

Eve walked forward steadily. Unhesitating, she put her foot upon the first of the shining prints.

A symbol leaped out in the fortunate field of the swinging globe. I heard a murmur, louder than before, go up from the darkened amphitheater. Satan watched, immobile.

She mounted, and set her foot in the next gleaming mark of the child's foot –

I saw Satan bend suddenly forward, glaring at the telltale, stark disbelief in his eyes. From the amphitheater the murmuring swelled into a roar.

A second symbol shone out in the fortunate field

She had won our freedom!

But how had it happened? And what was Eve doing –

She had mounted to the third point. She pressed upon it.

Out upon the telltale sprang a third symbol to join the other two!

Satan's face was writhing. The roaring at the back of the

Temple had become a tumult. I heard men shouting. Satan was fumbling frantically under his robe –

And now Eve sped up the intervening steps between her and the dais. As she passed them, she trod upon each of the gleaming prints. And as she trod, out upon the fortunate field appeared, one after the other, a shining symbol.

Seven of them – in the fortunate field!

None in Satan's!

The roaring had become deafening. Satan leaped from the black throne. The wall behind him opened. Out sprang Barker, automatic in his hand.

Now he was at Satan's side, the barrel of the gun thrust into his belly. The tumult in the Temple stilled, as though a cloud of silence had fallen upon it.

"'Ands up!" snarled the little man. "Wye up! Two ticks an' I scatter your guts h'over the map!"

Up went Satan's hands, high over his head.

I threw myself forward. The clamps of the chair gave so suddenly that I slipped to my knees. I reached back into the slit, and felt the barrel of a pistol. I gripped it – the executioner Sanchal was crouching, ready to spring. I shot from the floor, and with an accuracy that gave me one of the keenest joys I had ever known, I drilled Sanchal through the head. He fell sideways, flopping half down the steps.

The kehjt slaves stood dazed, irresolute, waiting command.

"One move o' them bastards, an' you're in pieces," I heard Harry say. "Tell 'em, quick!"

He jabbed the muzzle of the gun viciously into Satan's side.

Satan spoke. The voice that came from his lips was like that which one hears in nightmare. To this day I do not like to remember it. It was a command in the unknown tongue, but I had a swift, uneasy suspicion that it held more than the bare order to remain quiet. The slaves dropped their ropes. They slid back toward the walls.

I took the steps on the jump. Eve was beside Barker. I ranged myself at Satan's other side. She slipped behind him, and joined me.

The tumult in the amphitheater burst out afresh. Men were

struggling together in the semidarkness. There was a rush down from the seats. The edge of the brilliant circle was abruptly lined with figures.

Out from them stepped Consardine.

His face was chalk-white. His eyes burned with a fire that matched Satan's own. He held his hands before him with fingers curved like talons. He stalked forward like a walking death. And his eyes never left Satan.

"Not yet," whispered Barker. "Stop 'im, Cap'n."

"Consardine!" I called. "Stop where you are."

He paid no heed. He walked on, slowly, like a sleepwalker, the dreadful gaze upon Satan unwavering.

"Consardine!" I called again, sharply. "Stop! I'll drop you. I mean it. I don't want to kill you. But another step, and I drop you. By God, I will!"

He halted.

"You...will not...kill him? You will...leave...him for me?"

Consardine's voice was thin and high. It was Death speaking.

"If we can," I answered him. "But keep those others back. One move against us and Satan goes. And some of you with him. We've no time to pick friends from foes."

He turned and spoke to them. Again they were silent, watching.

"Now then, Cap'n," said Barker, briskly, "stick your gun in 'im, and move 'im over 'ere. I'm goin' to show 'em."

I thrust the automatic just under Satan's lower ribs, and pushed him toward the throne of gold. He moved over unresistingly, quietly, almost stolidly. He did not even look at me. I studied him, the vague apprehension growing stronger. He was intent upon Consardine. His face had regained all its impassivity. But the Devil looked out of his eyes, unchained. It came to me that he believed Consardine to be the archtraitor, that it was he who had set the snare! That we were Consardine's tools!

But why this apparently passive resignation? Even with our guns at his belly, it was not what I would have expected of Satan. And it seemed to me that besides the murder in his gaze there was a certain contempt. Had he, also, a final ace in the hole? My uneasiness increased, sharply.

"Now look, all o' you. I'm goin' to show you what the double-crossin' swine 'as been doin' to you."

It was Barker speaking. I did not dare turn my eyes from Satan to see what he was doing. But there was no need. I knew.

"Promisin' you this an' that," went on the cockney drawl. "Sendin' you to 'Ell! An' all the time larfin' up 'is sleeves at you. Larfin' fit to die, 'e was. An' you like a parcel o' trustin' h'infants. I'm goin' to show you. Miss Demerest, will you please walk down an' then walk up them prints again?"

I saw Eve go down the steps.

"Wyte a second." She halted at the bottom. "'Ere I am sittin' in 'is throne. I pull the lever. But h'after I've pulled it, I press on the h'edge of the seat. Like this. Now, Miss Demerest. Walk up."

Eve ascended, stepping upon each of the shining prints.

I could see, out of the corner of my eye, the telltale. Nothing appeared upon it. No symbol, either upon darkened field or lighted.

There was no sound from the watchers. They seemed dazed, waiting what was to come next.

"Didn't make a damned bit o' difference where you trod," said Barker. "It didn't register. 'Cause why? When I pressed on the h'edge of the throne, a little plate slipped down under there where the machinery is. An' at the same time, the cogs what myde the contacts what flashed the signals on the globe got moved over to another set o' contacts. The steps'd work all right when 'e wanted 'em to. They was always set right when 'e was off 'is throne. But after 'e'd set 'imself on 'is bloody black chair 'e'd 'ide 'is 'ands an' press an' disconnect 'em. 'Ell, a flock o' elephants could o' walked up 'em then an' they'd never give a blink!"

The tumult broke out afresh; men, and women, too, crying out, cursing. They surged forward, farther into the ring of light.

"Back!" I shouted. "Hold them back, Consardine!"

"Wyte!" yelped Barker. "Wyte! That ain't 'arf what the swine's done to you!"

The uproar died. They stared up at us again. Consardine had moved to the very bottom of the steps. His face was, if possible, whiter. His eyes glared upon Satan from rings, black as though painted. He was panting. I wished Harry would hurry. Consardine was near the end of his restraint. I didn't want to shoot him.

All of this I had seen incompletely. Suddenly I had the thought that Satan was listening, listening not to anything within the Temple, but for some sound far away. That he was willing, willing with complete concentration of all his unholy power for some certain thing to happen. And as I watched I seemed to see a flicker of triumph pass over the marble face.

"Now," came Barker's voice, "I'm goin' to show you. 'Ere on the syme h'edge is seven little plyces. Rubber, set in the stone. After 'e'd disconnected the contacts from the steps, 'e put 'is finger tips on each o' them plyces. Three of 'em was linked up to the contacts so's they'd flash the marks on 'is side the telltale. The other four was rigged up to flash 'em on your side. When any o' you tread on a print 'e'd press the button 'e wanted. Up'd go the mark, of the one 'e'd picked. You didn't make them marks show up. 'E did!' 'E 'ad you goin' and comin'.

"Wyte a minute! Just a minute!" Clearly Barker was enjoying himself. "I'm going to sit in 'is chair an' show you. Goin' to show you just what blinkin' bloody fools he myde out o' you."

"Jim!" there was alarm in Eve's voice, close to my ear. "Jim! I've just noticed. There were seven of the kehjt drinkers along that wall. Now there are only six. One of them has slipped away!"

At that instant I knew for what Satan had been listening and waiting. I had been right when I had sensed in his command to the slaves something more than an order to be quiescent. He had bade them watch for an opportunity that would let one of them creep away and raise the alarm.

Loose upon those who threatened him the horde of those soulless, merciless devils to whom Satan was a god since he, and only he, could open to them their Paradise.

In the absorption of us all in the drama of Satan's unmasking, a slave had found that opportunity. Had been gone – how long?

The thoughts flashed through my head in a split second.

And at that same instant the Hell which had been piling up slowly and steadily in the Temple like thunder heads broke loose.

Without warning, swiftly as the darting of a snake, Satan's arm struck down. It caught my arm. It sent my automatic hurtling, exploding as it flew. I heard Eve scream, heard Barker's sharp yelp.

I saw Consardine leaping up the steps, straight for Satan. Abruptly the whole Temple was flooded with light. Like an image caught between the opening and shutting of a camera shutter, I had a glimpse of Bedlam. Those who would have followed Consardine and those who were still faithful to Satan struggling for mastery.

Satan's hands swept in to catch me, lift me, hurl me against Consardine. Quicker than he, I dropped, twisting, and threw myself with every ounce of my strength against his legs.

He tottered. A foot slipped upon the edge of the dais. He reeled down a step or two, swaying in effort to regain his balance.

Consardine was upon him!

His hands gripped Satan's throat. The mighty arms of Satan wrapped themselves around him. The two fell. Locked, they went rolling down the steps.

There was a howling, like packs of wolves. At the back of the Temple and at the two sides, the panels flew open. Through them seethed the kehjt slaves.

"Quick, Cap'n!"

Barker spun me around. He pointed to the throne of gold.

"Be'ind it!" he grunted, and ran.

I caught Eve's arm and we raced after him. He was on his knees, working frantically at the floor. Something clicked, and a block slid aside. I saw a hole down which dropped a narrow flight of steps.

"Go first," said Barker. "Quick!"

Eve slipped through. As I followed I caught a glimpse of the Temple through the legs of the throne. It was a seething place of slaughter. The knives of the kehjt slaves were flashing. Men were shooting. From side to side was battle. Of Satan and Consardine I saw nothing. There were a dozen of the slaves rushing up the stairs toward us –

Barker shoved me down the hole. He jumped after me, landing almost on my head. The slab closed.

"'Urry!" gasped Barker. "Gord! If 'e gets us now!"

The stairs led into a bare and small chamber of stone. Over our heads we could hear the tumult. The feet of the fighters beat on the ceiling like drums.

"Watch the stairs. Where's your gun? 'Ere, tyke mine," Barker thrust his automatic into my hand. He turned to the wall, scrutinizing it. I ran back to where the narrow stairs entered the chamber. I could hear hands working at the block.

"Got it!" cried Barker. "'Urry!"

A slab had opened in the wall. We passed through. It shut behind us. I could see no place in the wall to mark where it had been.

We stood in one of those long and dimly lighted corridors that honeycombed Satan's house.

Clearly to us came the turmoil of the fighting above us.

There were five quick sharp explosions.

And, then, abruptly, as though at some command, the turmoil was stilled.

CHAPTER TWENTY

The effect of that abrupt silencing of the tumult overhead was disconcerting, to put it mildly. The five sharp reports had been less like pistol shots than those of a rifle. But who had been shooting, and how could so few bullets have ended such a melee as I had glimpsed?

"They're quiet! What does it mean?" whispered Eve.

"Somebody's won," I said.

"Satan – you don't think Satan?" she breathed.

Whether Consardine had done for Satan or Satan for him, I had no means of knowing. Desperately I hoped that Consardine had killed him. But whether he had or had not, my betting upon the general battle was with the kehjt drinkers. They swung a wicked knife, and they didn't care. If Consardine had choked Satan's life out of him, the kehjt slaves had in all probability sent Consardine's life after Satan. I didn't tell Eve that.

"Whether Satan has lost or won, his power is gone," I told her. "There's little to fear from him now."

"Not if we can get out of this blinkin' 'ole without gettin' scragged, there ain't," said Harry, gloomily. "It's only fair to tell you I'd a lot rather be 'earin' that Bank 'Oliday goin' on up there."

"What's the matter with you?" I asked.

"It'd keep their minds off us, for one thing," he looked askance at Eve. "But that ain't the 'ole of it."

"Will you kindly not regard me as a sensitive female, Barker," said Eve with considerable acerbity. "Never mind considering my feelings. What do you mean?"

"All right," said Barker. "I'll tell you stryte then. I don't know where the 'ell we are."

I whistled.

"But you knew your way here," I said.

"No," he answered, "I didn't. I took a long chance on that, Cap'n. I knew about the trap be'ind the gold throne an' the room under it. It's where 'e stows it, an' I been there, from up above. I took a chance there was another wye out. I was lucky enough to find it. But 'ow to get from 'ere – I don't know."

"Hadn't we better be moving along, somewhere?" said Eve.

"We sure had," I said. "We've only got one gun. Those slaves may come piling in any minute."

"I move we tyke the right 'and," said Harry. "We're somewhere close to Satan's private quarters. I know that. You keep the gun, Cap'n."

We moved along the corridor, cautiously. Barker kept scanning the walls, shaking his head, and mumbling. Something had been puzzling me ever since Eve had walked forth from the dark amphitheater to take my place at the steps. It seemed as good a time as any to satisfy my curiosity.

"Harry," I asked, "how did you work it so that all the prints registered only on that one side of the globe? What kept Satan from doing his double-crossing as usual from the black throne? He was trying hard enough. Did you get back into the Temple again after we'd left?"

"I fixed it before we went, Cap'n," he grinned. "You saw me fussin' with the machinery after we'd tried it out, didn't you?"

"I thought you were readjusting it," I said.

"So I was," he grinned more broadly. "Settin' it so the steps threw all the contacts on the lucky side o' the telltale. Settin' it so 'is little arryngement in 'is chair wouldn't myke no contacts at all. Took a chance, I did. Thought mybe the next Temple meetin' would be on account o' you. Only thing I was afryd of was 'e'd miss the noise when 'e pulled the little lever. I couldn't 'elp that. Thank Gord, 'e didn't. 'E was too mad."

"Harry," I took the little man by the shoulders, "you've surely paid me back in full and more for whatever I did for you."

"Now, now," said Barker, "wyte till we're out–"

He halted.

"What's that?" he whispered.

There had been another sharp explosion, louder than those we had heard before the silence had dropped upon the Temple. It was closer, too. The floor of the corridor trembled. Quick upon it came another.

"Bombs!" exclaimed Barker.

There was a third explosion, nearer still.

"Cripes! We got to get out o' here!" Barker began questing along the walls like a terrier. Suddenly he grunted, and stopped.

"Got something," he said. "Quiet now. Stand close be'ind me while I tyke a look."

He pressed upon the wall. A panel slid aside revealing one of the small lifts. He drew a long breath of relief. We crowded in.

"Down or up?" he closed the panel on us.

"What do you think?" I asked him.

"Well, the Temple's on the ground floor. We're just under it. If we go down, we'll be somewhere around that slyves' den. If we go up, we got to pass the Temple. If we can get by, an' keep on goin' up – well, it's 'ardly likely there'll be as many slyves over it as under an' around it, Cap'n."

"Up we go," said Eve, decisively.

"Up it is," I said.

He sent the lift upward, slowly. There was a fourth explosion, louder than any of the others. The frame of the elevator rattled. There was a sound of falling masonry.

"Getting close," said Eve.

"If we could bryke into Satan's rooms, we'd 'ave a chance o' findin' that private tunnel of 'is," Barker stopped the lift. "It's somewhere close by. It's our best bet, Cap'n. With any luck at all, we could come out syfe on the shore."

"I'll bet that by now everybody on the place knows what's going on, and is somewhere around here," I said. "We could lift one of those speed boats and get away."

"I smell something burning," said Eve.

"Cripes!" Barker sent the lift up at the limit of its speed, "I'll sye you do!"

A crack had opened in the wall in front of us. Out of it had shot a jet of smoke.

Suddenly Barker stopped the lift. He slid aside a panel, cautiously. He peered out, then nodded to us. We stepped into a small room, paved and walled with a dull black stone. On one side was a narrow door of bronze. It was plainly an antechamber. But to what?

As we stood there, hesitating, we heard two more explosions, one immediately following the other. They seemed to be upon the floor where we were. From below us came another crash, as of a falling wall. The lift from which we had just emerged went smashing down. Out of the open panel poured a dense volume of smoke.

"Gord! The 'ole bloody plyce is on fire!" Barker jammed the panel shut, and stared at us, white faced.

And suddenly I thought of Cobham.

Cobham, with his gentlemanly bomb that was to blow the bottom out of the Astarte. Satan had said that he had been driven into hiding near the laboratory. Had Cobham seen his chance to escape during the rush of the kehjt slaves to aid Satan? Had he found his way clear, gone straight to the laboratory, and was he now strewing in crazed vengeance the death and destruction he had garnered there?

I tried the bronze door. It was unfastened. Gun ready, I slowly opened it.

We were at one end of that amazing group of rooms, that shrine of beauty, which Satan had created for himself. That place of magic whose spell had so wrought upon me not so long ago that I had gone forth from it, half-considering the giving up of Eve, the placing of my whole allegiance in Satan's hands. There was a thin veil of smoke in the silent chamber. It dimmed the tapestries, the priceless paintings, the carvings of stone and wood. We crossed its floor, and looked into a larger treasure room. At its far side where were its doors, the smoke hung like a curtain.

From behind the smoke, and close, came another explosion.

Through the curtain stumbled Satan!

At sight of him we huddled together, the three of us. My mouth went dry, and I felt the sweat wet the roots of my hair. It was not with fear. It was something more than fear.

For Satan, stumbling toward us, was blind!

His eyes were no longer blue, jewel-hard and jewel-bright. They were dull and gray, like unpolished agates. They were dead. It was as though a flame had seared them. There was a red stain over and around them, like a crimson mask.

He was cloakless. Black upon the skin of his swollen neck were the marks of strangling fingers. Consardine's.

One arm hung limp. The other clasped to his breast a little statue of ivory, an Eros. Of all those things of beauty which he had schemed and robbed and slain to possess, that statue was, I think, the thing he loved the best; the thing in which he found the purest, perfect form of that spirit of beauty which, evil as Satan was, he knew and worshiped.

He stumbled on, rolling his great head from side to side like a blinded beast. And as he came, tears fell steadily from the sightless eyes and glistened on the heavy cheeks.

Through the curtain of smoke, following him, stalked Cobham.

A bag was slung over his left shoulder. It bulged, and as he emerged he dipped a hand within it. In his hand when he drew it out was something round, about as big as an orange, something that gleamed, with a dully metallic luster.

As Cobham walked, he laughed; constantly, even as Satan wept.

Cobham halted.

"Satan!" he called. "Stop! Time for a rest, dear Master!"

The stumbling figure lurched on, unheeding. The jeering note in Cobham's voice fled; it became menacing.

"Stop, you dog! Stop when I tell you. Do you want a bomb at your heels?"

Satan stood still, shuddering, the little statue clasped closer.

"Turn, Satan," jeered Cobham. "What, Master, would you deny me the light of those eyes of yours!"

And Satan turned.

Cobham saw us.

The hand that held the bomb flew up.

"Walter!" cried Eve, and leaped in front of me, arms outstretched. "Walter! Don't!"

I had not tried to shoot. To be honest, I had not thought of it. The paralysis with which the sight of Satan had touched me still held me. Eve's swift action saved us more surely than a bullet would have.

Cobham's arm dropped to his side. Satan did not turn. I doubt even if he heard. He was past all except his agony and the voice of his tormentor, and that, it came to me, he obeyed only to save from destruction the thing he was clasping.

"Eve!" some of the madness was swept from Cobham's face. "Who's with you? Come closer."

We moved toward him.

"Kirkham, eh? and little 'Arry. Stop where you are. Put your hands up, both of you. I owe you something, Kirkham. But I don't trust you. Eve, where do you think you're going?"

"We're trying to get away, Walter," she said gently. "Come with us."

"Come with you? Come with you!" I saw the madness fill his eyes again. "I couldn't do that. There's only a part of me here, you know. The rest of me is in a room full of little mirrors. A part of me in every one of those mirrors. I couldn't go away and leave them."

He paused, seemingly to consider the matter. The smoke grew thicker. Satan never moved.

"Disintegrated personality, that's it," said Cobham. "Satan did it. But he didn't keep me there long enough. I got away. If I'd stayed a little longer, all of me would have gone into the mirrors. Into them and through them and away. As it is," said Cobham with a dreadful, impersonal gravity, "the experiment remains unfinished. I can't go away and leave those bits of myself behind. You see that, Eve?"

"Careful, Eve. Don't cross him," I muttered. He heard me.

"Shut up, you, Kirkham. Eve and I will do the talking," he said, viciously.

"We could help you, Walter," she said, steadily. "Come with us—"

"I went to the Temple," he interrupted her, speaking quite

calmly, the shattered mind abruptly taking another path, "I had my bombs with me. I distributed a few of them. I used the sleep gas. Consardine was at the bottom of the steps. His back was broken. Satan was just getting up from him. He covered his mouth and nose and ran. I caught him. A little spray across the eyes with something I was carrying. That was all. He made for here like a rat to his hole. Blind as he was–"

The mood had changed. He roared his crazy laughter.

"Come with you! Leave him! After what he's done to me? No, no, Eve. Not if you were all the angels in Heaven. We've had a nice long walk, Satan and I. And when we go, we go together. With all the little bits of me in his damned mirrors going, too. A long, long journey. But I've arranged it so we'll have a swift, swift start!"

"Cobham," I said. "I want to save Eve. The tunnel to the shore. Will you tell us how to find it? Or is the way to it blocked?"

"I told you to shut up, Kirkham," he leered at me. "Everybody used to obey Satan. Now Satan obeys me. Therefore everybody obeys me. You've disobeyed me. Walk over to that wall, Kirkham."

I walked to the wall. There was nothing else to do.

"You want to know how to get to the tunnel," he said when I had reached it, and turned. "Go into that anteroom. Through the right wall there – listen to me, you 'Arry," he shot a malicious look at me. "Six panels left along the corridor. Through again into another passage. Go down the ramp to the end. Through it at the last panel, right. That's the start of the tunnel. So much for that. Now, Kirkham, let's see whether you're going with them. Catch."

He raised his arm and threw the bomb at me.

It seemed to come to me slowly. I seemed to have plenty of time to think of what would happen to me if I missed it, or dropped it, or caught it too roughly. Luck was with me. I did none of the three.

"All right, you go," grinned Cobham. "Keep it in case you meet any of the slaves. I think I cleaned them all out in the Temple. Gas bombs, Kirkham, gas bombs. They're lying up there asleep and toasting."

Again he roared with laughter.

"Get out!" he snarled suddenly.

We walked back through the other room. We did not dare look into each other's faces. At the door, I glanced back. Cobham was watching us.

Satan had not stirred.

We passed through the door, and closed it.

We got out of the little antechamber as quickly as we could. It was pretty bad with the smoke, and rather too much like a furnace. The first corridor was uncomfortably choky, too. The second was entirely clear. When we reached its end, Barker had a bit of trouble with the panel. Finally it swung open, like a door.

Before us was not, as I had expected, the entrance to the tunnel, but a bare, stone room about twenty feet square. Opposite us was a massive steel door closed with heavy bars. On each side of it was a kehjt drinker. They were big fellows, armed with throwing cords and knives. In addition to these they had carbines, the first guns I had seen in the hands of the slaves.

I had thrust Cobham's bomb in my pocket. For an instant I thought of using it. Then common sense told me that it might bring the place crashing down about us, at any rate seal the tunnel entrance. I dropped my hand on my automatic. But by that time the guards covered us with their rifles. The only reason that they had not shot on sight, I suppose, was that they had recognized Barker.

"'Ullo! 'Ullo! What's the matter with you?" Barker stepped toward them.

"What are you doing here?" one of the slaves spoke, and by the faint accent in the deadened voice I thought that he had been Russian before he had become – what he was.

"Satan's orders," answered Harry brusquely, and gestured to the guns. "Put 'em down."

The slave who had spoken said something to the other in that unfamiliar tongue I had heard Satan use. He nodded. They lowered their carbines, but held them in readiness.

"You have his token?" asked the slave.

"You got it, Cap'n," Barker turned his head to me quickly,

then back to the guard. "No, you 'aven't. I 'ave–"

I had read the message in his eyes. My hand was on the automatic. I shot from the hip at the second guard. His hand flew up to his breast and he toppled.

At the instant of the report, Barker hurled himself at the legs of the challenging slave. His feet flew from beneath him, and down he crashed. Before he could arise I had put a bullet through his head.

I felt no compunction about killing him. The kehft drinkers had never seemed to me to be human. But whether human or not, I had killed far better men for much less reason during the war. Barker dropped upon the guard he had tripped, and began to search him. He arose with a bunch of small keys and ran to the steel door. It could not have been more than a minute before he had the bars down and the door open. The tunnel lay before us, long, cased with stone and dimly lighted.

"We've got to tyke it on the double," Barker jammed the heavy valve shut. "I didn't like what 'e said about 'im an' Satan goin' awye together quick. I think 'e fixed it to blow up the lab'ratory. An' there's enough stuff there to move the northeast corner of 'Ell."

We set off at a run down the tunnel. After we had gone about a thousand feet we came to another wall. It closed the way, making of the passage apparently a blind alley.

Barker worked feverishly at it, going over it inch by inch with nimble fingers. A block dropped suddenly, sliding downward as though in grooves. We passed through the opening. And ran on.

The lights blinked out. We halted, in darkness. The ground quivered under our feet. The quivering was followed by a deep-toned roar like the bellow of a volcano. I threw an arm around Eve. The floor of the tunnel heaved and rocked. I heard the crash of stones falling from its roof and sides.

"Gord! There goes Satan!" Barker's voice was hysterically shrill.

I knew it must be so. Satan had – gone. And Cobham. And all those, dead and alive, in the chateau – they, too, were gone. And all the treasures of Satan, all the beauty that he had gathered about him –

gone. Blasted and shattered in that terrific explosion. Things of beauty irreplaceable, things of beauty for which the world must be poorer forever – destroyed for all time. Wiped out!

I had a sensation of sick emptiness. My very bones felt hollow. I felt a remorse and horror as though I had been party to some supreme sacrilege.

Eve's arms were around my neck, tightly. I heard her sobbing. I thrust away the weakening thoughts, and held her to me close, comforting her.

The stones ceased falling. We went on, picking our way over them by the gleam of Barker's flashlight. The tunnel had been badly damaged. If ever I prayed, I prayed then that no fall of stone or slip of earth had blocked it against us. If so, we were probably due to die like penned-in rats.

But the damage lessened as we drew further away from the center of the explosion, although now and again we heard the crashing of loosened stones behind us. We came at last to a breast of rocks, rough hewn, a formidable barrier that closed the tunnel, and must be, we knew, its further end.

Barker worked long at that, and I, too, and both of us at times despairingly, before we found the key to its opening. At last, when the flash was dying, a boulder sank. We breathed cool, fresh air. Close to us we heard the ripple of waves. Another minute and we stood upon that pile of rocks where I had seen Satan looking out over the waters of the Sound.

We saw the lights of the Cherub. She had come closer to shore. Her searchlight was playing upon the landing, sweeping from it along the road that led through the woods to the great house.

We crept down the rocks, and began to skirt the shore to the landing. At our right, the sky was glowing, pulsing. The tops of the trees stood out against the glow like the silhouettes of trees in a Japanese print.

Satan's funeral pyre.

We reached the pier. The searchlight picked us up. We went forward boldly. Barker dropped into a likely-looking launch that was fastened to the landing. Those on the yacht must have thought we were making ready to come to them. They held the light steady upon us.

The engines of the launch started to hum. I lowered Eve into it, and jumped after her. Barker threw the propeller into first speed, and then into direct drive. The launch shot forward.

There was no moon. A mist was on the waters. The glow of Satan's pyre cast a red film on the sluggish waves.

Barker steered for the yacht. Suddenly he swung sharply to port, and away from her. We heard shouts from her decks. The mists thickened as we sped on. They dimmed the beam. And then it lost us and swept back to the pier.

Barker headed the launch straight for the Connecticut shore. He gave me the wheel, and went back to nurse the engines. Eve pressed close to me. I put my arm around her and drew her closer. Her head dropped upon my shoulder.

My thoughts went back to the burning chateau. What was happening there? Had the great explosion and the glare of the flames brought outsiders to it as yet, volunteer firefighters from the neighboring villages, police? It was not likely. The place was so isolated, so difficult of access. But on the morrow, surely they would come. What would they find? What would be their reception? How many had escaped from the chateau?

And those who had been trapped in Satan's house? Those who had fallen before his slaves and Cobham's bombs? Among them had been men and women of high place. What an aftermath their disappearance would have! The newspapers would be busy for a long time about that.

And Satan! In the last analysis – a crooked gambler. Betrayed at the end by the dice he himself had loaded. Had he but played his game of the seven footprints straight he would have been unconquerable. But he had not – and all his power had rested on a lie. And his power could be no stronger than that which upheld it.

It was Satan's lie that had betrayed him.

Crooked gambler – yes, but more, much more than that –

Would his vengeance follow us, though he was gone?

Well, we would have to take our chances.

I shook off the oppression creeping over me, turned resolutely from the past to the future.

"Eve," I whispered, "all I've got is what's left of sixty-six dollars and ninety-five cents that was my sole capital when I met you."

"Well, what of it?" asked Eve, and snuggled in my arm.

"It's not much for a honeymoon trip," I said. "Of course, there's the ten thousand I got for the museum job. I can't keep that. It'll have to go back to the museum. Marked 'Anonymous Donor.'"

"Of course," said Eve, indifferently. "Oh, Jim, darling, isn't it good to be free!"

Barker moved forward, and took the wheel from me. I put both arms around Eve. Far ahead of us the lights of some Connecticut town sparkled. They evoked a painful memory. I sighed.

"All those treasures – gone!" I groaned. "Why didn't I have the sense to snatch that crown or scepter off the gold throne when I had the chance?"

"'Ere's the crown, Cap'n," said Barker.

He fished down into a pocket. He drew out the crown and dropped it into Eve's lap. Its jewels blazed up at us. We stared at them, and from them to Barker, and from Barker back to them – unbelievingly.

"Crown's a bit crumpled," remarked Barker, easily. "'Ad to bend it to stow it awye. Grabbed the scepter, but it slipped. 'Adn't time to pick it up. Picked up a few other tysty bits, though."

He poured a double handful of rings and necklaces and uncut gems over the glittering crown. We stared at him, still speechless.

"Split 'em two wyes," said Harry, "so long as you an' Miss Eve's goin' to be one. I only 'opes they're real."

"Harry!" whispered Eve, breathlessly. She leaned over and kissed him.

He blinked, and turned back to the wheel.

"Reminds me o' Maggie!" muttered Harry, forlornly.

I felt something round and hard in my pocket. Cobham's bomb! With a little prickling of the scalp, I dropped it gingerly over the side.

The shore lights had crept nearer. I scooped the jewels from Eve's lap and thrust them into Barker's pocket.

I clasped Eve close, and turned her face up to mine.

"Just like me an' Maggie!" whispered Harry, huskily.

I put my lips to hers, and felt hers cling. Life was very sweet just then.

Eve's lips were sweeter.

APPENDIX

THROUGH THE DRAGON GLASS

Herndon helped loot the Forbidden City when the Allies turned the suppression of the Boxers into the most gorgeous burglar-party since the days of Tamerlane. Six of his sailormen followed faithfully his buccaneering fancy. A sympathetic Russian highness whom he had entertained in New York saw to it that he got to the coast and his yacht. That is why Hemdon was able to sail through the Narrows with as much of the Son of Heaven's treasures as the most accomplished laborer in Peking's mission vineyards.

Some of the loot he gave to charming ladies who had dwelt or were still dwelling on the sunny side of his heart. Most of it he used to fit up those two astonishing Chinese rooms in his Fifth Avenue house. And a little of it, following a vague religious impulse, he presented to the Metropolitan Museum. This, somehow, seemed to put the stamp of legitimacy on his part of the pillage – like offerings to the gods and building hospitals and peace palaces and such things.

But the Dragon Glass, because he had never seen anything quite so wonderful, he set up in his bedroom Where he could look at it the first thing in the morning, and he placed shaded lights about it so that he could wake up in the night and look at it! Wonderful? It is more than wonderful, the Dragon Glass! Whoever made it lived when the gods walked about the earth creating something new every day. Only a man who lived in that sort of atmosphere could have wrought it. There was never anything like it.

I was in Hawaii when the cables told of Herndon's first disappearance. There wasn't much to tell. His man had gone to his room to awaken him one morning – and Herndon wasn't there. All his clothes were, though, Everything was just as if Herndon ought to be somewhere in the house – only he wasn't.

A man worth ten millions can't step out into thin air and vanish without leaving behind him the probability of some commotion, naturally. The newspapers attend to the commotion, but the columns of type boiled down to essentials contained just two facts – that Herndon had come home the night before, and in the morning he was undiscoverable.

I was on the high seas, homeward bound to help the search, when the wireless told the story of his reappearance. They had found him on the floor of his bedroom, shreds of a silken robe on him, and his body mauled as though by a tiger. But there was no more explanation of his return than there had been of his disappearance.

The night before he hadn't been there – and in the morning there he was. Herndon, when he was able to talk, utterly refused to confide even in his doctors. I went straight through to New York, and waited until the men of medicine decided that it was better to let him see me than have him worry any longer about not seeing me.

Herndon got up from a big invalid chair when I entered. His eyes were clear and bright, and there was no weakness in the way he greeted me, nor in the grip of his hand. A nurse slipped from the room.

"What was it, Jim?" I cried. "What on earth happened to you?"

"Not so sure it was on earth," he said. He pointed to what looked like a tall easel hooded with a heavy piece of silk covered with embroidered Chinese characters. He hesitated for a moment and then walked over to a closet. He drew out two heavy bore guns, the very ones, I remembered, that he had used in his last elephant hunt.

"You won't think me crazy if I ask you to keep one of these handy while I talk, will you, Ward?" he asked rather apologetically. "This looks pretty real, doesn't it?"

He opened his dressing gown and showed me his chest swathed in bandages. He gripped my shoulder as I took without question one of the guns. He walked to the easel and drew off the hood.

"There it is," said Herndon.

And then, for the first time, I saw the Dragon Glass!

There never has been anything like that thing! Never! At first all you saw was a cool, green, glimmering translucence, like the sea when you are swimming under water on a still summer day and look up through it. Around its edges ran flickers of scarlet and gold, flashes of emerald, shimmers of silver and ivory. At its base a disk of topaz rimmed with red fire shot up dusky little vaporous yellow flames.

Afterward you were aware that the green translucence was an oval slice of polished stone. The flashes and flickers became dragons. There were twelve of them. Their eyes were emeralds, their fangs were ivory, their claws were gold. There were scaled dragons, and each scale was so inlaid that the base, green as the primeval jungle, shaded off into vivid scarlet, and the scarlet into tip's of gold. Their wings were of silver and vermilion, and were folded close to their bodies.

But they were alive, those dragons. There was never so much life in metal and wood since Al-Akram, the Sculptor of ancient Ad, carved the first crocodile, and the jealous Almighty breathed life into it for a punishment!

And last you saw that the topaz disk that sent up the little yellow flames was the top of a metal sphere around which coiled a thirteenth dragon, thin and red, and biting its scorpion-tipped tail.

It took your breath away, the first glimpse of the Dragon Glass. Yes, and the second and third glimpse, too – and every other time you looked at it.

"Where did you get it?" I asked, a little shakily.

Herndon said evenly: "It was in a small hidden crypt in the Imperial Palace. We broke into the crypt quite by" – he hesitated – "well, call it accident. As soon as I saw it I knew I must have it. What do you think of it?"

"Think!" I cried. "Think! Why, it's the most marvelous thing that the hands of man ever made! What is that stone? Jade?"

"I'm not sure," said Herndon. ."But come here. Stand just in front of me."

He switched out the lights in the room. He turned another switch, and on the glass oposite me three shaded electrics threw their rays into its mirror-like oval.

"Watch!" said Herndon. "Tell me what you see!"

I looked into the glass. At first I could see nothing but the rays shining farther, farther – back into infinite distances, it seemed. And then.

"Good God!" I cried, stiffening with horror. "Jim, what hellish thing is this?"

"Steady, old man," came Herndon's voice. There was relief and a curious sort of joy in it. "Steady; tell me what you see."

I said: "I seem to see through infinite distances – and yet what I see is as close to me as though it were just on the other side of the glass. I see a cleft that cuts through two masses of darker green. I see a claw, a gigantic, hideous claw that stretches out through the cleft. The claw has seven talons that open and close – open and close. Good God, such a claw, Jim! It is like the claws that reach out from the holes in the lama's hell to grip the blind souls as they shudder by!"

"Look, look farther, up through the cleft, above the claw. It widens. What do you see?"

I said: "I see a peak rising enormously high and cutting the sky like a pyramid. There are flashes of flame that dart from behind and outline it. I see a great globe of light like a moon that moves slowly out of the flashes; there is another moving across the breast of the peak; there is a third that swims into the flame at the farthest edge – "

"The seven moons of Rak," whispered Herndon, as though to himself. "The seven moons that bathe in the rose flames of Rak which are the fires of life and that circle Lalil like a diadem. He upon whom the seven moons of Rak have shone is bound to Lalil for this life, and for ten thousand lives."

He reached over and turned the switch again. The lights of the room sprang up.

"Jim," I said, "it can't be real! What is it? Some devilish illusion in the glass?"

He unfastened the bandages about his chest.

"The claw you saw had seven talons," he answered quietly. "Well, look at this."

Across the white flesh of his breast, from left shoulder to the lower ribs on the right, ran seven healing furrows. They looked as though they had been made by a gigantic steel comb that had been drawn across him. They gave one the thought they had been ploughed.

"The claw made these," he said as quietly as before.

"Ward," he went on, before I could speak, "I wanted you to see – what you've seen. I didn't know whether you would see it. I don't know whether you'll believe me even now. I don't suppose I would if I were in your place – still – "

He walked over and threw the hood upon the Dragon Glass.

"I'm going to tell you," he said. "I'd like to go through it – uninterrupted. That's why I cover it.

"I don't suppose," he began slowly – "I don't suppose, Ward, that you've ever heard of Rak the WonderWorker, who lived somewhere back at the beginning of things, nor how the Greatest Wonder-Worker banished him somewhere outside the world?"

"No," I said shortly, still shaken by the sight.

"It's a big part of what I've got to tell you," he went on. "Of course you'll think it rot, but – I came across the legend in Tibet first. Then I ran across it again – with the names changed, of course – when I was getting away from China.

"I take it that the gods were still fussing around close to man when Rak was born. The story of his parentage is somewhat scandalous. When he grew older Rak wasn't satisfied with just seeing wonderful things being done. He wanted to do them himself, and he – well, he studied the method. After a while the Greatest Wonder-Worker ran across some of the things Rak had made, and he found them admirable – a little too admirable. He didn't like to destroy the lesser wonderworker because, so the gossip ran, he felt a sort of responsibility. So he gave Rak a place somewhere – outside the world – and he gave him power over every one out of so many millions of births to lead or lure or sweep that soul into his domain so that he might build up a people – and over his people Rak was given the high, the low, and the middle justice.

"And outside the world Rak went. He fenced his domain about with clouds. He raised a great mountain, and on its flank he built a city for the men and women who were to be his. He circled the city with wonderful gardens, and he placed in the gardens many things, gome good and some very – terrible. He set around the mountain's brow seven moons for a diadem, and he fanned behind the mountain a fire which is the fire of life, and through which the moons pass eternally to be born again." Herndon's voice sank to a whisper.

"Through which the moons pass," he said. "And with them the souls of the people of Rak. They pass through the fires and are born again – and again – for ten thousand lives. I have seen the moons of Rak and the souls that march with them into the fires. There is no sun in the land – only the new-born moons that shine green on the city and on the gardens."

"Jim," I cried impatiently. "What in the world are you talking about? Wake up, man! What's all that nonsense got to do with this?"

I pointed to the hooded Dragon Glass.

"That," he said. "Why, through that lies the road to the gardens of Rak!"

The heavy gun dropped from my hand as I stared at him, and from him to the glass and back again. He smiled and pointed to his bandaged breast.

He said: "I went straight through to Peking with the Allies. I had an idea what was coming, and I wanted to be in at the death. I was among the first to enter the Forbidden City. I was as mad for loot as any of them. It was a maddening sight, Ward. Soldiers with their arms full of precious stuff even Morgan couldn't buy; soldiers with wonderful necklaces around their hairy throats and their pockets stuffed with jewels; soldiers with their shirts bulging treasures the Sons of Heaven had been hoarding for centuries! We were Goths sacking imperial Rome. Alexander's hosts pillaging that ancient gemmed courtezan of cities, royal Tyre! Thieves in the great ancient scale, a scale so great that it raised even thievery up to something heroic.

"We reached the throne-room. There was a little passage leading off to the left, and my men and I took it. We came into a small octagonal room. There was nothing in it except a very extraordinary squatting figure of jade. It squatted on the floor, its back turned toward us. One of my men stooped to pick it up. He slipped. The figure flew from his hand and smashed into the wall. A slab swung outward. By a

– well, call it a fluke, we had struck the secret of the little octagonal room!

"I shoved a light through the aperture. It showed a crypt shaped like a cylinder. The circle of the floor was about ten feet in diameter. The walls were covered with paintings, Chinese characters, queer-looking animals, and things I can't well describe. Around the room, about seven feet up, ran a picture. It showed a sort of island floating off into space. The clouds lapped its edges like frozen seas full of rainbows. There was a big pyramid of a mountain rising out of the side of it. Around its peak were seven moons, and over the peak – a face!

"I couldn't place that face and I couldn't take my eyes off it. It wasn't Chinese, and it wasn't of any other race I'd ever seen. It was as old as the world and as young as tomorrow. It was benevolent and malicious, cruel and kindly, merciful and merciless, saturnine as Satan and as joyous as Apollo. The eyes were as yellow as buttercups, or as the sunstone on the crest of the Feathered Serpent they worship down in the Hidden Temple of Tuloon. And they were as wise as Fate.

"'There's something else here, sir,' said Martin – you remember Martin, my first officer. He pointed to a shrouded thing on the side. I entered, and took from the thing a covering that fitted over it like a hood. It was the Dragon Glass!

"The moment I saw it I knew I had to have it – and I knew I would have it. I felt that I did not want to get the thing away any more than the thing itself wanted to get away. From the first I thought of the Dragon Glass as something alive. Just as much alive as you and I are. Well, I did get it away. I got it down to the yacht, and then the first odd thing happened.

"You remember Wu-Sing, my boat steward? You know the English Wu-Sing talks. Atrocious! I had the Dragon Glass in my stateroom. I'd forgotten to lock the door. I heard a whistle of sharply indrawn breath. I turned, and there was Wu-Sing. Now, you know that Wu-Sing isn't what you'd call intelligent-looking. Yet as he stood there something seemed to pass over his face, and very subtly change it. The stupidity was wiped out as though a sponge had been passed over it.

He did not raise his eyes, but he said, in perfect English, mind you; 'Has the master augustly counted the cost of his possession?'

"I simply gaped at him.

"'Perhaps,' he continued, 'the master has never heard of the illustrious Hao-Tzan? Well, he shall hear.'

"Ward, I couldn't move or speak. But I know now it wasn't sheer astonishment that held me. I listened while Wu-Sing went on to tell in polished phrase the same story that I had heard in Tibet, only there they called him Rak instead of Hao-Tzan. But it was the same story.

"'And,' he finished, 'before he journeyed afar, the illustrious Hao-Tzan caused a great marvel to be wrought. He called it the Gateway.' Wu-Sing waved his hand to the Dragon Glass. 'The master has it. But what shall he who has a Gateway do but pass through it? Is it not better to leave the Gateway behind – unless he dare go through it?'

"He was silent. I was silent, too. All I could do was wonder where the fellow had so suddenly got his command of English. And then Wu-Sing straightened. For a moment his eyes looked into mine. They were as yellow as buttercups, Ward, and wise, wise! My mind rushed back to the little room behind the panel. Ward – . the eyes of Wu-Sing were the eyes of the face that brooded over the peak of the moons!

"And all in a moment, the face of Wu-Sing dropped back into its old familiar stupid lines. The eyes he turned to me were black and clouded. I jumped from my chair.

"'What do you mean, you yellow fraud!' I shouted. 'What do you mean by pretending all this time that you couldn't talk English?'

"He looked at me stupidly, as usual. He whined in his pidgin that he didn't understand; that he hadn't spoken a word to me until then. I couldn't get anything else out of him, although I nearly frightened his wits out. I had to believe him. Besides, I had seen his eyes. Well, I was fair curious by this time, and I was more anxious to get the glass home safely than ever.

"I got it home. I set it up here, and I fixed those lights as you saw them. I had a sort of feeling that the glass was waiting – for something. I couldn't tell just what. But that it was going to be rather important, I knew – "

He suddenly thrust his head into his hands, and rocked to and fro.

"How long, how long," he moaned, "how long, Santhu?"

"Jim!" I cried. "Jim! What's the matter with you?"

He straightened. "In a moment you'll understand," he said.

And then, as quietly as before: "I felt that the glass was waiting. The night I disappeared I couldn't sleep. I turned out the lights in the room; turned them on around the glass and sat before it. I don't know how long I sat, but all at once I jumped to my feet. The dragons seemed to be moving! They were moving! They were crawling round and round the glass. They moved faster and faster. The thirteenth dragon spun about the topaz globe. They circled faster and faster until they were nothing but a halo of crimson and gold flashes. As they spun, the glass itself grew misty, mistier, mistier still, until it was nothing but a green haze. I stepped over to touch it. My hand went straight on through it as though nothing were there.

"I reached in – up to the elbow, up to the shoulder. I felt my hand grasped by warm little fingers. I stepped through – "

"Stepped through the glass?" I cried.

"Through it," he said, "and then – I felt another little hand touch my face. I saw Santhu!

"Her eyes were as blue as the corn flowers, as blue as the big sapphire that shines in the forehead of Vishnu, in his temple at Benares. And they were set wide, wide apart. Her hair was blue-black, and fell in two long braids between her little breasts. A golden dragon crowned her, and through its paws slipped the braids. Another golden dragon girded her. She laughed into my eyes, and drew my head down until my lips touched hers. She was lithe and slender and yielding as the reeds that grow before the Shrine of Hathor that stands on the edge of the Pool of Djeeba. Who Santhu is or where she came from – how do I know? But this I know – she is lovelier than any woman who ever lived on earth. And she is a woman!

"Her arms slipped from about my neck and she drew me forward. I looked about me. We stood in a cleft between two great rocks. The rocks were a soft green, like the green of the Dragon Glass. Behind us was a green mistiness. Before us the cleft ran only a little distance. Through it I saw an enormous peak jutting up like a pyramid, high, high into a sky of chrysoprase. A soft rose radiance pulsed at its sides, and swimming slowly over its breast was a huge globe of green fire. The girl pulled me towards the opening. We walked on silently, hand in hand. Quickly it came to me – Ward, I was in the place whose pictures had been painted in the room of the Dragon Glass!

"We came out of the cleft and into a garden. The Gardens of Many-Columned Iram, lost in the desert because they were too beautiful, must have been like that place. There were strange, immense trees whose branches were like feathery plumes and whose plumes shone with fires like those that clothe the feet of Indra's dancers. Strange flowers raised themselves along our path, and their hearts glowed like the glow-worms that are fastened to the rainbow bridge to Asgard. A wind sighed through the plumed trees, and luminous shadows drifted past their trunks. I heard a girl laugh, and the voice of a man singing.

"We went on. Once there was a low wailing far in the garden, and the girl threw herself before me, her arms outstretched. The wailing ceased, and we went on. The mountain grew plainer. I saw another great globe of green fire swing out of the rose flashes at the right of the peak. I saw another shining into the glow at the left. There was a curious trail of mist behind it. It was a mist that had tangled in it a multitude of little stars. Everything was bathed in a soft green light – such a light as you would have if you lived within a pale emerald.

"We turned and went along another little trail. The little trail ran up a little hill, and on the hill was a little house. It looked as though it was made of ivory. It was a very odd little house. It was more like the Jain pagodas at Brahmaputra than anything else. The walls glowed as though they were full light. The girl touched the wall, and a panel slid away. We entered, and the panel closed after us.

"The room was filled with a whispering yellow light. I say

whispering because that is how one felt about it. It was gentle and alive. A stairway of ivory ran up to another room above. The girl pressed me toward it. Neither of us had uttered a word. There was a spell of silence upon me. I could not speak. There seemed to be nothing to say. I felt a great rest and a great peace – as though I had come home. I walked up the stairway and into the room above. It was dark except for a bar of green light that came through the long and narrow window. Through it I saw the mountain and its moons. On the floor was an ivory head-rest and some silken cloths. I felt suddenly very sleepy. I dropped to the cloths, and at once was asleep.

"When I awoke the girl with the cornflower eyes was beside me! She was sleeping. As I watched, her eyes opened. She smiled and drew me to her –

"I do not know why, but a name came to me. 'Santhu!' I cried. She smiled again, and I knew that I had called her name. It seemed to me that I remembered her, too, out of immeasurable ages. I arose and walked to the window. I looked toward the mountain. There were now two moons on its breast. And then I saw the city that lay on the mountain's flank. It was such a city as you see in dreams, or as the tale-tellers of El-Bahara fashion out of the mirage. It was all of ivory and shining greens and flashing blues and crimsons. I could see people walking about its streets. There came the sound of little golden bells chiming.

"I turned toward the girl. She was sitting up, her hands clasped about her knees, watching me. Love came, swift and compelling. She arose – I took her in my arms –

"Many times the moons circled the mountains, and the mist held the little, tangled stars passing with them. I saw no one but Santhu; no thing came near us. The trees fed us with fruits that had in them the very essences of life. Yes, the fruit of the Tree of Life that stood in Eden must have been like the fruit of those trees. We drank of green water that sparkled with green fires, and tasted like the wine Osiris gives the hungry souls in Amenti to strengthen them. We bathed in pools of carved stone that welled with water yellow as amber. Mostly we wandered in the gardens. There were many wonderful things in the gardens. They were very unearthly. There was no day nor night. Only the green glow of the ever-circling moons. We never talked to each other. I don't know why. Always there seemed nothing to say.

"Then Santhu began to sing to me. Her songs were strange songs. I could not tell what the words were. But they built up pictures in my brain. I saw Rak the Wonder-Worker fashioning his gardens, and filling them with things beautiful and things – evil. I saw him raise the peak, and knew that it was Lalil; saw him fashion the seven moons and kindle the fires that are the fires of life. I saw him build his city, and I saw men and women pass into it from the world through many gateways.

"Santhu sang – and I knew that the marching stars in the mist were the souls of the people of Rak which sought rebirth. She sang, and I saw myself ages past walking in the city of Rak with Santhu beside me. Her song wailed, and I felt myself one of the mist-entangled stars. Her song wept, and I felt myself a star that fought against the mist, and, fighting, break away – a star that fled out and out through immeasurable green space –

"A man stood before us. He was very tall. His face was both cruel and kind, saturnine as Satan and joyous as Apollo. He raised his eyes to us, and they were yellow as buttercups, and wise, so wise! Ward, it was the face above the peak in the room of the Dragon Glass! The eyes that had looked at me out of Wu-Sing's face! He smiled on us for a moment and then – he was gone!

"I took Santhu by the hand and began to run. Quite suddenly it came to me that I had enough of the haunted gardens of Rak; that I wanted to get back to my own land. But not without Santhu. I tried to remember the road to the cleft. I felt that there lay the path back. We ran. From far behind came a wailing. Santhu screamed – but I knew the fear in her cry was not for herself. It was for me. None of the creatures of that place could harm her who was herself one of its creatures. The wailing drew closer. I turned.

"Winging down through the green air was a beast, an unthinkable beast, Ward! It was like the winged beast of the Apocalypse that is to bear the woman arrayed in purple and scarlet. It was beautiful even in its horror. It closed its scarlet and golden wings, and its long, gleaming body shot at me like a monstrous spear.

"And then – just as it was about to strike – a mist threw itself between us! It was a rainbow mist, and it was – cast. It was cast as though a hand had held it and thrown it like a net. I heard the winged beast shriek its disappointment, Santhu's hand gripped mine tighter. We ran through the mist.

"Before us was the cleft between the two green rocks. Time and time again we raced for it, and time and time again that beautiful shining horror struck at me – and each time came the thrown mist to baffle it. It was a game! Once I heard a laugh, and then I knew who was my hunter. The master of the beast and the caster of the mist. It was he of the yellow eyes – and he was playing me – playing me as a child plays with a cat when he tempts it with a piece of meat and snatches the meat away again and again from the hungry jaws!

"The mist cleared away from its last throw, and the mouth of the cleft was just before us. Once more the thing swooped – and this time there was no mist. The player had tired of the game! As it struck, Santhu raised herself before it. The beast swerved – and the claw that had been stretched to rip me from throat to waist struck me a glancing blow. I fell – fell through leagues and leagues of green space.

"When I awoke I was here in this bed, with the doctor men around me and this – " He pointed to his bandaged breast again.

"That night when the nurse was asleep I got up and looked into the Dragon Glass, and I saw – the claw, even as you did. The beast is there. It is waiting for me!"

Hemdon was silent for a moment.

"If he tires of the waiting he may send the beast through for me," he said. "I mean the man with the yellow eyes. I've a desire to try one of these guns on it. It's real, you know, the beast is – and these guns have stopped elephants."

"But the man with the yellow eyes, Jim," I whispered – "who is he?"

"He," said Herndon – "why, he's the Wonder Worker himself!"

"You don't believe such a story as that!" I cried. "Why, it's – it's lunacy! It's some devilish illusion in the glass. It's like the – crystal globe that makes you hypnotize yourself and think the things your own mind creates are real. Break it, Jim! It's devilish! Break it!"

"Break it!" he said incredulously. "Break it? Not for the ten thousand lives that are the toll of Rak! Not real? Aren't these wounds real? Wasn't Santhu real? Break it! Good God, man, you don't know what you say! Why, it's my only road back to her! If that yelloweyed devil back there were only as wise as he looks, he would know he didn't have to keep his beast watching there. I want to go, Ward; I want to go and bring her back with me. I've an idea, somehow, that he hasn't – well, full control of things. I've an idea that the Greatest Wonder-Worker wouldn't put wholly in Rak's hands the souls that wander through the many gateways into his kingdom. There's a way out, Ward; there's a way to escape him. I won away from him once, Ward. I'm sure of it. But then I left Santhu behind. I have to go back for her. That's why I found the little passage that led from the throne-room. And he knows it, too. That's why he had to turn his beast on me.

"And I'll go through again, Ward. And I'll come back again – with Santhu!"

But he has not returned. It is six months now since he disappeared for the second time. And from his bedroom, as he had done before. By the will that they found – the will that commended that in event of his disappearing as he had done before and not returning within a week I was to have his house and all that was within it – I came into possession of the Dragon Glass. The dragons had spun again for Hemdon, and he had gone through the gateway once more. I found only one of the elephant guns, and I knew that he had had time to take the other with him.

I sit night after night before the glass, waiting for him to come back through it – with Santhu. Sooner or later they will come. That I know.